SOMETIMES THE WOLF

SOMETIMES THE WOLF

URBAN WAITE

WM

WILLIAM MORROW

An Imprint of HarperCollins*Publishers*

SOMETIMES THE WOLF. Copyright © 2014 by Urban Waite. All rights reserved. Printed in the United States of America. No part of this book may be used or reproduced in any manner whatsoever without written permission except in the case of brief quotations embodied in critical articles and reviews. For information address HarperCollins Publishers, 195 Broadway, New York, NY 10007.

HarperCollins books may be purchased for educational, business, or sales promotional use. For information please e-mail the Special Markets Department at SPsales@harpercollins.com.

A hardcover edition of this book was published in 2014 by William Morrow, an imprint of HarperCollins Publishers.

FIRST WILLIAM MORROW PAPERBACK EDITION PUBLISHED 2015.

Designed by Lisa Stokes

Library of Congress Cataloging-in-Publication Data has been applied for.

ISBN 978-0-06-221692-2

15 16 17 18 19   OV/RRD   10 9 8 7 6 5 4 3 2 1

For my father,
who has always gone his own way

You know, sometimes—for a long time at a stretch—it's like it hadn't happened. Not to me. Maybe to somebody else, but not to me. Then I remember, and when I first remember I say, no, it could not have happened to me.

—Robert Penn Warren, *All the King's Men*

THE BIG MAN STOOD in the cold watching the road. He wore an orange vest over his buttoned shirt and held a traffic sign in his hand that he flipped from time to time as he passed the minutes watching the road and waiting. Behind in the night a single blinking orange light marked his silhouette, causing his shape to shift and glimmer against the pavement on which he stood. There was the sound in the distance of jet planes landing and taking off, the high wheeling cut of their engines overhead as they made their turns through the clouds, dropping out of the air a couple miles away and moving earthward.

He had never been on a plane and all he could think of as he stood there was the way the wings seemed to drift open, the flaps bent down like a bird coming to rest on a lake. His mind taken back to a time forty years ago when, as a boy, he had sat out in the prairie grass watching chevrons of snow geese land on a pond in the Palouse. So many of them that the water appeared white as their feathers and the sound of the birds calling to each other deafened him.

He was half turned on his heels when the headlights broke from around the corner of the road and lit him full. The road fenced in on one side with the creep of blackberries and on the other by a stand of oaks that had long since lost their coverings. The dry rasp of leaves heard from within the stand any time the wind moved. He tried to remember what he was meant to do but it didn't come to him and he stood there in the middle of the road holding the sign. The car now drawn closer and the lights bathing his jeans in an unnatural shade of mercury blue.

There was no one around and as the car came to a stop he stepped forward and watched the window come down. "Construction?" the driver asked.

"Just up the road. Shouldn't be more than a few minutes."

With a flick of his hand, the driver brought a watch free from his shirtsleeve and checked the time. He wore a suit jacket and black pants. A black cap rested on the passenger seat with a shiny plastic half bill. He leaned forward on the wheel and looked toward the rounded curve of the road, where above at the bend the planes could be seen landing. He turned and looked behind him down the road from which he'd come. When he turned back around, he said, "It's late for construction."

"Best time," the big man said.

The driver looked up the road again. "Is there a detour? Some other way to get through?"

"You can go down the way you came but it will take you just as long. Maybe longer."

The driver leaned back in his seat and let the air out of his lungs in a long exhale. Somewhere in the oaks the leaves were moving again but there was no wind. And the driver, who sat slumped in his seat watching the road, heard only the hum of the car's engine and the soft putter of the exhaust.

"Hello," a voice said.

The driver turned and looked up not at the big man but into the face of someone much skinnier. His face hollowed out beneath the eyes where his cheekbones protruded in smooth orbs, the shadows beneath filling the length of his face all the way to his chin. The driver opened his mouth to respond but felt only the hard crack of metal come across his chin, and then on his forehead, repeated again and again.

When the skinny man brought his hand back from within the car it resembled a red candied apple. Rounded and shiny with blood. The black butt of a pistol visible at the base of his fist.

With the door open and the car still running, they carried the driver around to the trunk and placed him inside. The big man, who was still thinking about snow geese, had already thrown the vest and sign to the side of the road.

PART I

THE KILLING

Extraordinary Praise for *Sometimes the Wolf*

"A tremendous novel by a rising powerhouse of a writer. Waite tells tense, thrilling stories with thoughtfulness and emotional clarity, and his prose is simply astonishing. Anyone who is late to the party couldn't ask for a better entry point than this hybrid of crime drama and father-son story." —Michael Koryta, *New York Times* bestselling author of *Those Who Wish Me Dead*

"Riveting. . . . An engrossing, adventure-packed ride."

—*Publishers Weekly*

"Urban Waite is the rarest of writers: one who encourages you to turn the page to find out what happens while simultaneously forcing you to slow and admire the language and the tone he creates. In *Sometimes the Wolf*, Waite throws us into a rush of suspense and danger that tests the limits of the bond between father and son, and takes us on a thrilling trek through the Pacific Northwest he evokes so well. This is a book to read straight through."

—James Scott, author of *The Kept*

"It's a rare thing to balance a thriller plot on characters with such stooped shoulders, but Waite manages the feat with surprising dexterity. Another emotionally rich novel from a very special writer."

—*Booklist* (starred review)

"A brisk plot, well-developed characters, thoughtful reflections on the ebb and flow of family ties, and—most of all—Waite's eloquent language describing his setting's untamed beauty." —*Seattle Times*

"A father-and-son relationship, perhaps broken beyond repair, fuels Urban Waite's engrossing novel that skillfully exposes the complicated emotions that can stymie a once close family while also working as a superb action-adventure tale." —Associated Press

"Is the literary thriller a dying genre? . . . Fortunately . . . there are still thrillers like Urban Waite's *Sometimes the Wolf*, which seems to care—and care deeply, smartly—about the way it is written. . . .

The book's engine moves quickly, fired on, in part, by two somewhat spectral killers. They haunt the margins of the text, giving the story a wildness that only gradually comes into focus. But when it does, you start to see the masterful construction of the novel, as—one-by-one—the strands of the plot create a tense and memorable net."

—*The Oregonian* (Portland)

"A gripping tale of family intrigue, betrayal, lies, deception, kidnapping, murder, and even forgiveness. The story flows faster as the pace of action increases. Highly recommended for fans of Dennis Lehane and Elmore Leonard."

—*Library Journal* (starred review)

"Urban Waite keeps raising his own standards with each new novel and surpassing them with his next. His latest, *Sometimes the Wolf*, is one of those books that is totally engrossing as you are reading it and haunts your thoughts when you are not. . . . A beauteous and frightening joy to read from beginning to end. . . . It is violent and unsettling in spots, quiet and heartbreaking in others. . . . Waite is a marvel."

—Bookreporter.com

"I never thought I'd type the sentence 'better than Cormac McCarthy' but, oops, I just went and did. Waite's story about ex-con Dads, dangerous friends, and family loyalties peers into the same dark corners of the human psyche, but has a glimmer of warmth and humanity at its core which is lacking from a substantial portion of the noir genre."

—LitReactor.com

"Urban Waite has been getting some buzz as a writer to watch, often being compared to Cormac McCarthy, Dennis Lehane, and Elmore Leonard, and his latest novel, *Sometimes the Wolf*, shows why. . . . Taut dialogue, language that borders on poetry even as it describes murders and mayhem, artfully drawn settings, gripping tension, and believable, complicated characters. . . . Atmospheric, poetic, and hard to classify, *Sometimes the Wolf* is a page-turning thriller that invites the reader to savor the language and contemplate deeper issues than those on the surface of the plot. But with all its literary leanings, it's still a great story well told."

—ReviewingTheEvidence.com

THE DEER LAY A little way off the road at the bottom of the fence. The stomach opened on the cattle wire, with the skin peeled away and the viscera hanging loose in the predawn air. The sun had yet to crest the mountains and Silver Lake stretched away to the south for miles, dark and flat, with only the new wind that came with the morning to tousle the water and work the whitecaps. Gray slate all the way from one edge to the next, and the cattle wire and road running along it like a border. One piece of farm followed by another all the way around the top of the lake and into town, where the flatland ran out and the mountains began again, dense with fir and hemlock, sword fern and peat moss.

Deputy Bobby Drake stood beside the open door of his Chevy, toggling down through the contacts on his phone. Too early for anyone from Fish and Wildlife to answer. All of them had been out the night before—Drake partnered with one of the officers—as they worked to stop a string of poachings in the hills. The spotter plane high up over the mountains calling in positions as Drake and the local Fish and Wildlife officer rushed to catch up.

Now Drake waited in the growing morning haze with his breath curling before him in the twilight, the car hazards washing the scene in a slow pulse of orange, his fingernails cold on his face where he held the phone.

The message clicked on and he listened. When it was his turn he gave his name and then the location. "Pretty near cut herself in two," he said, looking to where the animal had caught on the cattle fence, the blood black and slick along the metal. He turned the phone away and looked at the deer, trying to decide if there was anything else he could say. A she-wolf had been at the carcass when he'd rounded the curve and caught the animal with his headlights. One rib gnawed to the white bone, and the wolf tugging at the deer, stretching the flesh along the wire.

For the past couple weeks the wolf had been in the hills, calling out for others. Haunting the mist that came off the lake at night and threaded its way up through the mountain valleys. Sheri, his wife, turning the volume up on the television and waiting till the howls faded away and all was silent again. No sound outside but that of the trees brushing against the siding of the house, and the familiar rattle of the wind as it shook through the naked branches of the apple orchard out back.

Drake took a step toward the fence. The head of the deer played back at a strange angle. The animal flipped over on its back, where it had come to rest, eyes black and wide, looking up into the sky. Belly all but eaten clean. He didn't know what else to say, the phone still open in his palm, and the message ticking down a second at a time. He gave the phone another moment of study before closing it in his fist.

He wondered how long the deer had lain like that before it was found, before the wolf came out of the darkness, pulled by the smell of blood and the bleat of fear. No way of knowing something like that, but a hope it had not been long and the deer had bled out along the wire before the scavenger arrived.

In the past couple weeks Drake had responded to three sightings. The wolf coming down out of the hills, tipping trash cans and chasing cattle. Only once had he seen her though, loping across a rancher's field, the gaunt hips slowing for a moment as she neared the forest. The wolf, winter worn and skinny, all bone and fur—turning to regard him where he stood. No pack to run with, or cubs to nurse. One of the first wolves to be seen in the valley in fifty years and Drake had no idea what he was supposed to do about it.

He raised his eyes and looked into the cool dark at the edge of the field. A pink light had begun to spread behind him over the edge of the mountains and in the grass the deep blue that came just before the dawn could be seen. He knew the she-wolf was waiting, shifting in the shadows beneath the trees, watching him where he stood.

He scraped a foot over the gravel at the edge of the road, feeling a dull tightness in his leg as he watched the forest. He checked the time on his phone and then ran his eyes to the south, where the sky was lightening with the sun. Out of uniform for the day, he wore a dress shirt and slacks on his thin frame. No desire in him to leave the carcass or the wolf. And a certainty that what lay ahead of him down the road was more threatening than anything lurking in the shadows beneath the trees. Nothing he could do but move on, an appointment he needed to keep and the simple fact that as soon as he rounded the next curve, the nature of the thing would continue.

THREE HOURS LATER Drake sat in his car watching the Monroe prison gates, waiting for his father's release. The clouds were breaking overhead and the moisture that had condensed inside the car now showed with the sunlight. The morning had been cold and as he'd driven up through the birch that lay around the recesses of the prison, he could see the rolling barbed wire clear down the line. Wrapping over and over again as it crested one wall and then fell ten feet to the next, layer after layer of it, and no chance of escape for anyone inside, except, Drake thought, maybe his father, Patrick.

It was almost twelve years to the day since his father had been sentenced. In the years past Drake had searched for some sign of his father in his own face, looking at himself in the mirror of his cruiser, or under the bright changing-room lights of the department. The genes there that all who met him said were evident in his face. A fine line dividing the two of them, a reason Drake had tried so desperately in the last twelve years to distance himself from the father everyone could see within him.

All that had changed in his life, Drake thought, and all that remained the same.

He checked his watch and then looked to the prison gate. He didn't know what to expect and he sat there in the lot watching the single pane of the steel door, searching for the shift of light or shadow from within that would signal Patrick's arrival. Twelve years ago the life Drake had wanted for himself at the age of twenty put up on the shelf. Everything after his father went away feeling like the life of someone else.

Fifteen minutes went by in this way, the cold seeping in through the seams of the late-model Chevy, before he saw the door push open from within and a guard emerge onto the small concrete path, holding the door wide. Drake didn't recognize his father at first, carrying a cardboard box in his arms, his breath curling away behind him as he walked. His beard grown full with white hair and a thin, almost animal-like mane, falling thick from his bald crown. He was over six foot, with the beginnings of a belly, and the well-built chest and shoulders he'd always had. The skin of his neck below the beard thickly veined in the cold.

Drake got out of the car and stood, waiting. The one time he had visited his father in prison, the man had just stared coldly back at him, his head shaved to the skin, and a slight tilt to his lips as he sat answering Drake's questions. The man locked away for a third of Drake's life. Sheriff Patrick Drake, a legend in his time with no other family left in Silver Lake except his son and daughter-in-law.

The deputy for years had not cared what happened to his father, shamed any time his father's name was mentioned. The family history in the hills and mountains around the lake nothing to be proud of, Drake's own grandfather, Morgan Drake, infamous for bringing booze and entertainment to the logging camps up and down the North Cascades, eventually settling the family in Silver Lake.

Looking at his father now, with his hair grown out and a beard matted across his face, his skin pulled flat in places and creased in others, Drake felt like he didn't know his father the way he should. So much time had passed with nothing being said between them. Patrick wearing the same clothes he'd gone in with twelve years before, outdated and now large on his thin, muscular frame.

Behind, the guard closed the door and Drake heard the latch fall as Patrick crossed the lot to where he waited by the car. The old canvas coat open at Patrick's chest, revealing the flannel shirt and jeans he'd gone in with all those years before.

"I see you've gone wild," Drake said, gesturing to his father's white mane.

Patrick smiled. He'd been in there a long time. And the creases on his skin looked all the deeper. "I've always been wild," he said.

In the lot behind them, Drake heard an engine start up, followed by the soft putter of exhaust, but Drake didn't think anything of it as he took the box from his father and loaded it into the backseat, watching how Patrick put a hand to the door and lowered his body down into the car.

IT WAS AN hour before they spoke again. The sound of the interstate moving beneath them, the thrum of the tires on the asphalt and the radio turned on low against the quiet. The absence of their voices like some living, breathing thing, tucked far back in the darkness waiting to appear.

"Pull off at the next exit," Patrick said, pointing ahead of them to an overhead sign.

There was still a good forty-five minutes before they would turn off the interstate and head east into the Cascades, threading their way up the mountain pass toward Silver Lake and the home that had been left for Drake and his wife when his father had gone in.

"You planning on knocking off a convenience store?"

"You know that's not what I was convicted of," Patrick said. His eyes flashed on Drake for a moment and then looked away again.

Drake had no idea why he said the things he did to his father. No way around what his father had done but to joke about it and hope it could be avoided for just another day. "You had a lot of people fooled," Drake said.

The old sheriff nodded but didn't look over at Drake again.

Drake took a hand off the wheel and ran it back over his scalp, feeling the close-cropped hair he'd gradually been losing since his midtwenties. Like his father he was built thick through the shoulders, with long legs and the thin, angular bones that had been passed down through their family for generations. "People still talk about it. That's all I'm saying."

"What people?"

"Silver Lake, the whole town."

"I never thought I'd be going back there."

"Well, I don't know where you thought you'd be. We had to sell a lot of the land just to hold on to the house."

"I never asked you to go back there."

"I never asked you to get thrown in prison."

His father shifted, then looked behind him, reaching for something out of the cardboard box in the backseat. "I'm not proud of what I did but at the time it seemed like the only option." He was sitting in the seat again, holding open a thin folder. "Look," he said. "I saved them, every one I could find. Even the ones that had my name in them."

Drake looked over at the clippings and then looked away. Some from before his father had gotten into trouble, some from years afterward. All of them he'd seen before and he knew they told something about Drake's past that he really didn't care for, that he wasn't proud of, but that he'd done because he'd thought at the time it would mean something.

Drake felt nauseous just thinking about those years. All he'd given up to come home and deal with his father's debts. A basketball scholarship to Arizona he'd had to leave behind. All the time he'd spent trying to make up for his father's crimes. To earn the name back. It wasn't Drake's fault. None of it was, and that point—most important to Drake now—had only recently occurred to him. Still, he had to remind himself that he was living for himself. For his wife, Sheri. He was living his own life in a way he hadn't for many years. And now with Patrick sitting beside him, trying to reawaken all the old memories, all the things that had occurred in the past, Drake knew he needed to look to the future.

"They're all here," Patrick said, holding a clipping up for Drake to see. "Even the newspaper articles from Arizona, from when you played basketball."

"Why would you keep those?"

"So I don't forget."

"Sometimes things are better forgotten."

Patrick paused, looking down at the clipping in his hand. Even with his eyes on the road, Drake couldn't help but notice. "I don't plan on making any problems for you," Patrick said. "Not anymore."

Drake looked over to where his father sat in the car, the green shift of the landscape going by, the backs of houses, run-down and scabbed with paint.

His father closed the folder and put it back with the rest of his possessions. "You don't need to worry about me," his father said, his eyes looking to the side mirror as the road went by in a flicker of light. "I just want you to know that I'll be fine. I want you to know that I have a plan. Whatever I did in the past, it's covered. You and me are going to be fine."

Drake nodded and watched his father. Now it's me and him, Drake thought. When did that happen? When has that ever been the way things were? Drake certainly hadn't played a part in the second mortgage Patrick took out on their house, on the money he owed. All that had added up after Drake's mother passed and there just wasn't anything in the bank for the bills.

"I was away for a long time," Patrick said. "I thought about a lot of things. I know going back to Silver Lake is what I have to do now. But someday I plan to build a cabin in the woods—live like your grandfather. Just disappear."

Drake shifted, rolling his shoulders back. "Don't disappear just yet. You're still out on parole. Plus I wouldn't be surprised if the forestry service had some sort of restraining order out against you after all the time you spent in the woods last time you were free."

"Very funny," Patrick said. He had his eyes on the side mirror and it made Drake look to the rearview, scanning the highway behind. Nothing to see but a tall line of semis and the daytime running lights of cars shining back on him.

Drake took the exit. He slowed into a stop sign and then turned to the east, where there were several gas stations and a McDonald's. Up the road he saw where a big warehouse store was going in, the skeleton of the place big as an airplane hangar.

"You need money?" Drake asked.

"No, just a bathroom."

Drake pulled in beside one of the pumps and watched his father go in. With his credit card Drake paid the machine and let the tank fill, sitting in the car with the door open and the sound of the engine ticking beneath the hood. With his hand he pushed into the muscle of his thigh and felt the tendons pull. Two years before he'd been shot in the knee while trying to help out a DEA agent by the name of Frank Driscoll, and there were pieces of Drake's patella still floating around through his insides. All of it the result of a bust Drake had tried to make on a man smuggling drugs over the mountains outside Silver Lake, a former acquaintance of his father's.

With the door open he brought his legs around, resting them on the pavement and working the muscle in his hands, the smell of gas strong in the air. There had been physical therapy for a year afterward, lessons on how to shift his weight, how to swing his knee, and try to minimize the limp he would have for the rest of his life.

All the people we try to be, Drake thought. All the people we will be in a single life.

On the weekends Drake still pushed the ball up the court at the local high school. Wearing a knee brace. His bad leg constantly losing the battle with his good leg. He'd had to adjust for how he shot, making sure he came off his good leg when he ran in for a layup. He had to think about it now, the way he couldn't jump as high anymore. He'd always been an outside shooter, playing point in college, he'd spent most of his time moving the ball around at the top of the key, or stepping back beyond the three-point line to line up his shot. But he'd put on weight since then. He'd slowed. And even keeping himself in shape he knew he'd never be the same player he once had been. Though he was teaching himself to be something different now, not worse or better, but something different. Smarter perhaps. Drake didn't know. The person he was then so far from the person he was now.

He sat in the car with the door open. The smell of gasoline dissolving in the air as he ran his fingertips over the muscles of his thigh, pushing the strain away. His fingertips digging for the familiar scars and wounds of his past.

A minute later his father came out of the gas station wiping his hands down the sides of his pants to dry them. "I worried about you when I read in the paper what happened," his father said.

"It's nothing now," Drake said. "It stiffens up on long drives."

"You were shot twice, weren't you?"

"Once in the knee and once in the arm," Drake said. His hand on his kneecap and the slight indentation left in the bone from where the bullet had passed through. He'd thought in that moment, two years before, he was a dead man, and that all he had tried to do in his life had been for nothing. A scar in the shape of a star on his forearm where the second bullet had gone in, and the dark purple sliver of tissue at the back of his left hand where he'd caught a knife through his palm. Thinking on it now he couldn't even begin to put it back together, or reason out why he was still alive. But he was. All that in the past and now he sat trying to wring the stiffness from his leg.

When he raised his eyes from his knee, his father was no longer looking at him, his head up, with his focus across the street. "You know those men over there?"

Drake turned and found where Patrick's gaze fell. A new-model Lincoln Town Car with two men inside, sitting in the McDonald's parking lot. "I don't think they care much about us," Drake said.

"They're a little too far for me to make out."

"I don't recognize them," Drake said.

"They pulled off the highway as we came up the exit," his father said. "They've been sitting like that ever since I got out of the car and went inside."

Drake stood and put his hands to the small of his back, working his shoulders until he heard the ligaments pop. "Is that why you were looking in the side mirror?"

Patrick stood watching the men. "Why are they just sitting there? Why don't they go in?"

"They could have gone in while you were in the bathroom."

"I wasn't in there that long."

Drake stared at his father and then looked back at the men. "Is there a reason they'd be following us?" The pump clicked off and Drake walked back to take the hose from the tank. "Are you feeling all right, Dad? You're scaring me a bit here."

Drake watched as his father's eyes quivered, something watery and loose in their stare before they broke away and met Drake again. "Just paranoid, I suppose. Too much time locked away in small places seeing things that aren't there."

Drake nodded, taking the receipt from the machine. Patrick stood on the other side of the car, the beard and stark white hair giving him a mythical quality, like some piece of history come to life from a book. "You sure you're okay, Dad?"

"I'm fine," he said. "Just feels different out here, I guess."

"That's fine," Drake said. He started the car and pulled it around to the road, feeling the engine work as he pressed his foot down and angled for the interstate.

In his rearview Drake watched the road, waiting to see if the Lincoln would round the corner and take the entrance with them. Nothing there to see, and only the semis out on the interstate as he pushed the accelerator again and headed north.

THERE WAS THE SOUND again of something hitting against the metal—the thump of an elbow, the beat of a foot, the hard strike of a palm against the inside of the trunk lid. The skinny man looked to the side where the big man sat and then he looked behind him, over the backs of their seats to where the leather—with every knock—seemed to palpitate like something alive.

He turned and ran his eyes to the gas station across the street. The car they'd been following since that morning now pulling out into traffic, headed toward the highway again. He watched it go, tracking it with his eyes as it went. And then when it was gone he got up from the Lincoln and walked around to the back where the sounds could be heard.

There were several children playing inside on the McDonald's play structure—twenty feet of slides and rope ladders, a bridge of netting from one plastic tower to the next. One overweight boy of eight or nine there at the edge, surveying the land, watching the skinny man where he stood in the parking lot. The two stared at each other for the beat of a second. The boy there and then gone, called away by his mother or by some other child.

The man turned and opened the trunk. The driver there in the belly, his face showed as only a mash of dried blood and broken bones. One side of his skull sagging like melted rubber, cheekbone to eye socket crushed inward. And the skin purpled and swollen from when he'd been beaten unconscious.

The skinny man took it all in quickly, looking to the McDonald's and then looking back on the driver. He dropped a fist fast into the windpipe of the man and crushed the driver's larynx. Then as the eyes opened wide, the driver's lungs struggling to breathe, the skinny man bent downward and with two hands took hold of the driver, breaking his neck as deftly as a farmer snapping the neck of one of his chickens.

YOU GOT SOME TIME?" Drake asked as they came into Silver Lake, the houses all strung together along the road. Prefabs with vinyl siding and patchy lawns farther out, and as they came into town, two-story clapboards with wood-frame windows and lopsided porches. A single yellow caution light dangling where the two main roads came together and then split apart again.

"Plenty of time," his father said, leaning into the windshield to take in the town. "Hasn't changed much, has it?"

"A few more logging outfits," Drake said. They came to the blinking yellow and Drake turned the steering wheel to the left, heading away from the lake.

When they came to the metal Quonset hut five miles up the road, Drake pulled into the gravel and set the brake. "This is new," Patrick said.

"Fish and Wildlife put it in a few years back. I've been helping them out. This morning on the way to pick you up I spotted a wolf just off the lake road."

"A wolf?"

Drake nodded. "Positive."

"No shit?" Patrick said, leaning forward to take in the hut like he might see the wolf standing there before them. "Your grandfather used to tell me stories about the old packs that ran in the North Cascades. Nothing like that when I was around. This must be the first wolf in fifty years."

"At least." Drake pushed the door open and moved to get out, pausing and looking back at his father. "You hear from him at all? Grandpa? Is he still crazy?"

"He wrote me a few times. Says he's getting old. Told us to come visit when we had a chance. Says he's been shooting gophers and prairie dogs. Sent me a recipe for chili a few years ago. Same crazy old man."

"What kind of chili?"

"It wasn't beef."

"Sounds about right," Drake said. "I'm surprised he wrote you."

"Living out where he does I think he gets lonely," Patrick said.

Drake told his father he'd be only a moment and then got up out of the car and closed the door. He could smell the tree pollen in the air. The first buds of spring showing on the stink currant branches off the road.

Nothing up the road but forest, and then eventually, thirty miles on, the border crossing into Canada. A single booth set in the middle of the road with red-and-white pole gates hanging off either side, like a trawler on the ocean. Drake took a breath and felt the sweet air at the back of his throat, cold and mineral as snowmelt. He nodded to his father and then went on to the hut.

He smelled the deer by the time he had the door open and he put a hand to his nose to quell the stench. "How long did she sit in the sun before you brought her in?" he asked.

Ellie Cobb leaned out from behind a metal cabinet. Eight years younger than him, she wore a pair of safety glasses over her dark eyes, her brown hair tied back and the green Fish and Wildlife uniform visible beneath a yellow rubber apron. With a gloved hand, she removed the glasses and stood. "When you left the message this morning you didn't say anything about the deer being half-eaten."

"She wasn't half-eaten when I left her," Drake said. He was standing close by Ellie now and he could see how the wolf had cleaned one of the flanks to the bone. A strong light focused down on the remaining muscle. The musk of the deer floated in the air, and an underlying smell of the wilderness.

The room they stood in a mix of salvaged wood furniture—culled from some government office in Olympia—and the more modern stainless examination tables toward the back, where a series of freezers lined the wall and filled the room with an electric hum. Each freezer containing the various remains of one thing or another, finds either Drake or Ellie had brought in over the last few months: a frozen coyote, a flattened porcupine, and the remains of a diseased elk.

Drake picked up a pair of surgical tongs and folded open the stomach cavity. The innards torn and the ribs snapped in a jagged fashion Drake knew had not been done with human hands. When he looked over at Ellie to tell her about the wolf, the Fish and Wildlife officer's eyes were looking past him.

Drake turned and found his father there, the big canvas coat on his shoulders and a hand held to his nose.

"Ellie Cobb," Drake said, "this is my father, Patrick."

"The convict," Ellie said, a playful smile on her face as she said it. "I'd heard your time was coming up."

"Ex-con," Patrick said, extending a hand to Ellie.

She looked down at it a moment and then gave him a weak wave with her gloved hand. "Sorry," she said. "Blood."

His father nodded and forced a smile. He was standing about two feet away from where Drake leaned over the carcass. "My son tell you I was getting out?"

"Actually, no. The sheriff, Gary, said you might be around soon. Bobby only told me about it when I pressed him a little."

"Gary is the sheriff now?"

Ellie looked to Drake.

"Gary was my deputy," Patrick explained.

Ellie's eyes locked on Drake. "I thought Bobby would have told you."

"Bobby doesn't tell me much of anything. I half expected I'd be catching the bus this morning."

"Bobby seems pretty good at keeping secrets. You have any advice for me if I decide to go rogue?"

Patrick ran his tongue over his teeth, thinking it through. His eyes dancing over her and then away again. "I can tell you what not to do," he said. "Don't smuggle drugs in across international borders. Don't let anyone know you're doing it. And . . ." He looked around the room in mock suspicion. "Don't get caught."

"I see you've been rehabilitated," Ellie said.

"Totally cured."

Drake watched Ellie to see how she was taking it. There was an undeniable level of sarcasm in Patrick's voice and it was hard to know what to do with it.

"You feel guilty about any of it?" Ellie asked.

"I'd take it back if I could," Patrick said. "I messed a lot up. I was the sheriff and I was arrested right here in town. I tried to run but I didn't make it far. I got cocky. Of course I didn't know it at the time. But sitting in Monroe for all those years I can see how it all spiraled out of control for me. I tried to sell too much at one time. People start to take notice."

"Those people being the DEA?"

"When I started out in this I didn't have a lot of options. No one wants to do business with a sheriff and I rushed into it. I needed the money. The DEA offered my contact down in Seattle a deal and that deal involved me. I walked right into it. I really didn't even need the money at that point."

"And you got out this morning?"

"Only three hours ago."

"It must feel pretty good, like a birthday or something."

"Yeah, a birthday I only get to celebrate every twelve years." Drake's father blew air through his teeth and looked around at the room. "Bobby told me about the wolf, I thought I'd come in for a second. I didn't expect to meet anyone like you in here."

"Is that a good thing?" Ellie asked.

"You're the best thing I've seen in twelve years."

"The state prison offering charm school now?"

"Yeah," Patrick said. "Just before shop class and after basic auto maintenance. It's real popular."

"I bet." Ellie looked from Patrick to Drake and then dropped her eyes to the half-eaten carcass on the table.

Drake turned and looked at his father. "You think you could give us a moment?"

"Yeah, no problem. I just came in to give the place a look." He nodded a good-bye to Ellie and then smiled toward Drake. "Bobby, I'll be out by the car when you finish up here."

Drake watched his father walk back toward the front entrance. When the door drew shut, Ellie said, "You definitely didn't mention he was such a smoothy." A playfulness showing on her face again.

"I didn't know you were into older men."

"Only if they're old enough to be my father," Ellie said. She gave Drake a wink. "That bad-boy thing really gets me going, you think he'd wear a leather jacket if I asked?"

"You can stop anytime, Ellie."

"Just having some fun. Just being polite. The guy has been locked up for twelve years."

"Uh-huh, and it's your job to cheer him up?" Drake said. He could feel the flush of blood on his cheeks. He didn't know why he felt this way about her, or what to call it. Protective? Maybe. Ellie was like a little sister to him. She'd grown up in the town and then left for college, later applying to Fish and Wildlife. She'd been something like twelve years old when everything had gone down with Drake's father. And just like everyone else in Silver Lake, she knew almost every detail about the case.

"He could probably use some good times," Ellie said.

Drake shook his head, trying to get a handle on it. He thought if he opened his mouth to speak his voice would break like a teenage boy's. He swallowed, wetting his throat, knowing it was all talk, and that Ellie was giving him a hard time like she always did. "You thought you'd just flirt with him a little?" Drake said. "Show him a good time?"

"The convict thing? It's the one thing he's known for, isn't it? That and knowing every inch of these mountains."

"That's what happens when you spend a couple years smuggling drugs over them." Drake laughed, but it felt forced, and he looked to the front door of the Quonset hut and wondered what his father was doing outside.

With one gloved hand, Ellie pushed the light back from the carcass and flicked off the power. "I didn't know it was for that long."

"Not everything was in the papers."

"I guess not."

"I tend to think people know things about our family before they've even met us. I'm surprised Gary never told you that part."

She took the gloves from her hands and threw them into the trash can beneath the table. A dappling of sweat showed at her hairline where the examination light had caught her. "Gary barely says a thing and you won't talk about him at all except to tell a few stories from his childhood. You're not exactly forthcoming with all the information sometimes." She walked over to her desk, where a topographical map of the surrounding mountains was spread. Little red marks all up and down the valley floor. "When you called this morning, you didn't say anything about our wolf."

Drake shrugged. "I didn't want you getting all excited about it."

"She's becoming a problem."

"Better the deer than someone's cow."

"That's the problem," Ellie said. "It's only a matter of time before one of those ranchers starts shooting at her. She's on her own and starting to look for the easy meal." Ellie put a hand to the map, running a finger from one red mark to the next. "These are all the places where she's been seen. She's not just passing through at this point. Wolves hunt in pairs. Without a pack she's pretty much just going to go for the easiest meal she can find. A calf, trash cans, or roadkill. All of which are related to humans."

Drake looked at the thin corridor of sightings, north to south along the lake, following the main road.

"I want to collar her and see where she goes," Ellie said. "When I can prove it's an individual wolf, and I have her movements worked out, I can start to put a plan together. I want you to help me out."

Drake looked around the room, wondering for the slightest moment if she might have been talking to someone else. "I'm a little busy being a deputy," Drake said.

"I'm trying to save her," Ellie said.

"That's all fine and good but I still don't see what it has to do with me."

Ellie got up from the desk and untied the yellow apron from around her waist. Standing she came to Drake's shoulders, petite with a swimmer's broad arms and sculpted legs. Her size alone reminded Drake of how young she was, and how brand-new to Fish and Wildlife she seemed. Nothing worn away on her or piled up against the surface of her skin, like a cabin in the winter under all that snow. No scars, or pieces of her missing. Drake wanted her to stay just the way she was, twenty-four years old, doing exactly what she wanted with her life.

Drake watched as she turned and hung the apron up on a hook by the door. By the time she turned back around she was already looking at him like something funny had been said. "I already talked this over with Gary."

"Christ," Drake said. "You want to go on a wolf hunt? I'm people police. You understand that, right?"

"He says you probably know the valley better than anyone."

"Christ," Drake said again, this time hoping a prayer might be answered. "When?"

"Tomorrow or the next day. Sooner the better."

"My father just got out."

"Bring him."

"No." Drake waved off the statement, both hands in the air. "No way."

"After all these years you'd think you'd want to spend time with your father."

"You might think that, but I don't."

"Like I said, he's famous for knowing every inch of these mountains."

"And for being a convicted criminal," Drake said. "Your words, not mine."

WHEN DRAKE GOT to the car his father was sitting in the passenger seat with the windows down looking toward the forest. The light slanting in through the trees, rich with pollen, and the sword ferns a nuclear green at the edge of the road.

"Gary is the sheriff now?"

Drake pulled open the door and then sat there looking at his hands on the wheel. Gary had been Patrick's best friend. And when Patrick went away Gary had stepped in to help Drake get situated, taking Drake fishing, even giving him the job at the department.

"He was the interim sheriff when you went away," Drake said. "And then he was elected a year after." Drake brought out the car keys from his pocket. "I thought you would have heard."

"I'm not surprised," Patrick said, turning to Drake. He smiled a bit, coming out of whatever place his mind had taken him.

His father had been gone a long time and Drake knew there were going to be times like this. Moments when the flash of a memory came across his father's face and then went away again. A decision that was made a long time before and that absence in time—what could have been—the only thing left to regret.

Patrick went on smiling and then he nodded toward the Fish and Wildlife hut as he came back to himself. "Did I cut in on your action?"

It took Drake a second and then when he saw what his father was getting at his face flushed. "That's not what that was about."

"Seems funny to me," his father said. "All this time since we've seen each other and the first thing you want to show me in Silver Lake is the young Fish and Wildlife officer."

Drake started up the car and turned out onto the road. "That's not it at all." In the rearview mirror Drake watched the Quonset hut disappear around a bend in the road.

"You know I haven't even met Sheri yet. Seems like she'd be the one you'd take me to see first."

"I hope you're not trying to be a dad," Drake said.

"She is your wife, right? Sheri?" Patrick smiled for a second and then looked away, watching the green thatch of the forest pass by out the window. Drake knowing that his father wanted him to say something, that the old man was just trying to egg him on like he had when Drake was a boy. His father trying to reconnect in the only way still familiar to him, like something lost long ago and then found.

Ten minutes later they passed through the yellow caution light and turned up the lake again, heading toward the house. Sheri would be away at work, but he'd told her they'd be home in time for lunch, and even if she didn't know, he felt an urge not to disappoint her. The sun above, almost directly over the lake. Nothing out on the water, and the thin glint of sunlight refracted off the chrome of a few logging trucks far down the other side of the lake.

"Ellie is a local girl, isn't she?" Patrick said. "Have Sheri and she met?"

"I'm surprised no one shanked you in prison," Drake said.

"She's young," Patrick said. "I recognize her. Didn't you go out with her older sister in high school?"

"Are you planning to blackmail me?"

"Just having a little fun," Patrick said. "You seem pretty familiar with her. You see a lot of her?"

Drake looked over at his father and then looked away. "You're relentless," Drake said. "I have to see Ellie for work, that's all." He wasn't looking at his father but he could feel his father's eyes on him and Drake was almost certain there was a grin to go along.

When they came to the opening in the forest leading toward their house, Drake waited for a couple cars to pass. When they'd gone by, rocking the Chevy on its springs, he turned the wheel and the car came off the lake road and bounced down into the rutted gravel drive. The house was another hundred yards on, hidden beyond a curve in the road and behind a patch of trees. "Sheri is meeting you for the first time. I know it sounds strange to say now that you're here, but it was sudden for us. Sheri's been under a lot of stress lately," Drake said.

"I was told the probation was dependent on your approval," Patrick said. "That was a month ago."

"I know," Drake said. "She's just nervous about it." They took the turn in the drive and came into the clearing before the house. The gravel drive ending and the house there before them. The Sheriff's Department cruiser Drake drove every day parked just to the side. The house a two-bedroom rambler, one story in height, with a few steps leading up to a red door. Drake taking it in fresh as he tried to see it through his father's eyes. Sheri and Drake had painted the house a few years back. The wood siding a light brown that the salesclerk at Home Depot had called sandstone. The trim around the windows painted white and the door a bright red color Sheri had said would make the house "pop."

Now Drake looked at it and didn't know what to say. He was thinking about Sheri. He was thinking about all the changes that had been made since his father had owned the place and Drake had been a child there. They had taken out much of the furniture, repainted the walls inside, updated the bathroom, all of it an effort to try to make the place seem more their own. Now, with Patrick there, Drake didn't know. He felt somehow like he'd been house-sitting all this time and as soon as he brought Patrick inside, the property would be his father's again.

Drake pushed the transmission up into park and sat looking out on the house. The red door and all that sat inside. "I meant to say that there's been some problems lately." Drake didn't turn in his seat. He kept looking up at the house. "I don't want you giving her a hard time. She really has always wanted to meet you."

"That thing about Ellie?" Patrick smiled. "I was just talking. I already told you I'm not going to give you any problems."

"That's good," Drake said. He opened the door and stood. He didn't know what he was trying to say to his father. Or even how to say it. Whatever had been said somehow not enough. Everything, lately, not enough.

DRAKE KNEW SHERI could keep a cool head about things. She'd been keeping a lot of things bottled up inside recently. But Drake didn't know how cool that head would be if he, or his father, told Sheri that the Fish and Wildlife officer he'd been working with till two A.M. was Ellie Cobb. A girl from Silver Lake with whom Drake had a little history.

Only the night before Ellie and Drake had sat up in the Fish and Wildlife truck for almost five hours. The truck pulled off the road, hidden beneath the trees, watching what passed for traffic in Silver Lake. Up above, circling high and wide over the valley, they occasionally heard the spotter plane Ellie had applied for a month before. The plane circling and looking down on the night forest below, marking headlights in the woods, and as soon as they had the locations they would go bouncing up logging roads or down old ranchers' paths, trying to figure who was out there.

Many of the places they'd found in the past month or so since the poaching had begun were just empty grass lots, barren of trees and thick with low-lying brush. Perfect for waiting out groups of grazing deer, spotlighting them with headlights, and then taking shots at them while they stood frozen in the light.

Poaching had been a problem lately on the weekends, and through the night they were called to four different sites, but each time they arrived there was little there to indicate the plane circling above had gotten the location right. At the third lot they came to Drake could see a clear track in the mud and nearby a set of boot prints leading down the slope into the grass.

About fifty yards in they found the bloodstain in the grass. A small depression made where the deer had gone down and then the poachers had lifted the animal and brought it back up the slope with them. There was no more sign than that and Drake knelt, looking the boot prints over, several of them there in the mud at his feet. Possibly two or three men from the size and shape of the tracks. Drake couldn't say for sure.

Ellie was back in her truck then, asking if the spotter plane had seen anything else, though Drake knew as soon as the poachers turned off their lights they pretty much disappeared beneath the trees.

Ellie and Drake sat for a long time, watching the clearing, their own lights out now, and Drake leaning into the passenger-side window. Ellie occasionally radioing up to the spotter plane for an update while Drake watched moths land on the glass. The insects drawn out by the light of the moon, dusty legs perched along the slant of the windshield. Their wings spread wide, fluttering for a moment, then moving on again to some brighter place among the trees.

They sat for another ten minutes before the radio crackled on again and the plane above gave them their next location. No more than a mile away. From where they sat looking out on the clearing, Drake could hear the crack of a high-powered rifle even from inside the cab of Ellie's truck.

"These guys are making a real night of it," Drake said.

Ellie turned the engine on and brought the truck around. "What are the chances they're still there when we show up?"

"Given what we've accomplished already, I'd say not very good." They were cutting back along the logging road with just their parking lights on, trying to keep a low profile, and in twenty minutes, when they found the location, they would see nothing but a bloody depression in the grass, just like what they had found every weekend for months now.

DRAKE SET THE keys on the counter and looked around. Sheri had left a note on the refrigerator telling Drake what time she would be home from work. The kitchen was completely clean, dishes put away, counter wiped down, a fresh set of towels hanging from the oven handle. Drake opened up the refrigerator and looked inside. Even the condiments had been organized inside the door. The leftovers from a few nights before neatly stacked in Tupperwares and the inside shelves soaped and cleaned. He closed the door without taking anything and went back to the counter.

The kitchen, dining area, and living room all one L-shaped room. Standing there he could see the small four-seat dining table, and then farther out around the bend of the L he saw part of the living room, where it led away to the bedrooms. After he'd married Sheri, they'd made a real effort to make the place their own, switching out his father's worn and mismatched furniture for a pair of sofas, a matching dining room table and buffet, and twin side tables for the living room. On one of the tables was the box his father had brought with him from Monroe. Drake stared at it for what seemed a long time, waiting until he heard the toilet flush and the door open down the hall.

Drake walked out and stood waiting for his father. Patrick stepped from inside the bathroom, pausing to flip the light off, and then wiping his hands down his pants to dry them. He was looking at all the pictures on the walls as he passed. Some that Sheri had taken, others that Sheri's mother had taken when Sheri was a girl. All black and white pastoral views of rolling farmland, or bent wood fencing. An artsy sort of thing that Drake had never quite understood, but that he'd grown used to and, truthfully, barely even noticed anymore. Everything, down to the two gray sofas in the living room, with their white piping, a sort of matching set.

Drake watched his father study one of the pictures for a moment before moving on. He passed his old bedroom, the one Sheri and Drake had taken for their own, and he paused, putting a finger to the door and pushing it open on its hinges. Drake tried to imagine what Patrick saw inside. The queen bed with the tall dresser nearby. The sheets pulled all the way to the top of the mattress and tucked beneath a collection of pillows, each a different size and shape, but somehow all appearing to belong. The whole scene put together that morning by Sheri. Her hands tightening down the corners of the bedding, running her palms along the topmost sheet, smoothing the wrinkles before pulling the comforter across it all.

Drake took a step and Patrick looked away from the room, noticing his son for the first time. "Different than you remember?" Drake asked.

Patrick didn't say anything and Drake wasn't sure if he'd even asked the question aloud. Lately it had been like that. Like Drake had tried to say something but forgotten to work his lips. Whole moments seeming to disappear from focus, then snapping back into a reality more clear and bright than anything before.

He watched his father step forward down the hall and push the door to Drake's childhood bedroom open. The door hinges heard in the silence as Patrick looked inside. It was the bedroom that Sheri and Drake had agreed to fix up for Patrick. The one he would have while he stayed with them.

Patrick turned and looked to Drake. "You didn't say anything about having a . . ."

Drake watched his father try to find the words. Two blank eyes looking back at him. "There was a complication," Drake said. "It's been almost a month now. She was pregnant, but we lost it."

Patrick turned again and pushed the door farther open. He was silhouetted in the hallway, the dark opening of the bathroom door behind him down the hall. "How far along was she?"

"Four months," Drake said. "After three they say you're in the clear." He hadn't moved from where he stood in the living room. He felt like he hadn't moved in weeks. "We painted the room those colors because we didn't know if it was going to be a girl or a boy. We thought we'd wait and see. Keep it a surprise." Drake heard the words come out of his mouth but he wasn't sure they were his. They were just words, mashed together, rushed, a series of observations, of hopes and thoughts on things that had never come to be.

"It was our office. We waited till after the third month to start buying things. To get the crib and find a changing table," Drake said. "I don't know why we haven't gotten rid of them now." He took a few steps and found he was standing next to his father. "We don't talk about it much. We keep the door closed."

What Drake didn't say was how he'd come into the room a week ago to put the single bed together for his father. He didn't say how he'd assembled it with the door closed and his back to the crib, trying not to look at the walls of the room, how they spread from light blue at the base, up toward the ceiling, where puffed white clouds were stenciled. The blue paint climbing farther up the walls, past the clouds, until it went pink, yellow, and orange like a sunset. The ceiling dotted with the same sort of glowing stars Drake remembered from his own childhood.

THEY STOOD AT the edge of the orchard, Drake and Patrick, looking down at the small patch of disturbed earth.

"Listen," Drake said. "She doesn't talk about it. We never even told anyone, we were going to wait until she started showing. Sheri didn't want people whispering about her at the restaurant. She didn't want to cut her hours until it was on her terms."

"So no one knows?" Patrick stood on one side of the little grave and Drake on the other. Patrick looked up at Drake and then looked away, across the orchard to where the house sat.

Drake checked his watch. Sheri's lunch shift ended in two hours. "We'd been seeing a doctor in Bellingham. She had some stomach pains one night and she went into the bathroom. She was in there a long time." Drake didn't know how to go on. He didn't know how to tell his father about how Sheri had locked the door, about the sound of her in there, the crying, the way her voice carried through the wood and came to Drake as if through the walls. The crying turning to sobbing and then the sobbing turning to silence. Drake having to ask again and again for her to open the door.

RECENTLY, THERE'D BEEN a lot of times when he had to remind himself they were going to be fine. That all would pass, and they could still have the future he had always thought they'd have.

Drake closed the refrigerator door and turned to look over at Sheri where she sat at the table. Patrick, sitting opposite, turned to look at Drake. "The lettuce," Sheri said. "There's a big plate in there with the cut tomatoes."

"Right," Drake said. He turned back to the refrigerator and opened the door. There it was, on the middle shelf. He reached in and brought it up and set it on the counter. It had happened again, he'd drifted, found himself just staring into space. The same thing had happened that morning, looking over the deer carcass, the cell phone in his hand and—for only a moment—no idea at all what to do.

He looked back at the table. Grilled hamburger patties, buns, a jar of pickles, potato chips, and all the condiments set out. Drake closed the door and brought the plate of lettuce and tomatoes around the counter and out into the dining room. Sheri trying to answer a question about her hometown, where her folks were from. Patrick leaning into the table with his forearms, his shoulders pushed forward as he listened. Drake set the plate down and asked, "Anyone want a beer?"

Sheri said she'd have one and when Patrick wanted one too, Drake went back to the kitchen and found three on the bottom shelf.

Everything with Sheri and Drake was in the open now. Sheri had come home after her lunch shift and met Patrick. Then she'd gone into the bathroom to take a shower as Drake unloaded the groceries Sheri had brought.

It was just before dinner when they were all outside by the grill at the bottom of the back stairs that Patrick brought up the changes to the house. The pictures and furniture. The way the house looked new to him. How well they'd taken care of it, painting the outside and updating the bathroom. Patrick and Sheri sitting on the stairs while Drake stood a few feet apart, spatula in hand as the burger meat spat and hissed on the grill. "It never looked this good when Bobby was growing up here." He gave Drake a quick glance before continuing. "I noticed the things you got for the second bedroom."

Sheri looked away toward the orchard and then turned back.

Patrick glanced at Drake again, almost asking permission. "Bobby told me about the baby. I wanted to say I'm sorry about what happened."

Sheri took a moment. "Thanks," she said. "We never told anyone about it and so when we lost it we didn't feel like we had anyone to talk with."

"I've felt the same way," Patrick said. With his fingers he worked a splinter up from the stair on which he sat and then flipped it away. "Bobby's mom and I tried for a while after Bobby started school here in Silver Lake, but with her getting sick we lost a couple pregnancies and then just figured we'd wait till she got better."

Drake was staring at his father. He'd never heard his father say anything like that to anyone. He'd never heard the man talk about anything personal, really. It was only when the burgers started to flame that he remembered they were there at all.

"They say it's common," Sheri said. "That's what they told us at least. They said it's just one of those things."

Drake flipped a few more burgers and let them cook. When they were finished he asked for a plate and waited while Sheri went inside to get one.

Now he stood looking into the refrigerator again, the beers suspended between his fingers. He closed the door and walked back to the dining room table. His father there with his wife, and Patrick telling Sheri about the day they'd had. Talking about how nice it was to sit at a table and have a burger, to drink a beer, to not have every day repeat itself like every day before.

"Did Bobby tell you about the wolf?" Patrick asked, taking the beer in his hand and twisting the top off. He didn't wait for Sheri to answer before going on. "First in the valley in fifty years." He was smiling now and for a moment he looked at Drake and then looked back to Sheri. "I bet he didn't tell you about the new Fish and Wildlife officer, either."

"HOW MANY DAYS will you be out?" Sheri asked.

Drake sat on the edge of their bed and slid one boot off, followed by the other. "Two to three, depending on how it goes." He looked back at Sheri. She was a few years younger than him, wrinkles just beginning to show around her eyes when she smiled.

They had met at the Chelan County Fair a couple years after Drake moved back to Silver Lake. Drake off for the weekend with one of the other deputies. Sheri with her friends, walking around the fairgrounds looking over the various prizes. The whole time Drake trying to catch her eye and missing every time. Watching her until he'd finally worked up the nerve to talk to her.

Now, turned on the bed, he looked back at her and thought over all the time that had passed in between. Sheri was already under the covers with her head resting on a pillow against the headboard. "The Fish and Wildlife officer wants me to take along my father."

Sheri turned in bed and moved her feet beneath the covers, digging one of her toes into Drake's side. "You mean the *cute* Fish and Wildlife officer that you didn't tell me about?"

Drake watched his wife for a second as he tried to decide whether she was playing with him, or if this conversation held any hidden pitfalls. He moved a hand down and caught her foot, pressing his thumb into the arch. She made a small animal sound. Her body curling up as she brought her other foot from beneath the covers and placed it on his lap.

"This how you passed the time last night?" Sheri said. "When you were out late on your stakeout?"

Drake screwed his face up, trying to look disgusted. He finished the massage on the first foot and started in on the other. "On Ellie? No," Drake said. "She's got horrible corns and the calluses on her soles cut my hands any time I try." Drake smiled back at his wife and Sheri dug her free foot into his side again, this time with a little more force, almost pushing him over.

"So she wants you to take your father along?" Sheri said.

Drake finished with the massage. "I haven't told him. I don't know if it's the best idea. Going along with us so soon after getting out." Drake pulled his T-shirt over his head and threw it to the corner of the room near a wicker hamper. "Seems like he's able to charm everybody except me."

"Pat has been perfectly fine," Sheri said, and Drake knew he had. Over dinner Patrick had asked Sheri questions about herself, where she worked. What she did at the Buck Blind, waitress or bartend. Who she knew in the valley. He complimented her on the garden out back and the line of time-warped mason jars she'd collected over the sink window. After dinner producing a gift from his little cardboard box of possessions, a whittled horse figurine he'd done for her in the prison shop. Sheri leaned in to kiss his cheek, and afterward asked, "How is it being back here in this house?"

"Strange," he said. "But in a good way. Everything is the same and everything is different. You know what I mean?"

Drake was leaning against the counter between the kitchen and dining area finishing his beer when Patrick looked away from Sheri, fixing Drake for a moment before going on. "Just strange, that's all." He looked back to Sheri and said, "It feels like I closed my eyes for a moment and then opened them again and twelve years passed." He shook his head, thanked Sheri and nodded to Drake, and said good night to them both.

Drake tried to put it all in perspective, but it just wouldn't go. For the next hour after his father had gone to bed Drake kept rolling around the idea of blinking away the past. Nothing like that had happened to him in those twelve years. All that time now seemed longer than anything. And everything before—when he'd been a boy in Silver Lake, then gone on to college—like water in his hand, bleeding through his fingers and then gone.

"The truth is," Drake said, "I can't trust him. I want to but I just can't."

"He's your father. I don't know what else you want from him. I'm sure he's sorry about it all."

"He's not the same person. He's not who I remember. Earlier, on our way home, he thought someone was following us."

"What do you want me to say?" She looked over at him, her eyes begging for understanding. "It's just nerves. When they told us he was getting out they said it might be difficult."

"Stop acting like you know him," Drake said, the words spilling out before he could stop them. "You don't know him like I do."

"Did you ever think that maybe *you* don't know him?" Sheri said. She'd pushed herself up on the bed now, her thin, fine-boned hands at her sides. The brown hair she usually wore at her shoulders, tied up in a ponytail, a smattering of freckles on her cheeks that would only grow darker as the season warmed. "You went to visit him only once in all his time away. At least I tried to write him and keep him in the loop. Telling him about you and what was going on here in Silver Lake, and he was good about responding, about wanting to hear about you. At dinner tonight you heard him yourself, talking about the land, about the hills and mountains, about how you two used to ride up into the valleys on horseback. It seems like going along with you would be something he'd want."

Drake shook his head. He knew already there was no point in going into it. He was being the asshole, but he didn't care, he was angry at his father, he'd been angry for a long time, and his father's coming home wasn't going to change that. He got up from the bed and crossed to the dresser, where he took out a pair of thin cotton pants and changed into them. For a little while, when Sheri had become pregnant—when they had stayed up late in bed, the lights off, making plans for the future and whispering to each other in the darkness even though there was no one else to hear—Drake had let himself forget about who he was, about where he'd come from and the reasons his life was the way it was. His father a convicted criminal, and anything Drake had wanted to be in his younger years no longer a reality he could ever hope for. "Don't you see that my life would be completely different if it wasn't for him?"

"You would have finished college," Sheri said.

"Yes."

"And you would never have come back to Silver Lake."

"Probably not."

"And you never would have met me."

Drake looked over at her; he didn't know what to say. It was the truth. He never would have met her. He started to tell her it wasn't true, but then gave up. He was being pigheaded. He loved her. He depended on her, knew she would never lie to him, that she would always give it to him straight. He felt bad for every unnamed thing that had been going through his head from the moment he'd woken up this morning, to this moment, here in their bedroom.

"I'm sorry," he said.

"I get it." Her voice losing some of the sharpness that had been growing in around the edges. "But it's not like you can invent a time machine and go back. Your life isn't going to change in that way. Not ever." The last few words beginning to tighten and catch in her throat as her voice broke.

"Hey," he said, and then, "Hey, hey, hey." His voice dropping to a whisper as he stood next to the dresser and looked back at her, knowing what she'd just said wasn't really about him alone. It was about them. It was about the baby they'd lost and a million other things that had been adding up to this moment alone.

She was crying now, softly, with her body turned away from him on the bed. The sheets pulled tight over her shoulders. He went around the bed and sat next to her. With his hand he tried to rub some warmth onto her back. "Hey," he said. "We're okay. We'll be just fine." But he didn't know it and he said it again, repeating it like a mantra.

For a while now he'd thought maybe they were both waiting to see who would leave first, and then when the parole board had called to tell Drake about his father's release, Drake had thought maybe they would stay together, maybe they would figure it out.

He knew losing the baby had hurt Sheri in a deeper way than he could understand. He hadn't been there for her. He'd been on the outside, listening through the bathroom door. Stuck between knowing what to do and not knowing. No clue. No training for a thing like this—for life to come at them out of the dark without warning. But hadn't that been it? Drake thought. One moment you're joking about calluses and corns and secrets and the next . . .

Drake sank into the bed and pulled Sheri toward him. Her wet face to his, warm and soft, strands of loose hair come free from her ponytail where they lay against her cheeks. She wasn't crying anymore and he listened to her snuffling breath. Her nose and mouth close into his shoulder and her hot breath on his skin.

"It's good," he said, taking his time, "that you were able to talk about it with my father today. That wasn't so bad, was it?" He felt her give the smallest nod. The crown of her head just below his chin. "We had to start talking about it sometime."

Everything Drake had thought or done in the last month felt like it was all coming together. His past life asking questions of his present. Still, he'd gone rigid when Patrick had started talking to Sheri about the baby. Drake just standing there holding the spatula, paralyzed. Everything inside telling him he needed to protect Sheri. But at the same time, realizing that he'd been waiting for this, waiting for this time of his life. The past meeting the future, Drake adding a new role, being a father, sweeping all the failures of the past away to make room for this new stage in his life. He'd wanted that baby more than anything he could remember wanting before.

Instead they'd lost it and now their marriage felt like something fragile, like an egg in the palm. Hold too tight and he'd crush the thin shell in his hand, too loose and he'd drop it on the floor.

He kept her close for a long time, feeling her breath whispering on his clavicle. He remembered the days after. Sheri home in bed, not wanting to move, not even bothering to take the medication the doctor in Bellingham had prescribed for her. He thought of this now and about how fragile she'd become in such a short time. So different from the person she'd become to him. The person he thought of as his wife. When she fell asleep he turned and flipped off the bedside light and lay there listening to the air in her lungs, feeling his heart beating in his chest.

He lay there until he was quite cold, feeling the chill on his skin but worried that if he moved to pull the sheets up and cover them both fully, she would wake. Eventually, when the goose bumps had risen and pricked his skin like chicken feathers, he got up from the bed and loosened the sheets from the bottom where Sheri had tucked them that morning. When he climbed back in, Sheri's breath had changed and he knew she was awake.

"I'm sorry," he said. "I feel bad about what I said to you. About another life. About things being different." He moved his fingers down the outside of her arm, feeling the little hairs that grew there, and for a while he wondered if she'd heard him.

"I thought tonight might be different," she said, eventually. "Meeting your father for the first time. Having him out of prison finally. To anyone else this would be a happy day."

Drake didn't know how he felt about it, either. He ran his hand down all the way to her fingers and squeezed them in his palm. He wanted to let her know he was there but he couldn't find the words to say it aloud.

"So you'll leave tomorrow?" she asked, her voice muffled by his arm.

"The next day," he said. "I need to go in to the department tomorrow. I need to talk to Gary about all this."

HE WOKE EARLY and made a pot of coffee in the kitchen. The sound of his father's snoring coming from beneath Drake's old bedroom door. All Patrick must have been thinking as he lay down in that bed last night, in that old room, painted now for a small child who had never arrived, while Sheri and Drake slept just down the hall in Patrick's old bedroom.

Drake poured a cup of coffee and tried to imagine what his father had thought before he closed his eyes. The unfamiliar becoming the familiar again. Like watching an old movie that hadn't been seen in years. The same lines replaying, the same scenes, and plot twists. A half-remembered life slowly coming back into focus.

Drake sipped at the coffee. He was barely awake. The thoughts in his head seeming random and disoriented, bumping around inside him with a sleep-starved stumble. After Sheri had drifted off, he'd slept poorly and in the morning he'd woken and dressed in his uniform. The light just up over the mountains and the back acre of their property—where the apple trees grew in unkempt lines all the way to the forest—bright with the morning sun.

He drank the coffee and watched the orchard. The year after his mother died, the apples had sat in the field unpicked. Drake, age nine, watching as a yearling bear wandered around, picking the apples from the ground. Going from tree to tree and eating what apples it could find. The bear drunk on rotting apples by the time it had reached the fourth tree.

His father had come to stand with him at the window as the yearling lay back against one of the apple trunks and rubbed its spine one way, then the other. Eventually falling back into the grass and rolling around with its arms half suspended in front of its face. The bear dozing for over an hour before lumbering off again.

Even now they didn't care for the trees as they should and half had gone wild, their tops lopsided and unkempt. The apples sagging on the branches in the fall, deer and elk showing up out of the forest to pick over the rotting apples on the ground, or as he had seen once or twice, put their hooves to the trunks and reach for the apples like giraffes extending their slender necks toward the most tender leaves.

Drake set his empty cup in the sink. He left the coffee machine on and collected his hat from near the door. When he'd gone a hundred feet down the wooded drive in his cruiser, he saw a Chevy Impala waiting out on Silver Lake Road. A man in a suit getting out of the car and closing the door behind him.

Drake pulled forward and when he came closer, he put down his window and said, "I was wondering if you'd show up."

The agent smiled and offered his hand. "How are you, Deputy?"

Drake took his hand and said, "Fine, Driscoll. It's been a long time."

Driscoll looked down the drive toward Drake's house. "How's the family? How's Sheri?"

"Still doesn't like you very much."

"She's got gentle sensibilities."

Drake watched Driscoll for a time, trying to figure the man out. There were only a couple reasons the agent would be waiting for him at the entrance to his drive. And none of those reasons meant anything good for Drake. "I'm guessing you didn't travel three hours from Seattle for a simple hello."

"Your father was released from prison yesterday, wasn't he?"

Drake thought of the two men who had been waiting in the McDonald's parking lot the day before. He hadn't thought much of them then but he was starting to reconsider. They hadn't looked like DEA men. "Driscoll, I hope you're here because you just wanted to make sure we got home all right?"

"Something like that," Driscoll said. A car went by on the road, the tires moving over the asphalt. Driscoll watched it go by and then when it was gone, leaned in again. "You think I could talk with you for a moment before you head in?"

"You got somewhere in mind?"

"Sure," Driscoll said, straightening up. "Follow me into town."

"YOU'RE SO FUCKING predictable," Drake said, looking around the doughnut shop.

"Just blending in. I thought all you small-town cops hung out in places like this." Driscoll took a seat in a far booth, away from the main windows. He gestured to the bench across from him.

Drake sat, throwing his hat on the table, and when the girl looked up from the counter, Driscoll ordered a black coffee and Drake asked for a maple bar. Their table far enough down the side of the doughnut shop that they wouldn't be noticed by anyone driving by.

When the girl brought the doughnut and coffee over, she nodded to Drake, and Drake said, "Thanks, Cheryl."

"I didn't know you were on a first-name basis here," Driscoll said, his head turning to watch the girl walk away.

"You've seen this town," Drake said. "We're all on a first-name basis. She probably even knows who you are—probably made you the moment you drove that unmarked Impala into town."

Driscoll waited for the girl to go into the back before he spoke again. He fingered his coffee cup with two meaty hands and looked down into it for a long time, like someone wishing into a well. "I need to talk to you about something," Driscoll said. "You remember how we first met?"

"Sure," Drake said. "You accused me of being a dope runner like my father."

Driscoll chuckled and looked up from his coffee. "I gave you a hard time, yes, but I wanted to make sure I could talk to you frankly. No beating around the bush. No leading you on, no feints."

"You're about to tell me why the DEA has been following me around."

Driscoll gave him a dead stare. "What do you mean?"

A strained laugh escaped Drake's lips as he looked around the doughnut shop like Driscoll was playing a joke on him. "The two men? The ones who followed us up the interstate yesterday morning in the black Lincoln. They were your guys, right?"

Driscoll took a sip from the coffee and then put it back on the table. He'd grown bigger in the two years since they'd last seen each other, his shoulders rounded and the jowls of his face thick on his jawline. White all the way through his hair in a way it hadn't been before. "Deputy, I didn't put any guys on you."

"Are you sure?"

"They were following you?" Driscoll asked. He had taken a small notebook from the inside pocket of his jacket and he wrote down "Black Lincoln."

"My father thought they were. I told him he was being paranoid."

"That's probably true," Driscoll said. "I'll check it out for you, though, just in case. You remember anything else about them?"

Drake went down the list, two white males, one larger than the other. He gave Driscoll the exit number and a more thorough description of the vehicle they were driving. He couldn't remember the license number. "Is this something I should be worried about?" Drake asked.

"Have you seen them since?"

"No."

"Then I wouldn't worry about it. You're probably right, your father is being paranoid." He tucked the notebook away in his jacket again and then sat forward with his forearms on the table and his fingers interlaced. "I think you know me and your father have a little history together. I think I made that pretty clear from the beginning. The thing I didn't tell you before is that I was part of the team that eventually brought him in."

"Just a little something you forgot to mention. Right, Driscoll?"

"I didn't want you blowing it out of proportion."

"You'd already accused me of being a criminal. How much worse could it have been?"

"I'm the guy who put the cuffs on him. Pushed his face into a table just up the street here."

"What the fuck, Driscoll?"

The agent raised his hands from the table. "I needed you to think we were on the same team, you know?"

"Jesus. We were on the same team . . . we are on the same team." Drake felt himself growing angrier, remembering how Driscoll had brought him into the interrogation room in the Seattle federal building and treated him like he was part of the problem, like he was the one smuggling drugs in from Canada. He reached down and straightened his leg, feeling his kneecap click. "I was shot twice," Drake said. "How many times have you been shot?"

Driscoll smiled, obviously enjoying this. "Let's not get into a pissing contest, Bobby."

"Why are you here, Driscoll?"

"Well, your father is out."

"Yes, and he served his time."

"What are his plans now that he's out?"

"So far his plans seem to be screwing with my life."

"Look, Bobby, I want to be straight with you here. We made an example out of Patrick Drake. We put him away for a lot of years. But if we could have proved everything we had on him from the start, he'd still be in prison. He did a lot of bad shit."

Drake took a bite of his maple bar, thinking it through. He didn't have a clue what Driscoll was talking about or what his father was doing. What his father had planned now that he was out. Coming north on the interstate Patrick had told Drake not to worry about him. It was all covered. "I'm not helping you put him back in prison," Drake said.

The smile spread across Driscoll's face again. "I thought you said we were on the same team."

"I remember now why my wife doesn't like you," Drake said.

"You could lose your house, Deputy. That's as straight as I can give it to you. You're in trouble, and your father is most certainly the root of your problems."

"What are you talking about?"

"I'm talking about the fact that before Sheriff Drake went to prison, two guys were found dead in a gravel lot north of Bellingham."

"That's a whole other county," Drake said.

"Well the thing about it is that they were two guys who had ripped off a lot of money from someone big. Someone your father worked for."

"Sounds like they had it coming."

"Who's saying that?" Driscoll asked. "You or your father?"

"I'm not my father."

"A lot of money went missing," Driscoll said. "Hundreds of thousands. It was drug money and—from what I hear—a portion of it was your father's. So, naturally, a big deal like this gets my attention, and I talk to my sources and they say Patrick was the one who tracked the two men down. Said they stashed the money before Patrick found them. Only I go around and start asking questions from the wives of these guys—real trashy sort of girls. Moss all over their houses, rent-to-own sort of lifestyle. You get what I'm saying?"

Drake nodded. His head turned toward the front windows, just looking at the sunlight outside, wishing he could be somewhere else.

"They say they don't know anything about the missing money. They admit to everything else. What their husbands were up to, how they did the job, who put them onto it, everything. Only they don't know anything about the money. Are you following me, Deputy? Twelve years later one of the wives is still living in the same house. She's paid off her rent-to-own couch, but there's still moss on her siding, and she's taking in welfare checks to pay for the kids. The other one isn't doing as well. Couldn't make her house payments, lost her place, and is living with her brother's family, working three jobs, all that horrible stuff."

Driscoll took a drink of his coffee. Drake knew he'd paused just to push the knife in deeper. A grin on Driscoll's face that heralded the coming twist of the handle.

"So you might want to ask: where's the money?" Driscoll said. "Well that's the interesting part. That's the part that gets me up in the morning and keeps me watching those two poor widows. Because you know what, that money is gone. It never made it back to the smugglers up in Canada. The widows don't have it. And little by little I start to wonder where it's gone and who has it. It's a lot of money to go missing, a lot of money that most anyone would do most anything to hold on to. And so I go to Monroe to ask your father this question a few years back. I tell him if he knows where it is and he's willing to point the finger at the people he works for, who sent him to do what he did, he can get out of prison right then and there. Time already served. He's off the hook. The murders weren't him, I know that. I just want to know where the money is and who sent it down this way in the first place. Hell, we went hard on him, too hard. And you know what, I don't think Sheriff Drake was in on it alone."

"You're saying my father didn't kill those men?"

"For now I'm giving Patrick the benefit of the doubt."

"How much are we talking about?" Drake asked.

"Two hundred thousand. Not much in this day, but twelve years ago it would have been a good amount. Enough to get out of the business. Maybe start a new life. For your father to settle his debts."

"You think that's what he was doing?"

"I don't know," Driscoll said. "That's why I'm coming to you. I'm asking for your help on this."

"Go talk to someone else. I'm certainly the last person my father would tell anything to," Drake said.

"That's right," Driscoll said. "But what I've heard and what I keep hearing is that your father and his deputies were pretty tight back in the day. Bend a few rules. Get away with a little here and there. Wasn't your current sheriff, Gary Elliot, one of his deputies?"

"That's taking it too far," Drake said. "Gary gave me my job after my father went away. For Christ's sake, he lives in a two-bedroom apartment over the Laundromat. He's not a rich man."

"I know where he lives," Driscoll said. "I even know how much money he has in his bank account. Look, we've gone through just about everything. Before you gave up being a basketball star and came back from Arizona we even went through your house."

"And you didn't find a thing, did you?"

Driscoll laughed. "This is just like old times, isn't it?"

"Yeah," Drake said. "I'm just waiting for you to accuse me of being a criminal mastermind. You got anything more you want to tell me?"

"That's it. That's all there is. I thought I owed you a talk at least. I thought you should hear it from me."

"Don't give it to me like that, Driscoll. What is it you really want?"

"I just want you to keep your eyes open. Stay sharp. Weeks from now I don't want to see you across the table from me in a federal interrogation room."

"You want me to tell you if my father starts spending ten-thousand-dollar bills."

"Just be careful, that's all I'm saying. We're friends, aren't we? I'm only asking you to keep your father close for a little while. If nothing comes of it, then I'll go back to sitting around the office, throwing the tennis ball at the wall. No harm done." Driscoll slid a card out across the table. "In case you lost the last one I gave you."

Drake picked up the card and read the title and name: Regional Director, Agent Frank Driscoll. "If you've got all this information on my father why didn't you just threaten him with life in prison for killing those two men?"

Driscoll smiled. "If there was evidence to prove it, I would have."

"You're out on a limb here, aren't you?"

"Doesn't mean I'm wrong."

"Doesn't mean you're right, either."

"I'm here to help you out, Deputy. I tell you about the fact that maybe you brought a murderer into your home and on top of that, your boss over at the Sheriff's Department might have been involved, and you think I'm the one doing you a disservice?"

"You're a fucking cheery guy, you know that, Driscoll? I ought to have you over for more barbecues."

"Yeah, well, tell that to your wife and see how it goes."

DRAKE GOT INTO the department thirty minutes late and went straight into Gary's office.

"I bet you're wondering why I set you up with Fish and Wildlife," Gary said. He was sitting at his desk, looking through the morning paperwork.

Drake nodded, his eyes casting out around the office like he might find a bloodstained sack of money in the corner. He had to check himself and keep his focus on Gary.

"I know you've been helping Ellie out with that poaching thing, and this didn't seem too much of a stretch," Gary said. A few years younger than Patrick, Gary had been like an uncle to Drake growing up. He'd given Drake his job, even loaned him money till Drake could sell off some of his father's land to buy groceries and pay for the mortgage on their house. Since then Gary had begun to show his age. The uniform rounded on his stomach and the hair that had once been red now gone thin on his pink scalp. Worry lines across his forehead deep and defined on the skin.

"The truth is," Gary was saying, "your fellow deputies, Andy and Luke, could have done it, but you know the valley better than anybody and you're the one who keeps getting the calls as it is." Gary shook his head like something was funny. "Hell, you're about the only one besides Ellie that gives a shit about that wolf. I think a lot of people would rather you just shot it, and to be honest, I'm one of them."

Drake had his hat sitting in his lap and as Gary talked he turned it slowly with his fingers. "You know my father is out?" Drake said.

"I know," Gary said. "I was the one who approved your day off."

"You ever visit him in Monroe?"

Gary cracked a smile, the flesh beneath his chin drawing tight. "You know I did. I haven't in a long while, but I did."

"Except for one time, I didn't visit him at all," Drake said.

"He's staying with you and Sheri?"

"He has my old bedroom."

Gary nodded; he leaned back in the chair and fixed his eyes on the ceiling. The office had been Patrick's at one time. Now all the pictures that had lined the walls were gone and Gary had replaced them with his own. Pictures from the fishing trips he took to Alaska, one with

Drake holding a king salmon and looking proudly at the camera. The trips a yearly vacation for Gary, sometimes on his own but often with one of the deputies from the department. And Drake knew, too, that if Patrick had never gone away to prison it would have been his father there in the picture instead of him.

"You guys were close when I was a kid."

"Yes, we were," Gary said. "It's a shame how it all turned out." Other photographs showed Gary in the Cascade foothills, kneeling next to big bucks he'd shot, their antlers turned up in his hand and the buck's eyes staring out at the camera, dull and black as those of the deer Drake had seen the other day. "You should tell Patrick we say hello. Me, Andy, and Luke, all of us, tell him that and say we'll get a few beers one of these nights."

"What I mean to say is that my father just got out yesterday. I don't know if I should be headed off into the hills on a wolf hunt."

"I can stop by and check up on him, if that helps you out at all," Gary said. "I don't think that wolf can wait more than a day."

Drake thought about what Driscoll had told him only thirty minutes before. The image in his mind of two old lawmen sitting on Drake's porch counting the cash they'd stolen twelve years ago. Drake was having a hard time keeping his focus. All the things Driscoll had said to him earlier at the doughnut shop were crawling up his spine like spiders through a tin pipe. "Maybe I'll just take Dad with us," Drake said.

"Is that you or Ellie talking? I already told her that was a bad idea."

"I told her the same," Drake said. "But I'm not going to leave him around the house doing who knows what."

Gary smiled. "Don't trust the old man yet?"

"Something like that," Drake said. He was having a hard time trusting anyone at this point. "Did Ellie mention when she wanted to head out?"

"She was thinking you'd go out tomorrow, early, as soon as the sun is up."

Drake collected his hat and stood. He was holding it in his hand and about to turn when Gary said, "Son, don't put too much faith in your buddy Driscoll. He was around here a good amount when your father went away. There was a lot of media and law enforcement throwing crazy theories around and he was one of the main guys throwing the mud."

Drake ran his fingers under the band of his hat. His eyes on the floor, feeling exposed.

"Andy's oldest daughter went to school with that girl over at the doughnut shop, Cheryl. Maybe it comes with the job, but the girl likes to get in people's business—she likes to talk, too, and it just worked its way up through the grapevine. It's the nature of a small town. I wouldn't think too much on it. I've been expecting we might see Agent Driscoll around here again at some time."

Drake let himself out and closed the door. Andy and Luke at their desks. Drake went and sat in his chair. He felt defeated. He had no clue what to think about any of it, but mostly he just felt pissed off. Until an hour ago he'd thought Driscoll was his friend, now he was saying one thing and Gary was saying another. Two people Drake had always trusted.

Drake sat at his desk and looked around the office. Whatever seed Driscoll had planted was growing. Roots coiling around his chest like a vine on a tree and Drake there in the office scared to see how it bloomed.

DRAKE MADE IT into the early afternoon before he went back into Gary's office and asked to take the rest of the day off.

When Drake pulled up to the house he saw his father one hundred feet away at the edge of the clearing where the apple orchard ran out and the alder fence had once sat. Patrick stood there for a moment and then bent a knee into the grass, where with one hand he seemed to be looking something over. He wore a set of jeans and one of his old flannels. His scalp and beard shaved clean. And the newly exposed skin white and puckered in places where the razor had nicked his neck and jawline.

Drake slipped the car into park. For a while he watched his father where he knelt at the edge of the clearing. He didn't know what to think about the man. And it was only when Drake got up out of the cruiser and closed the door that his father raised his eyes to Drake.

By the time he made it across the orchard to his father, Patrick was standing again. "I've never seen you in the uniform," Patrick said. His eyes on Drake, taking in the cop browns he wore.

Drake tried to smile. He looked Patrick over and then he looked back at the house, where he could see Sheri's profile through one of the kitchen windows.

"You get off early?" Patrick asked.

"Yes," Drake said, turning back to his father. "Gary let me go. I thought I'd just come home for a little while. What's been going on?"

"Sheri showed me around. We picked up some groceries, had lunch, really just took it easy."

"And now?"

Patrick bent and lifted something from the grass. "I came to look the fence over." In his hand was a rotted piece of alder. "I was thinking maybe I could help you build it again—maybe this weekend? With the two of us we could finish in an afternoon."

"Yeah," Drake said. "I don't see why not." He looked his father over one more time and then made an excuse about getting out of his work clothes. He said good-bye and then, halfway to the house, turned and saw his father still there at the edge of forest, picking pieces of rotten alder from the ground.

Later, dressed in a pair of jeans and a sweatshirt, Drake came into the kitchen and stood watching Sheri peel carrots over the sink. "You never left him alone the whole day?"

She told him that his father had slept until ten. Then they'd walked to the lake, and gone shopping for that night's meal.

"How long has he been out there?"

"Not long," Sheri said.

Drake took the few remaining steps to where she stood. Through the window he watched his father carry a load of wood and dump it into the burn pile out behind the house. "So you never left him alone the whole day?"

"He went to the bathroom on his own," Sheri said. "I didn't sign up for anything like that." Sheri was laughing now, looking to Drake like she thought the joke was so funny. Like she belonged on a stage in front of a packed house.

All Drake could think about was the money and if his father had somehow stashed it under the bathroom floorboards, or in a waterproof bag in the porcelain tank. All of his ideas ridiculous. He was turning into his father, seeing things that were not there.

THE MAN CAME IN wearing a black suit, ill fitted to his skinny body, and ordered two coffees and a Danish to go. While he waited he tapped his fingernails in rhythm to the stereo playing behind the counter and watched the girl walk away to the coffee machine, where she filled the two cups. When she came back he thanked her and paid.

He balanced the two coffees in the claw of his upturned palm. And as he went out the door, holding it with his hip, he already saw how the Danish had begun to stain the small paper bag. The paper turned waxen with pastry grease in the cold early evening air.

When he took his seat in the car again, he gestured to the glove box, asking the big man for a pen and paper, all the while watching the shop and drinking from his cup of coffee. As the minutes passed, they kept time by checking a prepaid cell phone they'd picked up at a convenience store and that they'd charged while driving.

They sat in the car for an hour before the girl closed the shop. When she was about a block up they started the car and pulled forward, coming even with the girl as she stopped at the corner.

The skinnier of the two men drove, slowing to make pace with the girl. He put the window down and called to the girl by name.

The girl paused, her eyes searching the face that looked up at her from the driver's-side window. "Hello?" she said, unsure at first. And then as she recognized the face staring out at her from inside the car. "How was the coffee?"

"It's Cheryl, isn't it?" the man said. His hair was slicked back and the suit was too big on his thin bones. He had one arm out the window and he moved his hand while he talked, gesturing to the uniform she wore. "It's right there on your name tag."

She turned and looked back toward the shop and then looked around her. The sun was almost gone down, a pale light now hanging in the air to the west and the street blue with shadow.

"You know Deputy Drake?" the man asked. "And maybe you met our boss Frank Driscoll today? They were in your shop earlier."

"You guys work for the DEA?" She shifted her weight from one foot to the other and then stepped forward, bending a little to take in both men.

"Have you seen either of them?" the skinny man went on. "Driscoll asked us to come up. He said there might be some trouble with Deputy Drake's father. Driscoll gave us the address but we're having a hard time." He held out a coffee-stained piece of paper for her to see. The address, written in blue ink, clouded and distorted with dried liquid.

She stepped up to the black car, a foot's distance from its open window, and took the small piece of paper from the man. She looked the address over and then gave it back. "I can see why you'd have trouble with this," she said.

"Some of the coffee spilled. It's important we find the deputy's place."

"Is Bobby in some sort of danger?"

"We don't think so but Driscoll asked us to come up. We heard they had coffee in your shop this morning. Would you mind showing us the address?"

The girl looked around on the street. The sound of plates and cutlery could be heard far down the block from the open kitchen window of the Buck Blind. The girl hesitated, looking to the restaurant a few hundred feet away. "You can't call your boss?"

"That's the thing," the skinny man said. "We're already late. He probably wouldn't be too happy."

She looked in at the two men and told them it was only a couple minutes away. The big man in the passenger seat was dressed informally in a worn pair of jeans and a padded flannel button-up. The last few buttons on the shirt left loose at the collar to allow for the rolls of skin that appeared below his jaw.

The driver turned and looked back down the street and then when he turned back, still holding the coffee-stained address between his fingers, said, "You show us where it is and we'll have you back in five minutes."

"Five minutes?"

"Yep, you'd really be helping us out." He reached behind him and pushed the door open from the inside. "Get in," he said. "We'll bring you right back."

She stepped in and brought the door closed behind her.

When they came to the intersection with the dangling caution light she told them where to turn and they followed the lake road. The shadow of the mountains over much of the lake, but far to the east a sliver of gold was still visible on the water.

"You heard what Driscoll was saying to the deputy today?" the man asked.

"Some of it," she said.

The man smiled up at her reflection in the rearview. "So you were eavesdropping?"

"No, of course not."

"It's okay if you were," the man said, kidding her still, his smile wide beneath his thin lips. "If the deputy is in trouble it's better we hear about it sooner than later."

"I didn't hear anything really. They were talking about his father," Cheryl said. "You're here about his father, right? So you must know the story about him."

"We've heard some stories."

The man watched her in the rearview and when they came to the driveway leading to the Drake property Cheryl pointed it out and told them how far up the house was. "Are you two here to take him back to prison?" she asked.

The man looked up at her in the rearview again and then broke away. He was driving on the lake road still, Drake's driveway now a quarter mile behind them. "What's up ahead here on this road?" the man asked.

"Nothing. Logging. A couple more houses."

"Can you keep a secret?" the man asked. His eyes were on her again and with his free hand he touched a button and dropped all the locks on the doors.

The sound made Cheryl jump, her fingers to the door handle before she knew she had placed them there. When she looked back to the front, the big man was climbing over the seat with one large hand outstretched toward her.

DRAKE SAT ON THE back stairs, drinking a beer and staring out on the orchard. The sky tinged a deep blue in the west and the first stars already showing. The little garden Sheri kept, dug out and lined with earth-turned rows.

He put the beer to his lips and tipped the bottle back. He'd given it a lot of thought through the day. What Driscoll had said, what Gary had tried to tell him, his father. It was all a mess. Drake kept running it around in his head. A footrace that never seemed to have an ending, just around and around until someone dropped dead.

He scuffed the heels of his boots over the dirt at the base of the stairs, digging a hole. The apple trees set in lines all the way to the forest. A patch of disturbed earth at the edge of the orchard where they'd buried their child in a grave the size of a shoebox. No one but them—and now Drake's father—knowing anything about it. All of their lives somehow entwined by this fact.

The new knowledge about his father adding to it all and piling on. He didn't think he would tell Sheri about Driscoll's coming to see him that morning, about what he had to say. He didn't want her trying to guess, as he was now, whether there was any truth in the story. He didn't want to add to the pressure. A feeling that had settled over Drake all through the day. Like everybody had agreed to take a ride on Drake's back—Driscoll, Patrick, and Gary—all at once and none of them offering to get off.

Drake took a swallow of the beer, tipping the bottle back, trying to calm his nerves. There was nothing he could do but wait it out, and when the spring on the kitchen door opened and then snapped shut, Drake already knew it was his father simply from the way the boards on the back porch took his weight. Drake didn't turn and he waited for Patrick to come down the steps and sit next to him. His father's hand on Drake's shoulder as he sat. The first time they'd touched in twelve years. The feeling strange on Drake's skin.

"Thinking some deep thoughts?" his father asked. He was holding a beer in one hand and he twisted the top off with his other. When Drake didn't respond, Patrick said, "This was always where I found you when you lost a basketball game."

"It's been a while since high school," Drake said. He finished the beer in one pull and set it on the step beside him. The smell of the yard all around him, fresh turned earth from a few days before, left to bake in the sun.

"Sheri asked me what she should plant this year," his father said. "I told her I don't have a clue about that sort of thing. Your mother was always the one who dealt with the growing season."

Drake nodded. A desire in him to just come out with it. To tell his father everything.

"You've made a life of it here," Patrick said.

"I've tried."

"Your mother kept a garden in the exact same spot."

Drake nodded again. "I remember." He felt dazed, his body thrown off balance as he looked into the rows of turned earth, avoiding his father's eyes.

"I know you didn't choose this life. Coming back here. Taking the job with Gary. I should have told you that earlier on," Patrick said. "I meant to tell it to you years ago. I'm sorry about that."

Drake nodded.

"It was easy money for me," Patrick said. "Your mom died and by the time you finished high school there was so much debt. I couldn't figure any other way. I was the sheriff, there was no moving up, there was no way to make more money. I really didn't know what else to do."

Drake turned and looked Patrick over. The clean shave on his face. The way he used to look when Drake was a boy. The same familiar way Drake remembered seeing him every day. His hand running over the skin of his cheek and along his jawline as he talked, his fingers searching out the small imperfections, the little scrapes he'd given himself.

"I could have waited," Patrick went on. "There were things I could have done. Legal things. But I didn't have the patience for it and the bank was telling me I needed to make my payments or they were going to take the house away. It felt like they were trying to take your mother away from me all over again." Patrick held a hand to his face, pinching the bridge of his nose. The sound of his breath amplified in his palm, whistling between his fingers. "I know it was wrong," he said. "It was all wrong . . ."

Drake didn't say anything, he didn't want to speak, even knowing it was his turn, that his father wanted him to say something, Drake couldn't do it. Patrick wanted him to tell him it was okay and the past was the past. At one time Drake thought maybe he could, but there just was no doing it now, not after everything he'd heard that morning. And now Drake feared if he said anything it would come out hateful, the words tearing up out of him like blood from a wound.

"When your mother got sick I knew things would be different. And when she didn't get better, when she kept getting worse, I knew the life we'd planned would never be." Drake listened as his father took a sip off the bottle and then set it back on the wood. "Somewhere in there we jumped the tracks," his father said. "One life going on the way it should have been, and another taking a completely different path."

"Dad, don't talk to me about this anymore," Drake said. His voice quivering in his throat. "I don't want to hear it from you." He felt the words slip up over his tongue and lash out. Nothing he could do to stop them, and a desire to simply spill it all out into the night air and be done with it.

So much hate for his father. For the last twelve years, and more, he realized, all the way back to when he was a boy and his father had brought him to see his mother in the hospital. Hours away. The clinic in Silver Lake not equipped to handle things like cancer, like people who needed to be held up on life support, wired up into the electricity while machines did the work the body no longer could.

Next to him on the stairs, he felt his father stand. "I needed to say that to you."

"You've said it."

"I'll see you inside, then."

Drake heard his father turn and move up the stairs, the grit working beneath his shoes on the wood. "Dad," Drake said. "I was going to tell you later, over dinner." Drake paused, trying to get the words right, trying to calm the dangerous beat he felt in his heart. "I'm headed into the hills tomorrow, west of the lake. We'll be tracking that wolf. Ellie asked if you would come. I think I'd like you there as well."

A long silence followed. Drake picked up the empty bottle next to him and ran a fingertip over the top, finding the slight imperfection in the glass where the two edges had been sealed together in the factory. He thought about his father twenty-five years ago, his mother in the hospital bed, he thought about the years that followed. He thought about all that had happened twelve years before. He thought about the money, about Driscoll, and Gary, and his father.

"Good," his father said. "I've been meaning to get up into those hills."

AFTER DINNER DRAKE lay in bed next to Sheri and tried to close his eyes. The thoughts in his head going around and around without end.

Sheri sat there with her back to the headboard. "You going to tell me what's up?"

"There's nothing to tell," Drake said. His eyes still closed and his arms crossed over his chest beneath the sheets.

"You didn't say much during dinner, and those questions you were asking me before, about your father and where he'd been through the day. He can't be that bad."

Drake turned away, opening his eyes and staring at the wall until Sheri put out the light. She was resting with her face to him and he felt her breath on the back of his neck and her body close into his. After five minutes had passed Drake asked, "What makes you trust him so much?"

"What makes you not trust him at all?"

"A lot has been said about him."

"You've heard it all before," Sheri said. "It's not like you haven't gotten used to the things people say."

"Not all of it."

"Well, you know him better than me," Sheri said, sarcasm in her voice.

Drake had his eyes open still, the dark room was coming back into focus and he saw the nightstand and the wall farther on. "What makes you so certain about him?"

"I just feel for him," Sheri said. "For where he's been and what he's had to do to get here with us. It took a lot for him to come back here after everything. To the house he used to share with your mother and you. For him to come to Silver Lake. I have sympathy for him, but I also think it takes a lot of courage."

Drake turned so that he could face her, hoping that she could see the smile on his face when he said, "You've got a soft heart, Sheri."

"Well, you've got a heart made of stone," she said, pushing at him a little beneath the sheets, her own smile now visible.

"He's here because he has to be. We said we'd take care of him, didn't we? It was one of the conditions of his release."

"I know he seems like a loner but he's not really to blame for what he is. Not totally."

In the dim light of their bedroom Drake lay watching his wife. He didn't know what else to say to her. The trip into the woods with Ellie was less than eight hours away. All the things people had said about Patrick Drake over the years and now he was here. Sleeping in the room down the hall, resting up for his chance at the mountains.

Drake lay there for a long time thinking it over. Sheri falling asleep and the thoughts in his head whistling around like leaves over an empty lot, nothing to catch them or anchor them to the earth as they moved. All the while, Drake simply trying to see the world through Sheri's eyes, but he just couldn't.

He didn't want his father to be any of the things people were saying about him. Mostly, though, he didn't want his father to be a murderer on top of everything else he'd already been convicted of.

PART II
THE HUNT

THE SUN WAS JUST up over the mountains when Drake pulled his cruiser past the cattle fence. The barbed wire stained black where the deer had been, but little else to say what happened two days before. Patrick sat in the passenger seat watching the houses go by as they rounded the lake. The smell of coffee thick inside the car from one of the old chipped cups Patrick held in his hands, amplified by the closed-in air packed tight between the windows.

Drake had half expected to see Driscoll at the end of his drive that morning, sitting there on the hood of his Impala, just waiting for them. Only he hadn't been there and Drake turned south along the lake and followed the road, feeling loose and untethered from his day and the expectations he usually had for himself. The home he'd made the last twelve years in Silver Lake shattered by what Driscoll had said. No way of knowing how any of this would turn out. His father next to him in the passenger seat and all they'd need for the wolf hunt loaded up in the back.

As he pulled past the field he saw the Fish and Wildlife truck waiting beneath the trees. The brown vehicle tucked into the shadows up a small access road that wound back into the forest and ran the perimeter of the property, ending at the farmhouse. Ellie standing there with the tailgate down and a rifle pitched skyward. The red tufts of tranquilizers sitting there beside her on the metal with the rest of her gear.

Drake parked the car off the side of the road and got out. He came and stood next to the truck with his arms resting over the top of the bed. A good amount of gear laid out below. "You really think you're going to take her down with one of those?" he said.

Ellie finished packing the tranquilizers into the case and then zipped it closed. "Why wouldn't I?"

"You're supposed to use silver bullets, aren't you?"

Ellie smiled. "You think this wolf is going to turn into a person after we catch up to her?"

"It might explain why she's all alone. The last of her kind."

"A wolf in these mountains is just about as rare as Bigfoot."

"Some might tell you a wolf is rarer than Bigfoot," Drake said.

Ellie laughed, hitching the strap of the rifle over her shoulder and leaning into the bed to grab up her pack. "Well, we'd probably have to put Bigfoot on the endangered species list as well, wouldn't we?" Over the uniform she wore a green fleece vest. Her hair, kept back from her eyes with a rubber band, bobbed from shoulder to shoulder as she moved one item after another out of the truck bed, setting them on the ground in a wide circle at her feet. "What about him?" Ellie nodded toward Patrick where he sat in Drake's backseat with the door pushed open, pulling on his boots. His coffee cup and pack on the ground near his feet. "Is he going to come over here and tell me to wear garlic around my neck and make sure to stab the beast in the heart with a wooden cross?"

"Don't be silly, Ellie. We may be talking werewolves here, but not vampires."

Ellie gave him a wry look, raising her hands in mock surrender. "Of course. But you know after all the rumors that have been going around the last dozen years, your father's probably going to be the scariest thing in these woods the next couple days."

Drake looked back to where his father sat, lacing his boots. In the last twelve years, he knew, Patrick had been called a number of things, which in their own way had reflected on Drake. He didn't know what to say about that. He knew Ellie was joking with him, and he wanted to laugh and play it off like it didn't matter, but the comment had hit too close to home and he was struggling to find anything to say.

He was still trying to find a way to keep the darkness out of their conversation when he heard gravel popping beneath tires as a car came down the ranch access road. The headlights cutting through the shadowed tree trunks for only a moment before they came around the corner and Drake saw the bubble lights on top of the car.

Ellie straightened at the sound and then moved some of her gear to the side of the road, close in to the wheels of her truck, leaving enough room for the cruiser to go past.

"You tell Gary where we would be this morning?" Drake asked.

Ellie turned and looked to Drake for a moment. "I asked Gary to go talk to the rancher for us. I thought asking for a spot to leave our vehicles would be better if it came from him. Fish and Wildlife aren't exactly the ranchers' favorites right now. They'd all rather see this wolf shot than have us out here trying to save her."

Drake glanced to his right and found his father up now, standing about three feet off, watching as the cruiser drew to a stop close by.

"It's been a long time," Gary said to Patrick through the open window. His arm up over the passenger seat as he spoke to Patrick. "I hope your boy told you Andy and Luke say hello. We'd like to have you down to the Buck Blind when you're finished here. We can catch up over a few drinks."

Patrick nodded. "Just like old times out here, isn't it?" he said, bending at the waist so that he could look in through the passenger window at Gary.

Gary glanced back over his shoulder to where Drake stood. "I don't want you to take this the wrong way, Pat. Going on a wolf hunt a few days after being let out of Monroe. I already told Bobby and Ellie how I feel about all this. Making you the third wheel. If you want, I can give you a ride back into town and we can grab breakfast.

You shouldn't be going up into the mountains your first week out."

"It's good for me to get back into the hills. Maybe it will help me tame some old demons."

"I guess it is just like old times, then," Gary said. "We'll catch up, don't worry. I wouldn't have much time today anyway."

"You sure you don't need me?" Drake asked, stepping closer to the car.

"No. It's nothing," Gary said. "Cheryl didn't make it home last night. Her parents called us pretty late. You know how this goes. She's probably shacked up at a boyfriend's somewhere." He nodded back toward Patrick and said, "You just watch out for your father, Bobby. I don't want anyone else going missing around here."

Drake nodded, watching as a thin smile slipped across Gary's face.

"I don't want it to be anything like old times out here," Gary said. "Make sure your father doesn't step out from behind a tree with a couple sacks of BC bud under each of his arms." Gary laughed. "See you both in a day or so, okay? Pat, let's grab that drink when you get back."

"Okay," Patrick said, stone-faced and impossible to read. "You and the boys." He moved back from the door and straightened up.

Gary laughed once more. "Happy hunting." Then he pulled away down the road and they watched him take the turn and head north toward Silver Lake.

SOMETIME AROUND NOON they lost the trail. No tracks in the moist ground. No broken branch, or scat, or tuft of hair. Nothing to go on. The forest all around them, dense and black with shadow. Sword fern and moss all across the forest floor. The large trunks of fir and hemlock stretching down from above and the sky only visible through slim blue cracks in the canopy.

Ellie stood and marked their location on the map. She was holding a GPS in her hand and as she looked around at the forest, she measured their bearings against the map. Drake found an old deadfall. The bark beneath his fingertips, grown thick with rough moss, felt spongy to the touch. He put his full weight to it and sat, the log buckling slightly as the rot compressed.

On his knee he wore a metal brace, with Velcro ties and padded fittings. The material beneath wet with his own sweat. For nearly five miles they'd been making a straight line upward through the mountain, veering often before coming back on path, heading almost parallel to the lake below, but always climbing.

Next to him, Patrick swayed on his feet, his hands tucked under the straps of his pack and a half circle of sweat stained into the shirt below his neck. "So what's the plan here?" he said, raising his eyes to Ellie. "We're just going to track this girl, shoot her, and then put a collar on her?"

"You make my job seem so easy," Ellie said.

"Well, there is the hiking part."

Ellie grinned and studied her map. When she looked back up, searching the hillside above, she said, "And the finding her part."

Drake worked the muscles beneath the brace, feeling the familiar pain. He knew this was good for him, all of it, pushing himself till the new muscles formed over the old, cutting out the scar tissue. He carried with him his old .270 hunting rifle, the gun strapped to the side of his pack, and a scope zipped into one of the pockets. He wasn't expecting to use it, but he was nervous about this whole thing and had packed it that morning, thinking about stories he knew were myths, but that somehow had worked their way into his reality. When he looked back up at Ellie she had walked off a ways and then come back, GPS in one hand and her own rifle in the other.

"How long since the last wolf sign?" she asked.

"It's been a while now," Drake said.

Ellie turned and looked to Patrick. "You see anything?"

Patrick had produced a water bottle from his pack and stood

drinking. When he was done he passed it along to Drake and said, "What did you think? This wolf was just going to pop out of the woods so we could shoot her?"

"That wasn't exactly it," Ellie said.

"You bring any kind of bait?"

"This one seems to be attracted to dead bodies."

"That why you had us come along?" Drake said. "Human sacrifices?"

"The way you're both breathing it'll probably turn into something like that," Ellie said. "I brought along some urine from a male wolf, and a distressed-elk call. I figure between the two we can hope to get her coming our way."

"Where to now?" Patrick asked.

"Your guess is as good as mine," Ellie said. She ran the back of her palm along her hairline to wipe the sweat away. "You got any hideouts for us to hole up in?"

"Not that I recall."

"Two years smuggling drugs over these mountains and you got nothing, huh?"

"Well, the idea was not to leave a trail."

"Makes sense," Ellie said. "I'm just starting to think about how it took them two years to find a guy in these mountains and we're looking for one wolf who's only been here a few weeks."

"Well, I wasn't exactly howling at the moon, either," Patrick said.

Drake finished drinking from the water and then offered it to Ellie. When she turned it down he handed it back to his father. "Still," Drake said. "You did get caught."

OUT IN THE darkness they heard the wolf call.

Drake and his father sat around a small fire Ellie had allowed them to make on Forestry land. The two tents they'd set up just beyond the light in the shadowed forest. Ellie already asleep in her tent and only

Drake and Patrick sitting up with the fire. No words spoken between the two of them in thirty minutes or more as they sat looking inward. Transfixed by the dance of the flames while out in the forest the wolf called and called without response.

The feeling Drake had carried with him through the day brimming at the edge. The simple question he feared to ask. He felt it all circling around them in the night. The threat out there and all it held with it. His father returned to the valley for only a few days and already Drake's life felt more tenuous than perhaps it had ever felt. But still he wouldn't say a thing, fearful of what response might come, of what truths might be revealed. Miles from home in the middle of the woods it was either the best or the worst place to confront his father.

From the pile by his feet Drake grabbed a piece of wood and threw it into the fire, the sparks dancing for a moment and then settling again. The fire small but strong where the coals burned bright and iridescent in the belly. Nothing to be said. In the morning they would bury the black coals in the ground and move on.

The wolf called again and Drake raised his head, trying to fix a location. The night all around them now and the cold that came with it. A bright half-moon above in the sky and the pathways of moonlight visible on the ground in all directions. The flicker of the fire reaching only so far into the forest, where the blue-black light began and the ferns feathered out of the shadows. No idea how far or close the wolf might be. Only the lonely rise and fall of the howl trailing through the trees.

DRAKE WOKE IN the morning with the air thick around him. The tent he'd packed for his father and him zipped up and stale with the smell of their breath. In the night he'd dreamed about Ellie. The two of them sitting up in her truck on another night, waiting, not for poachers this time but for something else, something that had gone—like most dreams—painfully unnamed. What they'd said to each other and how they'd acted as indistinct as fresh ink smeared on paper. Words only half-legible. His hand at one time during the night held toward her.

Rolling over, remembering it all, he brought his arm up and lay looking at his hand as if it had acted alone in some brutal conspiracy that implicated them all. Above, through the thin tent walls, a pale light came streaming down. A slight hiccup to his breathing as he tried to calm whatever thoughts had been churning inside him. It was a full minute before he realized his father was missing.

Unzipping the tent, Drake stood up into the forest. The trees all around him as they'd been the night before. His eyes skipping over the landscape, settling on their packs for only a moment before skittering on. No sign of his father. The question he'd wanted to ask the night before never having come to his lips and the two men simply watching the fire until it died away and they, too, went to sleep.

He stood now with his feet bare on the forest floor, the dry needles like a mat beneath his heels, and the green moss over everything else. The sun was up, slanting in sideways from the east, and where the sun did not touch the shadows felt cold and damp with mountain dew. The only thing to hear was the slight breeze roaming in the branches high above, washing the treetops one way, then another.

He didn't have an idea where his father had gone and he looked from their packs to the opening of the tent, only a few feet behind him. He sat in the entrance to the tent and pulled his knee brace on, then his socks and boots. He didn't want to worry Ellie, and in some way he knew, too, he wasn't ready to admit to her the unease he'd felt all through the night and the guilt he now felt for bringing his father along.

When he checked the packs a minute later he saw that Ellie's rifle was gone. He looked around the camp, trying to remember if she had stashed it somewhere, or if it was in her tent. No memory of either, and a certainty he'd seen the rifle right here, strapped to the side of her pack when Drake had gone to sleep.

For a moment his eyes scanned the dense forest. The camp made in a little clearing among the trees. Dark soil beneath his boots and nothing but the endless wall of tree trunks in any direction. A slope to the ground about twenty feet east of the camp, where the valley opened up below and the lake sometimes could be seen through the trees.

Taking his eyes off the surrounding forest, he unstrapped his own rifle from his pack and slung it over his shoulder. Driscoll's words from the day before playing in Drake's head and not the first idea which way his father had gone, or why he'd wanted to come along with them in the first place.

There was a small stream a tenth of a mile downslope and this is the way Drake went, hoping his father had simply gone for water. He could feel the breeze strengthen as soon as he came off the even ground. The valley floor far below him down the slope, and the rush of air felt rising upward through the trees.

With his boots loosely tied, the land fell away quickly and felt dense and fragile beneath his feet. The deep scent of fungus and turned soil rising from the ground any time he took a step. His heels landed heavily on the downward slope, sinking in as they pushed a mixture of detritus that clumped and fell away before him.

The rifle felt heavy on his back as he walked, the butt bouncing against his waist. No sound in the forest except for his own footsteps and the rush of wind in the trees. Farther on he heard the stream, a slight gurgle of water, endless as the slope he now found himself descending.

As he came down and found the bottomland before the stream, he saw his father a hundred feet on. Crouched with his back to Drake and his arms outstretched over a deadfall. A bright green wall of salmonberry leaves and currant bushes separating the streambed from the dark undergrowth of the forest. Patrick so still that it forced the words to Drake's mouth before he quite knew he was saying them. Throwing his voice forward as he called to his father.

Only then did Drake catch the movement far down the stream,

the brief wheel of fur as something bounded up from the water and moved for the forest. He saw too the quick snap of his father's arms and the red dart flush out of the gun. The sound loud in the silence of the forest, as the wolf sprang up, visible for a second in the morning sun, yelping in pain. The red dart now hanging from her hindquarter.

THE WOLF LAY on her side fifty yards from the stream. The slight pulse of her lungs as she took air and then gave it back, moving the dirt beneath her snout. She was bigger than Drake had thought. A full six feet from tail to head, standing on her hind legs she would be as big as a man, and looked to weigh between ninety and a hundred pounds. Lying there, drugged, under all that fur it was hard to say. Drake knew just by looking at her that she was older, or perhaps sick, the gray and white fur matted in places where she had ceased to care for herself.

"A hell of a shot," Drake said. It was the first thing he'd said to his father since he found him at the edge of the stream. A sheen of sweat visible on Patrick's skin. The wolf leading them up a steep grade before collapsing under the power of the tranquilizer.

With Ellie's rifle still in Patrick's hands he pushed the barrel into the side of the wolf, testing her. "You didn't make it any easier."

"They keep a rifle range in the prison for you to practice on?" Drake saw his father smile for a moment. His teeth there, then gone again in a flash. "How'd you even know the wolf would be down there?"

"I followed her."

"Followed her from where?"

"From the camp," Patrick said, glancing back in the direction they'd come from. "She was out there circling us most of the night."

"I don't believe you."

"Believe whatever you want," Patrick said. "You get real used to picking up on small sounds when you're locked up in prison. Especially if you're an ex-cop."

"I still don't believe it," Drake said, shaking his head.

Ten minutes later he came back with Ellie and the three of them got the wolf weighed. Ellie put a GPS collar around the neck, then started down through the list, taking samples of fur and blood, swabbing the mouth and checking the teeth. To Drake it seemed like there were a million things she had to do, checking them off on a laminated sheet as she came to them. The animal unconscious through it all.

Drake helped Ellie as she worked, pulling the fur away for her as she took the blood, or holding a small penlight to better view the wolf's dark pupils and yellow corneas. The whole while Patrick squatted close by, keeping to himself as he watched.

Afterward, when Ellie had finished and Patrick had gone back to camp ahead of them, Ellie said, "You have any idea what he was up to?"

"My father?" Drake asked, watching the animal from about fifty feet away, waiting for it to wake up. "He said he heard her outside the tent last night."

"Could you have made that shot?" Ellie asked.

Drake shook his head. He knew shooting a tranquilizer wasn't like shooting a bullet. It was slower. The shot had to allow for the lag. If an animal stayed still at that distance, there was a chance of getting the dart in where you wanted it. If the animal was running it was a lot harder, and if the animal was surprised, as this one had been, it was nearly impossible. "It was a hell of a shot," Drake said.

DRAKE'S FATHER HAD been the one to teach him how to shoot. Nine years old with the rifle raised over the alder fence out behind their house, aiming at apples. The echo of the shots carried far up the valley, bouncing from one slope to the other. Silver Lake much smaller then, simply a few houses, a general store, and one diner. No one to care about the sound of a hunting rifle carried in the air. The yellow-white flesh of the apples spread everywhere in the grass. One shot out of three hitting its mark. And his father telling him how to hold the gun, how to keep it cradled into the meat of his shoulder, where his deltoid met the muscle of his breast.

The skin bruised from one weekend to the next. More apples and more shooting until he missed only one shot out of six, and then one out of seven. The apples bursting up out of the grass with every shot, and the rich warm smell of the dirt beneath coming to him out of the orchard. His own boyhood encompassed in this.

The smell of Ivory soap on his hands, the tang of gunpowder in the air like the crack of fireworks on the Fourth of July. And always the deep sweetness of the apples everywhere as he shucked one shell and loaded another, taking aim where his father pointed. Wanting more than anything for his shots to fly true.

IT WAS FOUR hours before Drake came in the door with his father close behind. The hike down had taken them less time than the day before; they stopped fewer times as they moved down the slope with the blue sheet of the lake laid out before them. The wolf somewhere behind, groggy but awake, the GPS collar already sending its signal to a satellite far overhead.

With the door open, Drake let the air into the house. Crisp spring air smelling mineral as cracked rock, and the cool feel of the lake air spreading through the house. The windows all closed up and a note from Sheri telling Drake she'd gone in to cover a shift for one of the other girls.

Drake ran the water from the kitchen tap, watching the sun filter in through the windows. His father in Drake's boyhood room and the packs left out on the living room floor with their boots. When the water was cool enough, Drake put a hand beneath the tap and cupped the water to his face. The grit coming off in muddy whorls that showed like tree knots in his palms.

He washed his hands and dried them by running his fingers up over his thin hair. All through the forest he'd thought about how he'd picked up his rifle that morning, ready to use it. But ready to use it for what? The wolf? His father? He didn't know what he had been afraid of. He knew only that he had been.

He looked in on the living room. The rifle still there, still strapped to his pack as it had been all down the mountain. His father's pack and boots not far off. His own boots tucked away by the door, the toes caked with forest mud, and the laces frayed from long use and many days away in those same hills his father was so familiar with.

There wasn't a thing Drake could say about what he was feeling. No one he could talk to. What Driscoll had told him about Patrick, about Gary, it wasn't right. None of it was, and Drake knew it would eat away at him until he knew the truth. He couldn't go on like this, mistrusting his own father, feeling like every minute of every day he needed to know exactly where Patrick was.

Drake turned away from the packs and boots and went down the hallway. He stopped outside his old room and looked in through the open doorway. Patrick lay on the bed in his hiking clothes, his feet dangling off the side of the bed as if he didn't want to sully the sheets.

Drake stepped inside and sat at the computer desk, looking across the room at his father. "I want to ask you something."

"Go ahead then." The same smile on his face that Drake couldn't read. Crooked and then gone again before Drake got a feel for it.

"When I picked you up from prison you told me you wouldn't cause me any trouble. You said you were done with that." Drake took his time. He was trying to get the words right. He needed to know the answer, but first he needed to know how to ask the question. Something he'd wanted to ask his father ever since Driscoll had met him at the front of his driveway. "You meant what you said to me?"

Patrick stared mutely back at him from the bed. He raised a hand and rubbed his cheek, feeling the white scruff that had covered his face in the last day. "I don't plan on being around here long," Patrick said, "if that's what you're asking. I'd like to make my own way. I don't need to depend on you and Sheri. This place hasn't been mine for a long time now and I see you two have made a home here."

"That's not what I meant," Drake said. He felt embarrassed. He hadn't meant to make his father feel unwanted. "This is your house, too."

"We both know that's not true anymore."

Drake looked around the room, if only to focus his thoughts. Sky-blue paint and the colors of sunset. "I meant to say you're welcome here."

"I just need a few days," Patrick said; he was up now, sitting on the bed with his feet on the floor, moving his hands as he talked. "There's outreach programs for people like me. If I stay in town I can chop logs, or I can maybe see if there's some work with the Department of Forestry. I don't know if they'd take me, but I'd be willing to give it a try."

"That sounds fine," Drake said. He tried to imagine who his father would have been if he hadn't gone to Monroe, if he'd just stayed the sheriff of a little town in the North Cascades. The thought seeming foreign even to Drake. Patrick's whole identity wrapped up in the fact that he'd smuggled drugs, that he was a crooked sheriff from a place no one had ever heard of until Patrick put them all on the map.

Drake went on trying to discern a future for his father as he looked at the man, sitting there on the bed. Worn out. Burned out. Busted up from a life that hadn't been meant to be. There were programs for people like him. Support groups, ways for men like Patrick to make their own way in this world. Even with a history like his father's.

"I never meant to say you weren't welcome here," Drake said. He knew he was backpedaling but he couldn't help it. He got up from the computer chair and walked to the doorway, putting one hand on the frame.

"I'll talk to some people," Patrick said. His words hesitant, stumbling one after the other. Patrick just sitting there looking up at his son where he stood at the entrance to the room. Drake knowing he'd come in to talk to his father about one thing, but, in the end, forced the issue of another.

"That sounds fine, Dad." Drake could feel himself shrink back inside as he watched his father. The man seemed oblivious to what Drake was hinting at. Desperate, too. The veneer of his words beginning to crack and Drake wishing he could make what he'd said disappear.

"We okay?" Patrick asked.

"Yes," Drake said.

HIS FATHER WAS in the shower when Drake came back to the room. For a good minute he stood there in the doorway looking everything over. Forcing himself to see the crib and changing table, the bands of color on the walls and the pale stars fixed to the ceiling.

Down the hall he could hear the shower through the bathroom door. The water going and the sound of his father in there.

All the dreams Drake had had for the room. All they had filled it with. All that it was now.

He knew there were other times he could come to the room, when his father was out with Sheri, or away looking for work, but Drake couldn't wait any longer. He didn't want to believe what Agent Driscoll had told him. He needed to know whether his father was guilty or not. He needed to know for sure.

The changing table was opposite the bed. Patrick's clothes kept in the drawers beneath. Drake went through this first, opening each drawer and going through them top to bottom. By the time he finished he was on his knees with every drawer open in front of him. He turned and looked around the room. Not sure what he was looking for, but knowing he had to look, that if he didn't he would always wonder.

It was only when he came to the bed that he saw the cardboard box pushed in under the frame. The container of mementos barely visible from the darkness.

Drake got up and went to the bed. Sitting, he removed the box and pulled it out onto the floor. Twelve years of his father's life in one container, wooden figurines made in the prison shop, the letters Drake's grandfather, Morgan, had sent to Patrick. A few letters from Sheri, a couple worn paperbacks without their covers, and the manila folder Patrick had tried to show Drake on the drive up from Monroe.

Drake pulled this up and opened the folder, looking down at the aged clippings. The newsprint gone yellow, cracked and dotted with pinholes or marked with tape at the corners where his father had probably secured these relics to his cell wall. Patrick said he'd kept them all, every article. And Drake went through them one by one. All of them in order, from the ten-page *Silver Lake Weekly* announcing Drake's basketball scholarship to Arizona, to the *Seattle Times* article the day after he got himself shot in a North Seattle neighborhood.

He laid them on the bed as he came to them. Articles he didn't even know existed. A high score from when he'd shot twenty-eight in one game. Speculations by the local papers on the team's chances for a tournament, or even who among them might go on to a higher level of play. All of this carefully stacked, one after the other, in the folder. The clippings aged and yellowed, kept together with paper clips and bits of tape. All like some sort of family album locked up for years in the basement safe.

It was a long time since Drake had allowed himself to think of those years. When he'd been a young man, a couple years past high school, living in another state, in a city a hundred times bigger than Silver Lake, playing basketball.

Drake loved it all. The running endlessly, one end of the court to the other. The quick shots, the passes from player to player, the fade, the rebound, the way the world never seemed to pause in all that time and one action fed into the next like a flood of water carrying everything else along.

It was the beginning of his third year when he went into his coach's office to tell him about the trouble back home. Telling his coach all the things the newspapers were saying about his father. And the coach standing up from his desk and walking around to sit facing Drake, trying to work through it all, trying to tell Drake he would always have a place on the team. Though Drake knew—no matter what the coach said—that the offer could wait only so long.

Drake sat in his father's room, a room that had once been his own, and looked the articles over. Many of the clippings were about him, but the majority of them were about his father, about his arrest and then later conviction. That time in Drake's life almost a complete wash. Like he'd been there and not there all at the same time. Gary had come to the airport to pick Drake up and told him how Patrick had been led into the courtroom for his sentencing. How even in the week since he'd been arrested, Patrick seemed to have lost weight, shrunk back into himself. The jumpsuit too big on his frame and the shuffling, almost hesitant, steps he took as he came out into the court, his eyes downcast on the floor.

Drake had tried to picture it all then, but he couldn't get a grasp on it. The man Gary was describing so unlike the man Drake had grown up with, leading him on horseback through the hills. Camping in the high meadows in the years before he'd left for Arizona and listening to the rut of elk as they brought their antlers together late in the evening. Drake and Patrick rising from the small butane stove to stand watching as the big animals clawed the earth a hundred yards away, diving at each other with lust-filled abandon. The clash of their fighting echoing off the rocks high above while Drake and Patrick looked on.

Later Drake would sit in the courtroom with his grandfather and listen to the charges laid against Patrick. The trial going on for five days and then the judge waiting as the jury gave their verdict, listening to the foreman go down through the charges. Guilty. Guilty. Guilty.

Drake shuffled the articles in his hand. He'd read them all. He'd been a part of many of them, seen most of it with his own eyes as the reporters sat a couple rows back scribbling notes on paper. All of it taking shape. Drake's vision of his father slowly cracking, until finally it had all crumbled, flake by flake, as his father was led away and Drake sat watching.

The articles dropped off until Drake saw his own name mentioned again in the Seattle paper. The story not about his basketball career anymore, but his role as a deputy, his father's history, and the arrest Drake had tried to make in the mountains outside Silver Lake ten years after his father had gone away. An attempt that would eventually get him shot, leaving him as close to death as Drake ever cared to be.

He looked at them all, shuffling back through each clipping on the bed, trying to make sense of it. His life in this valley. His father's life. The two so dissimilar from each other, but in many ways the same.

Everything his father, Patrick Drake, had ever done. Every highlight and failure. His rise as sheriff, the death of his wife to leukemia, and his eventual fall, outlined there for the world to see. And not a single article in his father's collection mentioning the two dead men outside Bellingham.

What had Patrick said to Ellie on his first day out? Don't get caught.

Drake looked up from the articles and saw his father staring in at him. His bald scalp still wet from the shower. His eyes red and worn from the water. "Is this why you came in here earlier?" Patrick asked.

Drake followed his father's eyes to the open drawers beneath the changing table, all of the clothes in disarray, hanging loose over the sides. The cardboard box on the bed next to Drake with the articles spread everywhere on the mattress.

"You don't trust me," Patrick said. He was wearing a towel around his waist, standing there in the doorway. He was staring at Drake with an intensity Drake could only remember from when he'd been a child.

"There have been things said about you that I can't ignore," Drake responded, keeping his eyes focused on the door frame near his father's head. Looking but not looking.

"By who?"

Drake took the box off the bed and set it on the floor again. "The DEA has been following you around."

"Is that a fact?"

He met Patrick's eyes. "They say you had something to do with two men getting killed outside Bellingham before you went away."

"And you want to know if I did it?"

"I want to know if it's true in any way. If you knew these men, or had anything to do with their deaths."

"I told you a long time ago when you visited me that I wasn't going back in."

"I know what you told me," Drake said. "What I want to know is if you killed those men."

Patrick looked at the open drawers again and then looked back at Drake. "I didn't do anything to those men."

"But you know of them?"

"I know of them."

"Then you know about the money, too."

"Yes," Patrick said. "There's a lot of people who've heard about the money."

"That's how you got into all this, isn't it? For the money. So that you could pay off Mom's medical bills."

"That's what I've always said. I took on that second mortgage and never was able to pay it."

"You did it for the money then?" Drake didn't know why he was repeating himself. The emphasis he put on the end of the sentence more of a command than any kind of question and he realized he really didn't want to know.

"There was no other reason. That was it, that was all there was," Patrick said. "I never did intend to do that type of work for long, and I don't intend to do it now that I'm out."

Drake moved his hand over the articles. Gathering them up and putting them back into the folder. He knew he should let it go. His father had said he didn't kill those men. Drake knew that should have been enough. But a lot of time had passed since Drake had gone away to college and his father had made the decision that would ultimately change both their lives.

"I'm a deputy now," Drake said. "I know it's been twelve years, but there are still plenty of people who probably question what I knew about you, and what I know now. I don't want you to put me in that position again. If the DEA is still looking into this then there's a chance Sheri and I could lose the house."

"The only way that would happen is if I was stashing money or drugs on the property."

"Are you?"

"Who do you think I am?"

"A convicted drug smuggler," Drake said.

Patrick laughed. "You *really* don't trust me."

Drake stuffed the folder back down into the box and turned away from the bed. "I don't know how I'm supposed to."

"You're supposed to because you're my son."

"That's a lot to ask," Drake said.

"You'll see," Patrick said. "I'm not going to be a bother to you. I'm going to be out of your hair just as soon as I can. Living my own life." He walked over and took a set of clothes from beneath the changing table, taking his time.

"I don't think the DEA is going to give up just because you say you didn't do it."

"I'd be disappointed if they did," Patrick said.

DRAKE TOOK A long shower. Letting it run cold before he allowed himself to shut off the water and pull the curtain back. Standing in front of the mirror he listened to the house beyond the door. Outside the sun was setting and the light came through the bathroom window with a low pink hue. The slight movement of air felt on his bare feet where the cool air from the hallway slipped in beneath the door. He half expected his father to be gone when he came out of the bathroom, never to be seen again. Simply to have walked off into the woods, where the darkness might eat him.

Drake ran a hand up his forearm, pressing his thumb to the purple scar tissue. One hole all the way through. Clean and simple. It felt like nothing now, just a raised circle of skin. Only really identifiable to those who knew the story that went with it. He rubbed his thumb up his forearm several more times, watching the pink flesh go white, then fade away again as his thumb moved on. Nothing he could do about it now.

When he came out of the bathroom Patrick was sitting in the living room drinking one of the beers Sheri had bought a few nights before. Patrick's attention turned to one of the catalogs that came every month in the mail. One of the home magazines Sheri liked to dog-ear and leave around the house even though they barely had enough money to buy groceries some months.

"You want to go by the Buck Blind?" Drake asked. He was standing at the entrance to the hallway in a pair of jeans and a flannel shirt, his towel over his shoulders and his hair mussed. "Sheri can get us a good price on a pitcher."

"Yeah," Patrick said, "we can do that."

WHEN THEY GOT to the Buck Blind Sheri was just finishing up her last couple tables. She gave Drake a kiss and sent him and his father ahead to the bar. "I'll be just another forty-five minutes," she said. "Gary and Luke are in there if you want to say hello."

Drake led his father through the doorway into the bar. Dim compared to the restaurant, the bar had been built when the grocer next door went out of business and the restaurant decided to expand. The walls all brick and mortar, and a doorway from restaurant to bar opened up halfway down the wall. Tables ran one side, while opposite, a wooden bar took up almost the full length of the place. Only open for five years, the bar already had the smell of spilled liquor, sweet and dusty in the air, while in the summers the air felt thick and closed up by the brick walls. Everything, even the random kitsch along the walls, gave the feel of a bar in someone's home basement.

"I heard you guys caught your wolf," Gary said. He was sitting midway down the bar with his face turned toward them as they came in. Luke sat on the stool beside him, still in his uniform.

"My dad actually got her," Drake said, motioning back over his shoulder toward Patrick.

"You let the ex-con shoot the wolf?" Gary asked. "With a gun?"

"Come on, Gary," Drake said. "You know it was a tranq gun. There's nothing to that."

"Just warning you. Because that's not how the court will see it."

"I know the rules," Patrick said.

They sat in a line down the bar next to Gary. Luke raised his head to look at Patrick and then eased off the stool for a moment to shake the old sheriff's hand. "Good to have you back," Luke said.

Drake watched and after Luke sat back down he asked about Cheryl.

"False alarm," Gary said. "One of her friends thought she remembered Cheryl saying she planned to go down to see a boy in Seattle."

"And the parents?"

"She's done this a few times now. Andy is still out looking for her but we're thinking she'll show up tomorrow or the next day."

The bartender came by and they ordered a round, and then Drake ordered two more for Gary and Luke. Gary kept smiling, running his fingers over the edge of the pint glass and looking at Patrick. Finally saying, "You don't recognize the bartender?"

"No," Patrick said, turning to follow the man as he tended to a customer at the other end of the bar.

"It's Jack."

Patrick leaned farther into the bar, trying to get a good look. "Bill's son?"

"Yeah, same kid. Only a dozen years older now."

When Jack came over their way again Patrick caught the kid's eye. "You're the bartender here?"

"He owns the place," Gary said.

"No shit."

"I'm a partner," Jack said. "I don't own it." He was leaning against the back bar now, his arms crossed. Skinny with acne scarring along the line of his jaw. Drake had known him his whole life. He was a little older than Drake. They'd been in high school together.

"Jack is one of my hunting buddies. Aren't you, Jack?" Gary said, looking to Jack where he stood on the other side of the bar.

"If you call going up into the woods to drink a fifth of bourbon and stare at some trees hunting," Jack said.

"Sounds about right," Patrick said. "How's your father doing? How's Bill?"

"Passed away five years ago. The money he left me went into this bar, though, so it seems fitting. He was always putting his money into booze as it was."

"Sorry to hear that."

"Yeah, well it happened. That's how it goes," Jack said. A man at the other end of the bar signaled for service. Jack was off the back bar and beginning to walk away when he turned to Patrick and Gary. "Look, next round is on me, okay? It's good to see you, Pat." He was already halfway down the bar before any of them could say anything.

They moved over to a table after they finished the round Jack bought them, sitting for a long time bullshitting about the weather and giving Patrick a hard time about being back in the world. Luke making several prison-shower jokes that never got any of the other men to laugh, but Patrick nice enough to smile and let the comments roll past him. One of the old loggers down at the other end of the bar was playing Lynyrd Skynyrd on the jukebox and they listened to "Free Bird" for what seemed like twenty minutes.

"So you're the sheriff?" Patrick said. He whistled a bit as he said it, letting the air escape from his lungs for a long time. "How's that working out for you?"

Gary looked up from the beer in his hands. He'd been listening to the song playing on the jukebox. "To be honest: it's tiring," he said. "I chase down every little thing people have any concern over."

"A cat goes missing I bet you're on it," Patrick said. He was smiling now and Drake could see he didn't envy the man.

"Something like that. Luke and I spent half the day looking for that girl from town. She never was much for staying around here as it was."

"She'll turn up," Luke said, his voice a little loose with alcohol. "She always does."

When Sheri came in they'd finished off two pitchers and were ordering a third. Whatever tension Drake had felt between Gary and Patrick at the trailhead was now gone. The two of them telling stories that Drake barely recalled from when he was a child. Gary doing most of the talking as Patrick nodded his head and filled in all the little details Gary had skipped over.

Sheri pulled a chair to the end of the table and sat with her purse in her lap, the strap still on her shoulder, ready to go.

"You want a glass?" Drake asked, raising his hand to signal Jack.

When the next pitcher came Sheri said she'd just share with Drake. The guys crowded up around the table as the logger at the end of the bar started in on some Zeppelin. Nobody left in the place and Jack—with his arms crossed over his chest and a distant look in his eye—kept watch over the logger at the opposite end of the bar.

"You want to get out of here soon?" Sheri asked quietly.

Drake turned and looked at the three other men and nodded. Luke halfway through the story about a young bear that had gotten itself stuck in an outhouse the summer before last.

"If I leave," Drake said to his father, "you think you'll be fine to get home on your own?"

"You're going to trust me?" his father said, a smile half cocked on his lips.

"It's fine," Drake said, feeling a little loose with the alcohol. "You know the way home. We'll leave the door open for you."

Drake was tired, too, and they left the three men talking over their beers, saying good-bye to Jack and giving the logger a wide berth as they went by. The man singing along to the music now and Drake wondering how much more Jack was willing to take.

A LITTLE PAST one A.M. Drake got up to answer the door. It was about the time he estimated that his father would have been kicked out of the bar, give or take fifteen minutes for the walk home. The door had been left unlocked so that Patrick might let himself in. But Drake got up anyway, figuring maybe his father was drunk and hadn't even tried the doorknob yet.

Drake came into the living room a little fuzzy from the pitchers they'd drunk, leaning his weight on the handle and pulling back on the door. He was dressed in a T-shirt and a pair of his old basketball warm-ups, planning to go right back to bed as soon as he let his father in.

Agent Driscoll stood on the porch when Drake opened the door. He pushed through and came into the living room, giving the room a quick once-over and then coming back to Drake. "Is he here?" Driscoll asked.

Drake studied the Impala parked in their drive for a quick second, looking to see if anyone else was inside before he closed the door. Driscoll was standing in the middle of the living room, the hallway light on behind him. His suit jacket crumpled at the armpits and along the sleeves.

"Your father?" Driscoll said.

"No," Drake said. "Not that I know of." Drake walked by Driscoll and went down the hallway to his father's room. He opened the door and flipped on the lights. No one there and the sheets looking just as they had earlier in the day when Drake and Patrick had sat talking.

Drake came out of the room and went into the bathroom, throwing on the lights. He even went as far as to pull the curtains back on the shower and look in on the tub.

Driscoll was there in the bathroom doorway when Drake turned around. "I lost him about thirty minutes ago," Driscoll said.

"You've been following him?" Drake came out of the bathroom and looked down the hallway toward his own bedroom. There was a light on under the doorway.

"You thought because I told you to keep an eye on him, I'd just hand it off?"

Drake led Driscoll back into the living room. He spread his fingers up into his hair and brought them down across his eyes. "He didn't do it, Driscoll. He's not the guy you're looking for."

"You told him?"

Drake turned and looked at Driscoll, the man waiting on a response. "What did you think I was going to do?"

"I thought you'd remember your duty as a law officer."

"He's my father, Driscoll."

"Christ."

"He didn't do it."

"Two years ago, when we first met, you were ready to throw away the key. Now you're acting like he never put you in this position."

At the far end of the hallway Drake saw the bedroom door open and Sheri come out wearing her robe. She was looking at Drake, but her eyes darted toward Driscoll for a moment and Drake saw the surprise in them, followed quickly by disgust. The last time they'd had a full conversation together Driscoll had said something about not wasting taxpayer money on repeat offenders, preferring instead if they just got offed beforehand. Drake liked to think that Driscoll had been joking. Sheri had never seen the comedy in it.

"Long time no see," Driscoll said to Sheri as she took a seat on the sofa and kept a steady watch on Drake.

"What's this about?" she asked Drake.

Drake shrugged, wishing his father would walk in and they could all just go back to bed.

"Your father-in-law has disappeared," Driscoll said.

"What do you mean disappeared?" Sheri asked.

"He's missing. Gone. Vanished off the face of this earth," Driscoll said. "Though I think the better definition of what happened is he's on the run." Driscoll had his arms crossed and each of his hands buried in his armpits. He was bouncing slightly on the heels of his feet.

"What is this man doing here?" Sheri asked Drake.

Drake didn't have an answer for her that would make the situation any better and he asked Sheri if she would stay up and wait to see if Patrick came home, and if he did to call Drake straightaway. Drake led Driscoll out onto the porch and closed the door.

"She still doesn't like me very much," Driscoll said.

"It's late," Drake said. "She's tired."

"I don't know about all that," Driscoll said, "but thanks for trying."

"So what happened, Driscoll?"

"I was waiting on your father when he came out of the bar and halfway home he goes running into the woods."

"Did he see you?"

"I don't know. I don't think so."

"Then why did he run?"

"I was walking behind him, two or three hundred feet back. I don't know how he would have noticed me."

"You didn't try to go after him?"

"Of course I chased after him. I was shining my light around. It's a fucking funhouse in there, everything looks exactly the same: tree trunk, fern, tree trunk, fern . . . you want me to go on?"

"I get it," Drake said. "He really took off running?"

"I've called in a favor with some of my guys from Seattle, but they won't be here for a couple more hours."

"You don't need to do that," Drake said. "I'm here. I can help you find him."

Driscoll looked to be thinking that over. "Fine," he said. "It would take them too much time to get here as it is."

"What channel are you using on your radio?"

Driscoll told him the channel and where Patrick had gone off the road.

"I'm going to take my cruiser out," Drake said. "I want to shine the spot around a bit and see what I can see," Drake said.

"I know he's your father but I want you to be careful, Drake. Don't do anything stupid and get yourself hurt. I want you to call me on the radio if you see anything. Even if it's just a flicker of something, you'll let me know first."

"I know," Drake said. He was watching the forest beyond the fall of the house lights. The gravel shining white under the reach of the exterior lights, and the dark forest all around, circling them in. "Maybe he saw you, Driscoll. Maybe he just spooked? He'd been drinking a lot at the bar. This could all be one big mistake."

"If he's not guilty, what does he have to hide?" Driscoll said. He was down at the Impala now with the door open. "No heroics, Drake." Driscoll closed the door and pulled away. His red taillights still visible up the drive when Drake got in his own vehicle and brought it around toward the lake road.

Drake ran a circuit around the lake, as far south as he was willing to bet his father could get on foot, then again north. When he'd finished, he turned up into the forest and followed the road past the Fish and Wildlife Quonset hut, shining the spot all over the parking lot and down the sides of the metal exterior. He went all the way up to the border crossing and talked with the guard there, giving the man a description of his father. Not a single car gone past in the last two hours, either south or north.

When he came into town he was feeling frustrated and betrayed. His father was out there and he was running. There was no other explanation.

Driving past the Buck Blind he eased the car to a stop. He sat there with the engine running. The dash lights giving the inside of the car a green aura of light and the bar shut down with its windows dark. Drake got out anyway just to feel the air on his skin. Cool in the night with the smell of pine resin like menthol on the wind.

He sat back down in the cruiser and took the radio in his hand, intending to contact Driscoll, but as he sat there his eyes caught the reflection of an upstairs window in the rearview mirror. The window was a block down on the opposite side of the street and Drake knew it right off as Gary's place over the Laundromat.

Drake knocked and waited. He was standing at the top of the wood stairs that led to Gary's place, a good view back toward the lake and the moon shining on the water. No one came to the door and he looked around at the window with the light still on and then he pounded the door several times with the heel of his palm.

Gary came to the door almost as soon as Drake finished. "I figured it was you," Gary said. He stepped aside and let Drake into the crowded apartment.

"You know he's gone, then?"

"I know."

"And you were waiting to tell me . . ."

Gary shook his head. "More of a feeling," he said. He crossed to the kitchenette and took a beer from the fridge. He offered it and then when Drake wouldn't take it he opened it himself. "Driscoll wasn't going to leave him alone. You know that."

"That doesn't mean he can just run out on his problems."

Gary grinned. "That's what you think?"

"What else is there?"

"You sure you don't want a beer?" Gary asked. He stood waiting for an answer and when none came he walked back into the living room and sat heavy in the solitary lounge chair. "Driscoll's fucking obsessed with the man."

"Should he be?"

"Your father's trying to make things right, that's all I know. He fucked up."

"Where is he?" Drake asked, his eyes darting over the apartment. Pictures on the wall that had been there as long as Gary lived in the place, a gun rack against the back wall, and the old television in a corner below the kitchen counter. The whole place lit dull yellow by a single floor lamp standing at one end of the room. "He's not here, right?"

"Be my guest." Gary waved at the open room, telling Drake to have a look.

When Drake came back into the living room Gary was still sitting there sipping from the beer. "I think I might be going crazy," Drake said. He rested his back on the door and then slid to the floor, cupping his face in his hands and rubbing at his eyes with his fingers.

"It's okay, son. Driscoll has that effect on people."

Drake looked up. "My father has that effect on people."

"Don't worry about Patrick. He knows what he's doing."

"He said nothing to you?" Drake asked. "He just took off? He doesn't have a car. He doesn't have more than twenty dollars in his wallet."

"Honestly," Gary said, "I don't know where he is. All I know is he's a resourceful guy."

For a time, after coming out of Gary's apartment, Drake sat in his cruiser listening to the blank fuzz of the radio, not knowing what to do. Every once in a while he took a call from Driscoll, relaying his position, and then letting the radio go silent again. No one was out on the streets, and Drake didn't see a single car pass in all the time he sat watching the road. Eventually Driscoll got Drake on the radio and told him to go home.

Sheri was still up. A pot of coffee steaming on the counter when he came in, Sheri sat on the couch waiting on him to say something. He shook his head and went through to the kitchen and poured himself some of the coffee. The clock on the stove said it was three A.M.

"I'll wake you up if anything happens," Drake said. He was back in the living room now and he put a hand out for Sheri and helped her up off the couch.

"How long have you known about Driscoll?" Sheri asked.

"A few days now."

"Do you believe whatever he's saying about Patrick?"

"No," Drake said. "But Driscoll is saying things about other people besides my dad. I don't know what to think, really."

"Like who?"

"Like Gary," Drake said.

Sheri shook her head and he knew she didn't believe him. "Patrick is smarter than this."

"I hope so." He led her back through the hallway and closed the door behind her. After a time he saw the light go out under the door and he walked back to the living room. His coffee cup sat steaming on the table. He picked it up and drank a quarter of it in one long gulp. He was sitting on the couch with the television turned on low to the late-night infomercials when he began to nod off. His eyelids falling once, then twice, and his chin diving onto his chest for a moment before rising once again. The clock on the stove said four thirty A.M. There were birds chirping in the trees outside, but the sky was still dark.

WHEN HE WOKE up there was a big man wearing a padded flannel—eating milk and cereal from a bowl—in Drake's kitchen. Another man, blond and slightly built, sat across from Drake on the opposite couch wearing a black suit. Both were staring at Drake.

"Help yourself to some Frosted Flakes," Drake said.

The man in the kitchen took another spoonful and stood chewing it like a cow with its cud. He was much larger than the other man, the muscles beneath his pink temples working in parallel motion with his jaw. His forehead glistening slightly with oil or sweat and his dark eyes appearing like two pinpricks beneath the girth of his brows.

"You Driscoll's guys?" Drake said. "I told him we didn't need the help." Drake could feel a little drool at the corner of his lip from where he'd sat sleeping. His neck ached from resting his head on his chest and he was aware for the first time that no one except for him was making any effort to speak. "You just let yourself in?"

"It was open," the man behind the kitchen counter said. He took the cereal box up and poured another helping, then walked to the refrigerator and poured some more milk, leaving the carton out on the small bar that divided the living room from the kitchen. "We didn't want to wake your wife." He was back behind the counter now and he was watching Drake.

Drake wiped two fingers across his lips and then wiped the drool on his pants. The television was on and an old TV star from the eighties was trying to sell a juicer to an audience of retirees. Drake was still dressed in the same warm-ups from the night before. Outside he heard rain falling. The sound of big drops hitting against the roof above. "You guys find my father yet?"

"We were hoping you might have something to say about that," the skinnier man said.

Drake looked at him for a long time trying to judge the man's age. Blond hair slicked tight to the edges of his skull, with irritated eyes and a rough unshaven quality to his cheeks and neck. Where his hands rested in his lap Drake could see scars on every one of his knuckles, like he'd spent years punching through glass windows or grinding his fists into cement. The skin strangely pigmented at the back of his hands. Drake kept staring at him, trying to figure it out until the man crossed one hand over the other, then raised his eyes to Drake.

"You do a lot of bare-knuckle boxing when you were a kid?" Drake asked.

"We always heard you were a smart guy," the skinny blond said.

"You guys work for the DEA, right? You're Driscoll's guys?"

"We know Driscoll," the big man said from behind the counter, taking another bite of cereal and sucking on the spoon.

Drake ran his eyes back and forth between the two men. The clock on the stove said six A.M. When he moved to get up, the blond raised a Walther pistol from where it had rested, out of sight, on the other side of his lap. He was pointing the gun at Drake's chest.

"Tsk, tsk, tsk," the big man said, waving his spoon back and forth in his hand like a finger.

Drake's eyes were on the gun and then they went searching down the hallway toward his bedroom.

"She's fine," the skinnier man said. "She's asleep. She doesn't even know we're here and if you want to keep her safe you'll be quiet as a mouse. You can do that, can't you?"

"Who are you guys?"

The big man made a wave of his spoon in the air, taking in the room and speaking through a half-finished mouthful of cereal and milk. "Old friends of your father's."

"I see," Drake said. "You guys were in Monroe."

The skinny one smiled and looked back at the big man. He never let the gun waver. "Your father was right about you. He always did say you were a smart boy."

"I didn't see this one coming," Drake said.

"Recently, a lot of people have made the same mistake," the big man said. He put his bowl of cereal down in the sink, watching Drake.

In the background, the eighties TV star was telling the audience he woke up every morning feeling twenty years younger. "You won't regret it," the eighties star said, the enthusiasm surging through his voice like an incoming tide as the audience applauded.

"You've got to smarten up, Deputy," the blond man said from the opposite couch. "Was your father wrong about you all these years? I don't know if you've noticed but he left you holding the bag."

Drake looked away toward the door and the sound of rain beyond. "The bag is empty," Drake said.

"I hope you give some thought to the situation you're in. It's not a good one and it can get a lot worse if it's ever going to get better."

"Does it get better?"

"That's up to you." With the Walther he motioned toward the door. Drake got up and walked across the living room. He could hear the rain again. Falling heavy on the gravel outside, eating up any sound he might be able to make. Behind him, he heard the big man move out from behind the counter.

Drake walked outside and stood in the gravel at the base of the stairs, his back to the porch as he watched the edge of the forest beyond the drive. The rain falling hard on his bare head and the water running on his face. No idea what would happen to him, or what he could do about it.

Nothing out there in the night and the sound of gravel crunching under the feet of the skinnier man as he trailed Drake out onto the drive. His breath curling past Drake's left shoulder and the barrel of the gun felt on his spine.

"You have any idea where your father has gotten to?" he heard the skinny man say behind him.

"I don't have a clue where my father went. I don't think he planned on telling me, either."

"That's too bad," the skinny man said. "We need your help on this but if you're not willing, well, we can take this another way."

"What way is that?"

"Any way we like," the skinny man said. "But I don't think your wife would like it very much."

Drake shivered for a moment with the night air, the tremor going up his back in a wave and shaking his shoulders. Wind was coming off the lake and he smelled the minerals in the water. Cold as an incoming storm, the energy in the air charged with electricity.

The skinny man put the pistol to the nape of Drake's neck and the barrel felt solid and heavy against the base of his skull.

No one spoke for a long time and Drake listened to the rain. The wind moved in the tops of the pines and the shadows at the edge of the clearing seemed to flutter with darkness.

Drake shuddered with the cold. He heard the big man come down off the porch now and he listened to the shuffle of the man's weight on the gravel as he drew closer. "You get snow geese on this lake?" the big man asked, only a few feet behind.

Drake stood in the rain, getting soaked, feeling the water seep into his clothes and his skin bristle with the cold. The lake only a hundred yards away. His mind turning thoughts over like stones in an ancient dried-out riverbed, something lost beneath that he couldn't find.

"Most beautiful thing you've ever seen," the big man went on.

The thoughts in Drake's head had come to a stop and it seemed there was nothing but silence waiting for him. He moved to turn. The house lights spread out along the gravel, the old glass jam jars Sheri had collected lined along the kitchen window.

"It's a pity you can't help us," the skinnier man said. Drake heard the gravel shift for a second. A blinding pain at the base of his skull. The trees around him falling away, the house, the light, all shattering into pieces before everything went black.

DRAKE WOKE IN darkness, liquid and heavy around him. The cold tingling at his scalp and his whole body feeling weightless as a cloud, something tethered to his shirtfront holding him in stasis.

Fighting the darkness for air, he breathed in only water as his body flared and convulsed, aware finally of what surrounded him. The dull sound of rain above on the surface like hail on a roof fifty feet above.

He came up out of the water a man newly born. The thick hand of the big man held tight to Drake's shoulder and the other to Drake's chest. Water splashing the surface of the lake where he struggled and the early morning dark all around them.

There was a pain at the back of his head but he didn't quite understand it. He felt turned around, beyond himself, not dead, but slowly dying. The big man let him breathe. On shore, standing below the bank of the lake road, he saw the other skinnier man through the rain, watching the two of them. The big man up to his thighs in the water and Drake on his back, his heels touching the silt at the bottom of the lake.

He was breathing hard with the shock of the water. His lungs constricted in his chest from the cold, one hand held to the underside of the big man's arm, as if clutching a life preserver. "There's something you're . . . ," the skinnier man said from the shore. Drake felt himself pushed under. The big man's hand pressed to his chest as he went down, fighting for air, his legs kicking at the muddied bottom of the lake, gripping at nothing but the soft detritus below. He came up gasping. ". . . not understanding, Deputy," the skinnier man went on. "We're looking for Patrick."

"I don't know anything," Drake managed to say. He went under again. His eyes open, taking in the murky shape of the big man's oval face above.

He came up spitting water. There was water in his sinuses and he felt it trickling down the back of his throat. "Until a few days ago I hadn't talked to him in years." He coughed. "I can't tell you more than that."

He was under again, trailing bubbles, the dark all around. "You better get familiar," the man said from the shore as Drake came up. Water glassing over Drake's skin and dripping from his earlobes. "You get familiar and you find your way after him or things will not be good. You think you can handle that, Deputy?"

Drake nodded.

"There you go," the skinnier man said. "We just want to ask him a few questions now that he's out. See if he remembers us, or the money he owes. We don't need to make it complicated."

Drake nodded again, his heels resting on the lake bottom below. "Complicated?"

The big man dunked him and Drake came up sputtering. "How many times you going to put me under?" Drake yelled. Water running cold on his face.

"As long as it takes," the big man said, pushing him under again.

Drake came up gasping for air, his shirt clenched tight in the big man's fist.

The skinny man bent on his knees and squatted next to the shoreline, picking over the small rocks there. When he satisfied himself he flicked one out over the water, watching as it skipped along the surface and then disappeared within the rain. "Don't call on the law and expect it to turn out for you, Deputy," he said, cleaning his palms by rubbing one on the other. "Don't complicate things for you and yours."

Drake looked at the man till he saw him turn away and climb up the bank toward the road. The big man still holding him there and Drake cold all the way through, his body shivering in the water and wavelets shaking out around his shoulders and head. "What do you mean 'you and yours'?"

The skinnier man didn't look back. Drake called after him again and then he looked to the big man. "What does he mean?"

"Find your father," was all the big man offered, his fist gripped tight to Drake's shirt.

"If I find him, what then?" The cold was all the way through him now, his clothes like lead, dragging him down.

The skinny man was at the edge of the road looking down on them. No cars or light anywhere Drake could see. "We have your cell number," the skinny man said. "We won't be far off."

He felt the big man's hand tighten and then send him down through the water again, the grip coming loose on his shirt and Drake out of his depth. He came up treading water, adrift in the lake, watching as the big man waded to shore and stepped onto land like a creature out of the swamp, bent on some unknown destruction.

DRAKE HEARD THE doors clap shut and then somewhere in front of him a car engine start. He was halfway up the incline when he saw headlights flare out over the water and then turn south on the lake road. The red taillights of the car already distant by the time he stood on the road, cleaning the grit from his hands. His clothes soaked through and a tired, frozen feel to his muscles.

They could have killed him but they hadn't.

For a time he stood there trying to steady his heart in his chest. The night air filled with the sound of falling rain as he tracked the taillights around the lake. He spit a mixture of saliva and water onto the pavement and turned, searching down the road to either side. He was a hundred yards south of his driveway and as soon as he found his bearings he was running.

The wet clothes grated on his skin but he didn't stop. He took the turn to the driveway and ran, increasing his speed as he came to the house. Drake's Chevy was missing and Drake turned and looked back down the drive. He spun and took in the clearing, his lungs heaving in his chest and a vein in his neck beating a constant rhythm under the skin. His cruiser was still there and as he passed he saw that the shotgun had been taken from the stand between the passenger's and driver's seats. He cursed under his breath and went up the stairs, still rushing to get inside.

He called his wife's name as soon as he was through the door. Only the television there to greet him. A rerun of some show from the seventies playing dully on the screen. Drake called his wife's name again as he crossed the living room and entered the hallway. There was no response. When he came to the bedroom door and pushed it open he found out why.

"Sheri?" he said. Slower now, letting the name linger there like he expected a response. None came.

PART III

MISSING. GONE. VANISHED OFF THE FACE OF THE EARTH

IN THE EARLY LIGHT of morning the old man, Morgan Drake, crossed the grass field and went down into the hollow before the house, then up through the cottonwoods. His breath hard to come by and the beat of his pulse thumping in the thin flesh of his forehead. On a string he carried two prairie dogs and a small rabbit over his shoulder, all swaying to the cadence of his walk, slow and labored as he climbed toward the house. His balance measured with caution as he moved his weight to the next foot, making his way up out of the hollow. The creek there barely an inch deep and the water flowing fast and cool from the rain the night before. His pant legs wet to his knees from the grass and sage he had passed through just before morning, the sun inches below the horizon and the eastern sky glowing red like a cold thin fire along the prairie.

He came up out of the cottonwoods and stood catching his breath. The little house there before him. Two front windows and a door. A porch of wood slats and the tin roof he'd put on himself five summers before. The rolling plains all around spotted with bunch grass and deepening growths of cheatgrass. Grown almost to his hips and darkened with the rain.

Morgan crossed the last hundred or so feet and came out of the grass. He'd lived in the place for fifteen years. Through snowstorms that left drifts up to his windows, and through summers where the air thickened to the color of charcoal and huge plumes of smoke could be seen coming off the distant mountains, climbing dark into white clouds. Every morning his porch dusted with gray ash as if from some volcanic explosion.

Except for the septic he'd done most of the work on the small house himself. The dirt road almost a mile in length patched and repatched with gravel he brought in on the bed of his pickup every spring. The grasslands all around slowly trying to take it back by growth or destruction. Mud holes and wallows forming in the depressions and corners when the land softened away from winter and the snow melted and bogged every low point on the plain. Often he stood on the porch and watched how the sun moved across the land, catching the light on the pools of water. The creek loud in the hollow and the leaves of the cottonwoods green with the snowmelt.

Morgan left only once a month to run errands at the store. Buying those things that he could not grow or hunt for himself. His shopping list always much the same: propane, cigarettes, flour, butter, powdered milk, bacon, and whatever fresh greens were on hand. At times he bought things like chocolate and jam, and once a year he made a trip into the big Walmart outside Spokane for birdshot, trapping wire for snares, soap, shaving razors, and kerosene. Often taking his time to wander through the aisles, getting a sense of the way the world had changed around him in the year since.

He was always alone and had grown used to it. At eighty-six he was older than most of the people he met at the little store in town and certainly older than even the retirees who greeted him at Walmart. Three summers before he'd met an old veteran from the Second World War who was eight years older than him and the two had sat on one of the benches outside the Walmart pharmacy for an hour comparing their lives. The next year he looked for the veteran but did not see him, and asking around, he heard that the man had passed sometime that spring.

For a number of years Morgan's only regular connection to the world had been his son. The two sending each other letters that Morgan would sit up and read again and again by the kerosene lamp he kept on his table, or by the light of the small iron stove. The words dancing on the page as the firelight in the belly of the open stove lit the room.

The old man's life had not been good and for a time he had felt that his son's would be better. Only it hadn't, and the same things that had seeped slowly but accurately into Morgan's life had seeped into his son's as well. Guilt and disappointment, hope for something better that never came, and a desire for relief that always seemed just beyond. This feeling of dissatisfaction the old man had come to understand, because it was how the world sometimes worked and he knew—through reading his son's letters—his son had not yet concluded.

DRISCOLL KNEW THE girl as soon as he saw her. The neck broken and the skin bruised a deep purple just beneath her jawline. They were a quarter mile up the lake on one of the muddy logging tracks. The early morning light starting to break through the trees and slip down among the trunks into the undergrowth. To the side of the road one of Gary's deputies was vomiting and the other stood back a ways with a roll of police tape he hadn't yet fed across the road, but that he was supposed to.

"You recognize her?" Gary asked. He stood to the side of the open trunk, giving Driscoll his room.

"She worked at the doughnut shop in town."

"Yes she did." The deputy dry-heaved once more and Gary went on. "Andy's daughter grew up with her. They graduated high school together."

"You wanted me to see this?"

"I called you, didn't I? You had a conversation with Bobby in this girl's doughnut shop. I want to know what you talked about. I want specifics. I want to know why this girl goes missing the very same day."

Driscoll could feel Gary's eyes on him. He could feel the hate, the way the man seemed to blame him for this. Driscoll didn't know what to say. He didn't know if this was his fault. He just kept staring down at the girl, her chin pointed up and to the side like some sort of seabird washed up on a beach. Only it wasn't a beach, it was the trunk of a black Lincoln Town Car.

"How far is this from Bobby's place?" Driscoll asked. He was looking over the girl still, unable to take his eyes from her. Behind, pushed back within the shadows of the trunk was another body. A man stripped to his boxers. His face a bloody mash, the cheeks and nose so swollen that the eyes were pinched shut.

"Close," Gary said. "It's the next drive south of here."

"Did you call Bobby about this? Have you seen or talked to him this morning?"

"I went by there on my way out here. No one was home. With Patrick gone I don't blame them for keeping up the search."

Driscoll turned and looked to where the other deputy was tying the police tape off at the side of the road. The forest to the south now visible and the shadows gathered dense between the trunks. The big pines for a hundred yards almost a singular living thing. And then, kneeling with his calves pushed into the backs of his thighs, Driscoll squinted and saw farther on the first of the apple trees in Drake's orchard. "We need to get over there right now," Driscoll said.

MORGAN DRAKE DID not have a phone nor any way to get ahold of him except the mail, and when he went into town for his necessities he stopped by the small post office and picked up his letters. He was a reader of books and many times when he picked up his mail there would be a number of packages from the store up in Spokane he subscribed to. His letters and packages bound together with twine usually amounted to no more than a couple inches altogether. It was only through the books that he had made his first friend in a long time. A woman who worked at the post office and who was fifteen years younger than him, a widow, who had started quizzing him about the books he received. They started an exchange in this way. Every month, talking about books on her lunch hour. Trading stories.

She'd been to his place only once and he made her a rabbit stew with wild onions and carrots he'd grown himself, browning the rabbit first in bacon grease and flavoring it finally with some of the sage that grew on his property. He'd been proud of it at the time. Though it was nothing special to him, it had made the woman very happy and they'd sat in front of the woodstove for an hour after to talk over books as they did on her lunch hour. Afterward he walked her out onto the small drive where she'd parked and for a moment he thought he would kiss her. But the moment passed and he regretted it deeply, knowing he had let something slip by that he could not replace.

It was the woman he was thinking about as he came up out of the cottonwoods, the rabbit and two prairie dogs on a string over his shoulder. He wanted to cook her something and he was planning it out in his head as he walked. Stopping to catch his breath again, he leaned a hand to the porch railing and kicked the mud from his boots before going into his house.

There was little light inside and he could see that the coals in the stove had burned themselves to white ash, almost dead except for a small pocket of red deep in the belly. He broke kindling and stoked the fire. Leaving the rabbit and prairie dogs in the sink to be skinned and washed in the next hour, he went out onto the porch and sat in a chair watching the way the road wound away from him over the rises of land. Grass everywhere turning from winter gray to something like gold.

From inside his jacket he brought up a pack of cigarettes and shook one out. He put it to his lips and lit it, letting the smoke into his lungs and watching the world around him. It was nearly as cold in the house as outside and he pushed the lapels of his hunting coat up and pulled the collar close around his neck. Holding it there with one hand and smoking with the other.

After a few minutes he went in to check on the stove, threw more wood on, and then came back outside. He liked to sit there in the morning and let the heat build inside the house as the dawn light spread through the sky. The two seeming linked in some cosmic way. He was smoking another cigarette when he saw the sheriff's deputy car break over the far rise in the road and come down the long slope toward his house. It was a car he had seen a few times before and he only stirred slightly as it drew to a stop and the young man got out. The face older than Morgan remembered but still recognizable.

PATRICK SAT FOR an hour in the old logging truck, watching the sun crest the mountains to the east. The lake fog everywhere in the trees and a haze of it floating like a slow river over the fenced-in asphalt parking lot. Through the night he'd kept himself warm with a wool blanket he'd found in the doghouse off the back of the truck's cab. Too worried to climb up into the bunk, he'd sat watching the road through the windshield most of the night. The Silver Lake Sheriff's Department cruiser going past twice while he sat there, and the unmarked Impala patrolling the streets like a shark through clouded water, feeling its way around.

He hadn't meant to run, but he had. The decision coming on him all at once, just like that, there for only an instant and then his feet moving, veering off the road into the forest, jumping thick stands of sword fern and dodging past tree trunks as he went into the darkness. The rich peat smell of the spring earth released with every step, soft and silent as his feet went. A good fifty yards gone by in only a matter of seconds before Patrick turned and watched a single golden flashlight beam spring up behind him.

It was Gary who told him about Driscoll. Both Gary and Patrick waiting for Luke to leave before they could talk. Those two men dead all those years before outside Bellingham. Something terribly wrong about the whole thing, about how it had been handled by both Patrick and Gary. And the bleak promise for the future that had been left for Gary and Patrick when it was done.

"You know he'll never let it lie," Gary was saying. The two of them in the Buck Blind sitting close over the last of their beers.

"I know he won't," Patrick said. He'd already looked toward the door twice, and now he did it a third time, watching for movement, expecting any minute for Driscoll to come through that door and force Patrick's face to the table as he had twelve years before. "I'd be disappointed if Driscoll gave up that easily. All this time he's had his nut out for us."

"Wouldn't you?" Gary asked.

"Those men had wives," Patrick said. "They had children. It's a hell of a legacy we left them."

Gary shook his head and looked off at the bar, where Jack was starting to clean up. "It was an accident," Gary said. "I was all nerves. I didn't mean to shoot them."

"I know you didn't, but that doesn't change the fact that it happened."

"He's telling things to your kid."

"I know," Patrick said.

"Well," Gary said, drawing the word out long before going on again, "what are we going to do about that?"

"Christ, Gary," Patrick whispered. "That isn't on the table. He's a fucking federal agent."

"I've shot bigger animals with my hunting rifle," Gary said. He was grinning and he looked away at Jack where he stood clearing glasses from a far table. The logger who had been playing the music was long since gone from the bar. When his eyes came back to Patrick, Gary said, "It's just a joke. I'd never suggest something like that. I was just asking the question."

"Good," Patrick said. "I didn't go away for twelve years just so I could go back in."

"He's telling stuff to your kid, doesn't that get under your skin? Doesn't that piss you off?"

"I know what he's saying. I know all about it. I wouldn't have left anything around to get Bobby in trouble and I wouldn't do it now."

"You should tell that to Driscoll," Gary said.

"I'd say it to him and he'd go through Bobby's place regardless." Patrick laughed. "If there's anyone I know after being gone for twelve years, it's Driscoll. He came to see me every year. Like we had an anniversary."

"He's a real sweet guy," Gary said.

The man had thought one thing about Patrick for twelve years and he'd been right. Patrick had stolen that drug money. Driscoll wasn't going to give up just because Patrick said he didn't do it.

"Fuck," Patrick said. He finished the last of the beer and sat waiting for something from the universe, anything, some sign to tell him what he should do. Nothing came and he looked over his shoulder at the bartender and watched the son of their old friend Bill bring the glasses behind the bar, then go back to the table and wipe the wood laminate down with a towel. They were the only ones left in the Buck Blind. "I'll call you from the road," Patrick said to Gary.

"I can come with you."

Patrick made a watery circle on the table with the bottom of his glass. "How would that look? Twelve years away and I haven't screwed you over. You think I'll do it now?"

"It's a lot of money," Gary said.

"That's about the only thing that got me through," Patrick said. "My life's already gone, Gary. I wish I could say it to you another way, but that's it. All I'll ever be has already come and gone. And now all there is *is* the money. It's the only thing I can look forward to. You've still got your life."

"You're going to run?"

"Do the smart thing, Gary. Wait it out. The money will be there for you when you retire, just like it's been there these last years. Nothing is going to change. You've still got a life here. I don't have anything like that and I don't see Driscoll giving up on me any time soon."

"You know that kid Jack over there?" Gary said, gesturing to the bartender. "He's a good kid. You need me for anything you give the bar a call."

"He *is* Bill's son," Patrick said.

"He is that." Gary tipped the last of his beer back, then waved to Jack for the total.

Five minutes later they were standing outside the bar. No stars above in the sky and the moon visible only as a faint orb of white light behind the clouds. Rain coming. Down the street Patrick saw Driscoll's Impala waiting for him in the shadows.

Gary turned and followed Patrick's gaze. "You don't think Driscoll will ever give up, do you?"

"I don't think he has it in him," Patrick said.

They said their good-byes and when Patrick was halfway home, he went into the woods.

The truth was that the life he'd led in Silver Lake was gone. It had disappeared the moment Patrick had tried to run twelve years before and Driscoll had been waiting for him, forcing his face down onto a restaurant table. Possibly the life Patrick had always wanted had disappeared even before, when he'd sat in the Seattle hospital listening to the machines pump life in and out of his wife. And it was sure enough gone as soon as he cut through the woods only hours before. Climbing the fence of the logging outfit and waiting inside the cab of the semi.

Patrick saw, too, that his son and Sheri had done good with what was left to them. He could see that just as plainly as he could see his own situation. The land Patrick had shared with his wife was no longer his. It never would be again, never needed to be, and Patrick expected that his presence there would always be a reminder of what had once existed. What had once been his life there and what he had lost.

With the set of keys he'd taken from the steel box at the end of the lot, Patrick started the logging truck. The sun now completely up over the mountains and a sheen of water from the night's rain visible on the asphalt. No sight of a Silver Lake cruiser or Driscoll's Impala for two or three hours. He shifted the gears until he had a feel for the big semi and then he moved out of the line, bringing the front of the truck around and aiming for the gate.

He came out onto the road dragging the chain link beneath him, the sparks visible in the mirrors as he made the turn toward the lake and ground the gears up through second and into third. He knew he could make good time before anyone showed up at the lot, and he hoped he could make the interstate before the first call came in about the broken-down fence and missing truck.

MORGAN QUARTERED THE rabbit, separating the skin first and then running the knife along the joints to break down the carcass. He boned out the legs and pounded the meat flat on the cutting board, leaving it lean and opaque as chicken thighs. When he was done he warmed a pan, letting the grease grow smoky with heat before laying the rabbit sections down against the metal. The oil spitting in the ancient cast-iron pan.

His grandson, Bobby Drake, sat behind him at the table, watching the window that looked toward the road and the slight rise a quarter mile away.

"You hungry?"

Drake turned and looked at the old man and then looked back to the window.

Morgan stood there at the stove listening to the snap of the grease in the pan. He salted the rabbit and turned it, listening again for the familiar sizzle. When he was satisfied he covered the pan, turning the propane down to let the meat cook.

They ate on the porch and watched the road. Morgan smoking a cigarette and letting the meal cool. Drake, with the plate in his lap, picking the meat apart with his fingers. The morning still cold around them and a slight haze beginning to rise off the dew-covered grass with the sun.

"There's more if you want it," Morgan said. "A few pieces of fry bread I made yesterday by the stove as well. I could heat them up." He finished his cigarette and ground it out on the railing.

Drake shook his head. He rubbed his hands over his thighs several times, cleaning the grease from his fingers.

"There's still two pieces of rabbit left," Morgan said.

Drake looked over at his grandfather and then away again. They had said little more than a greeting to each other since he showed up, and Morgan hadn't expected much more. Drake's wedding was the last time they had seen each other. Morgan sitting off to himself for much of the time, smoking cigarettes at a steady pace, at times acknowledging what others said to him, but never offering comment. He was on the road again, headed back east over the mountains and down into the plain, before the wedding had even come to a close. Thankful for the return to the life he'd accustomed himself to.

Besides the widow from the post office, he hadn't had another human being on his property in more than ten years. The chair Drake sat in having to be pulled from inside so they could both sit on the porch.

"You going to tell me what this is about?" the old man asked. He had begun to pick at his own rabbit, careful to keep the plate level on his lap and the juices from staining his pants.

Drake opened his jacket and brought out a series of worn envelopes. Bound with a single rubber band and collected in a stack just the same way Morgan received his mail once a month. Morgan sucked the grease from his fingers and set the plate on the porch again. He leaned forward and took the collection of envelopes from his grandson and turned them over in his hand. He recognized his own scrawl there on the outside of the envelope and looked back over the postmark dates. More than ten years of letters written in his own hand.

"How long has he been out?" Morgan asked.

"A few days. He's been staying with me."

"But he's gone now?"

Drake turned to take in the old man. "A couple men have been looking for him."

Again, Morgan looked down at the collection of letters. "Who has been looking for him?" Morgan asked.

"They said they knew my father from Monroe. They'd like to talk with him."

"In what kind of way?" Morgan asked.

"In the bad kind of way."

Morgan slipped one of the envelopes from the rubber band and opened the letter within. Blue ink and paper yellowed with time.

"I'm hoping you have the other end of those letters," Drake said.

"That's why you came?"

"Those two men almost drowned me last night. They came into our house," Drake said, his voice straining. After a while he went on. "They say he promised them some money."

"Patrick?"

Drake shrugged. "If my father did have some money he didn't trust me with it. I was wondering if he said anything to you. I'd like to see those letters he sent."

Morgan rose from his chair. He tried to think about the letters, bound up with twine. Aged. Sitting away in a hidden place. How many times had he gone through them? Late at night with just the light of the fire burning deep in the stove. Feeling the paper beneath his fingertips, the way the creases had begun to wear and the ink to fade. Months since he'd received the last. He was at the door when he turned. "They're going to hurt Patrick if they find him," the old man said.

"Probably."

"You don't care?"

"They took Sheri."

"Your wife?" Morgan stood looking back at Drake, his body half turned in the doorway. "Did they hurt her?"

"I don't know," Drake said. "I don't know anything."

"You could call someone."

Drake shook his head.

"You don't want to?"

Drake didn't say anything, he'd fixed his eyes on a place at the old man's feet and he looked to be trying to find the bottom.

"They have to know hurting her isn't going to help them," Morgan said. "They have to know that."

"I need to get her back. And in order to do that I need to find my father," Drake said.

DRISCOLL STOOD IN the doorway and looked inward at the bedroom. The comforter lay on the floor with two of the pillows. A single red sheet was still attached at the bottom of the bed, though it, too, had been yanked down and stretched along the floor like blood dripping from a wound.

He turned and went out into the living room and found one of the deputies fingering a half-full milk carton on the counter. "Don't fucking touch that," Driscoll said. He stood watching the deputy till the man put the carton down. "Where's Gary?"

The deputy pointed outside.

They'd found the front door unlocked after they came out of the woods, Driscoll in the lead with Gary close behind. The logging road, where the deputies had found the Town Car early that morning, only a hundred yards through the forest. Driscoll's leather shoes wet from the night's rain as he came out of the trees and stepped into the orchard.

Driscoll found Gary looking at the driveway a few feet past the bottom of the stairs, a pair of long scrapes in the gravel like parallel rows in a garden. The gravel raised on either side and the dirt showing brown beneath. "Did you try Bobby again?"

Gary looked up and nodded. "No answer."

"Try Sheri."

Gary pulled his phone out and put the call through. Driscoll watching. From somewhere inside they heard a phone begin to ring. The deputy came to the door and Gary told him to look into it.

Twenty seconds later the deputy was back with the news the phone was on a charger in the bedroom.

"These are drag marks," Gary said. "I didn't even think to look for them this morning, but now . . ."

Driscoll raised a hand. "I know," he said. "They're both missing now and I don't think they left by choice. The television was on when we came in, there's a half-full carton of milk just sitting on the counter, and the sheets in Bobby and Sheri's bedroom look like someone fought pretty hard to stay in bed."

"And a hundred yards away there's a Town Car with two dead bodies in the trunk," Gary said.

"There's that, too."

Gary's phone began to ring and Driscoll watched him answer. When Gary finished he put the phone away in his pocket and told Driscoll a foreman had just called in about a broken-down chain-link fence and a missing truck.

"WHAT WILL YOU do when you find Patrick?" Morgan asked. He stood by the window, looking out on his property.

Behind, at the table, Drake stirred, pushing one foot across the wood floor. The sound of grit beneath the sole of his shoe. "Arrest him, I guess."

"You don't seem sure of that."

"I'm not."

SHERI WOKE IN darkness with a thin prick of light the only thing visible before her. Her hands were bound and the arm resting on the floor had gone numb. Still she could feel the movement of the car and for a while she lay there trying to think back on how it had all happened. Waking to the sound of someone in her bedroom. The figure of a man moving toward her in the darkness.

She closed her eyes and felt the swelling over her left cheekbone. The flesh raised and tight. The slim prick of light like the only star in a dead sky shining back at her. There was the dusty smell of the trunk and the creak of the springs any time the car moved from one cement panel to another. She didn't know how long she'd been out but she guessed it had been a while.

With her tongue she wet her lips and tasted blood like flaked, rusted iron. A dry crust of it lay along her upper lip, softening as she brought her tongue across the skin again. She was in trouble and for the first time she thought about Drake. She didn't know where she was or who had come into their house.

She moved closer to the light, lifting her neck to get one eye over the hole. With one lid closed she could make out a long country road, cattle wire running both sides, and fields of wheat stalks shining gold on either side. No cars behind and only the yellow dividing line feeding away from her as the road went on underneath the tires.

She let her head drop. The muscles in her neck tight from the effort and the constant thump of the car wheels moving over the concrete. Again she thought of Drake. She was alone and she was scared. She raised her head and placed her eye to the small hole. The road went on behind just as it had before. No one was there, and though she hoped for it, she knew no one was coming.

THE OLD MAN came away from the window and sat in one of the chairs across from his grandson. "That's all of them there." He reached a hand out to touch the worn top of an old shoe box sitting on the table. The feel of the cardboard soft beneath his fingers. "If it's not in there I don't know where it is."

"It?" Drake said.

"Whatever you're looking for."

Drake opened the box and removed the stack of letters. He flipped through the envelopes one after the other, examining the dates before laying them on the table. "What will I find in these?" Drake asked.

"I don't know. Something, but I can't tell you what that something is."

"You can't?"

"I have a friend in town I exchange books with. I read a book and then I give it to her. Some of the things we see in these books are the same, but a lot of it, scene to scene, page to page, is always different. You understand?"

"But you could describe the book for me, couldn't you?"

"Yes."

"Then what would you say?"

"I would say Patrick was sorry about the way things turned out. He worried over the past. He worried over the present. Mostly, though, he worried over the future. What would happen to you. To him."

"That's what's in here?"

"That's what fathers always worry about."

Drake let that sink in before he opened one of the letters and scanned the words. Morgan watched him for a time before he got up and walked to the stove, where he'd left the remaining rabbit to braise over low heat. He lifted the top of the pan and touched the meat with one of his fingers, feeling the bones move beneath.

He was at the sink skinning the two prairie dogs when Drake's phone rang. The old man turned and watched his grandson look at the number on the display, then slip the phone back into his pocket.

"You don't want to get that?"

"It's nothing," Drake said. "I'm waiting on a call but that wasn't it." He was bent over the table, reading one of the letters. It was the third letter Morgan had seen him open.

"What call are you waiting on?"

"The call that tells me Sheri is okay," Drake said. "The call that tells me what I can do."

"I'm sorry about this," Morgan said.

"I'm sorry, too." He held one of the letters up to the light. Something there he was trying to make out. "What are the dates and times at the bottom of each letter?" Drake asked.

"Times when I could see him," Morgan said.

Drake turned and looked at his grandfather. "You went to Monroe?" Drake's phone rang again and he looked at the number and then put the phone away. "How often did you see him?" Drake asked.

Morgan cut a piece of sinew away and brought the skin down another inch. "When I could. Almost any date you see there in the letters. Sometimes I had to wait a bit for the guards to find him but he usually showed within a half hour or so. I brought him things. Books, cigarettes, things he needed."

"I didn't know he smoked."

"I don't think he does, not like me at least. But he could use them. They helped him avoid trouble."

Drake was staring at his grandfather in total disbelief when the phone rang again.

DRISCOLL STOOD IN the orchard. He had his phone out and he listened to the message click on a third time and Drake's voice asking him to leave a number, and then he hung up. Driscoll didn't have a clue and he kept wondering why Drake wouldn't pick up, or if it was Drake at all who had the phone.

The night was starting to come together. Thirty minutes earlier Driscoll had returned from the truck lot, where the foreman had played the closed-circuit cameras back for him. From one angle they saw Patrick climb the fence, then go over, slipping into the lot. From another angle they picked out Driscoll's Impala as it passed by and then came back. They saw Drake's cruiser several times as well. The ghost in the

shadows—Patrick sitting there in the truck cab—watching each vehicle pass. By the time Driscoll returned to the house a set of prints had
come back and two U.S. marshals were on their way out to see them.

The prints belonged to two guys from Monroe. Convicts, Gary
said, who had spent time with Patrick when he was inside. Two violent men who had escaped a week before while being transferred
from Monroe to Walla Walla, killing a guard and taking his hand-
gun with them.

Driscoll looked at the phone in his palm once more. He figured he
had an hour before the marshals showed. An hour before they came in
and took the scene over and Driscoll went back to sitting in an office
in Seattle.

He began to walk to the house. The sun above shone pale beneath
a thin layer of clouds. The heat in the grass causing the dew to rise and
the apple trunks—obscured in places—seeming to float a foot above
the ground.

One night and everything had changed. Two people murdered
and stuffed in the trunk of a car. Drake, Patrick, and Sheri all missing.
And now two escaped prisoners.

He didn't know where any of them were and even seeing Patrick
take the truck, Driscoll didn't know whether Patrick was working
with these men or against them. He had an hour to figure it out.

PATRICK CAME OUT of the Indian casino onto the lot, looking back
over his shoulder as he went. He knew they had cameras in there but
he'd kept his head down, trying only to get through the casino floor
and then out the opposite door.

It had taken only two hours for the police to track down the big
semi. The biggest thing in the lot except for the few RVs that had set
up on the perimeter where the cars were fewer and something as big
as an RV or a semi could be parked sideways across several spaces.

If he'd really wanted to hide the thing he would have dropped it by the cranes and container ships down by the Port of Seattle, but he hadn't had the time to get south, the semi too big and too visible among all the cars on the highway.

Now he walked across the lot, weaving between cars as he went, looking behind him every thirty seconds or so. His nerves going like little electric shocks inside his chest, and an awareness to his movements that he had to force on himself, counting the seconds before he could turn again to look behind toward the semi and the growing flicker of police lights.

Certain that he could not turn around, and that all he'd left behind was waiting for him in the lot by that semi. Prison and possibly worse. There was no going back, and he felt himself committed to whatever would come next, and what that would hold for his future.

Ahead, he saw the cars were beginning to thin. The lot surrounded the casino on all sides. A building that hadn't even existed when he'd been put away, at least not in the form it was now. Ten stories tall, like something off the Vegas Strip, all glass and neon lights.

All down the access road off the highway, he'd passed fast food joints, cell phone stores, and even a Safeway. He looked to these now. The Safeway the closest building. If he was going to make the big grocery store, he'd need to get out of the casino parking area and move across two lanes of traffic and a wide open lot that looked ready for development. It was too much ground to cover.

Looking behind him, he saw two of the officers had already broken away from the rest and were headed toward the casino doors. For a long while he just stood and stared at them, both officers a good hundred yards away across the lot, their attention not on him at all, but on the casino doors.

Patrick was standing between a big Ford pickup and a smaller Toyota. No idea what to do. If he went any farther he'd be on open ground, obvious as a flashing beacon to anyone looking.

He knelt between the two vehicles and felt his chest beating. Moving low on his haunches he made his way through the small alleyways between the cars. At first trying every door he came to, and then, after finding them all locked, he stood for a second and canvassed the nearby lot with his eyes. Most everything a new-model car with a computer doubtless inside and an alarm ready to spring.

When his eyes fell on an old Camry three rows up, he made his way to it with caution, watching for people or cars before scuttling from one row to the next. With his elbow he took out the glass and waited for the alarm. When none sounded he eased the lock up and let himself in. The car model just as he remembered it from before he'd gone away to prison. The number one stolen car in America for almost his entire time as sheriff.

Working quickly, he pulled the harness down from behind the steering column and found the wires he needed. With the sharp edge of the key from the semi, he stripped the rubber sheathing and then dashed them together. The engine came on right away and he put the car in reverse and came out of the parking spot, cautious not to move too fast. The officers he'd seen heading for the casino nowhere in sight. When he let himself look again, he was already on the access road, heading for the highway. The lights still flashing by the abandoned semi.

DRAKE LOOKED AT him and then brought up one of the letters. "What does this mean?" He held the letter in one hand and even without Drake pointing it out to him, Morgan knew the date on the letter and why it had been sent.

Morgan walked the few steps to the table and sat opposite. He took the letter and scanned down through the writing. Patrick had sent it two years ago, just after Drake had come to visit him for the first and only time.

"He was messed up when he wrote this," Morgan said.

"He didn't seem all that messed up to me," Drake said. "He didn't seem like he even gave a shit I'd come to see him."

Morgan shook his head. He wanted to drop the letter, to push it away and dismiss it. But he couldn't.

"I know they censor the letters," Drake said. "I know that's part of it—that sometimes you can't say exactly what you mean."

Morgan's eyes dropped to the letter again. He scanned over it, picking out the text:

> *The boy has come to see me. It's the first time . . . He's grown.*
> *I know you haven't seen much of him but I . . . I need to make*
> *sure everything is set. If I can . . . I'll be out in two. I need to*
> *know that you'll watch over your half.*

Morgan knew that was as close as it came. He knew, too, whatever Patrick had expressed in that letter was still important to him. Drake. Any future Patrick might have with his son.

"You know what he's talking about?" Drake asked. "Your half?"

Morgan looked up. He could see the desperation in Drake's eyes—the need for answers.

"Tell me," Drake said. "If you know something—tell me."

Morgan wet his lips. He wanted to tell Drake everything. All there was to know, however it might help. But he didn't know if it would. The letters were filled with sentences about the future. Patrick had filled his life with them. What he would do when he was out, where he would go, the man he was meant to be. They were simply plans that had not come to be and Morgan did not know if they ever would. But, like Patrick's letters, Morgan hoped one day for something more.

"Please," Drake said.

Morgan looked up at his grandson. A long time ago he'd promised to protect him. Whatever that meant.

DRISCOLL STOOD IN the casino security office looking over the television screens. There were twenty of them total, all showing different angles of the casino. The head of security stood next to Driscoll and he had one of the clerks play the video back a third time.

"You know him?"

It was Patrick. The cameras showed him by the north doors and then seeing the police in the lot next to the truck; they showed Patrick cut across the casino floor and exit through the south entrance. "Can you zoom in on that?"

Using a joystick the clerk brought the image up. It was of an old Toyota Camry in the south lot. "We've put it out over the PA system already but no one's come forward."

"You don't have the license?"

The head of security shook his head. He had straightened and he was looking down at Driscoll where he hunched over the television screen, now working the controls himself. It was no good.

Even if Driscoll had been wrong about the man, the semi made the connection back to Silver Lake. The tape showed Patrick parking and then getting out. No one else had been inside. Which meant Drake and Sheri were still out there. It meant the killers were out there, too.

Driscoll pushed himself up. "Do me a favor. There's going to be two marshals out this way in thirty minutes. If you get a license for that car, I want to be the first to have it." Driscoll found a card and gave it over to the man. He tried to smile but it came off a little loose and desperate. He was clutching at straws and he knew it.

Looking once more at the displays there he couldn't help but feel some relief. If that's what Driscoll could call it. There on the monitor was proof that he'd been right. All those years ago—all those trips to Monroe to see Patrick. It was all coming together. It was the reason Driscoll had come up to Silver Lake to see Drake, to tell the deputy what he suspected. Patrick was running.

PATRICK THOUGHT ABOUT it for a long time. Just sitting there in the stolen Camry and watching the house before he finally pulled away.

He parked the car five blocks over and then walked back through the lengthening shadows. The sun almost down in the west and the street-lights beginning to pop on overhead.

When he came to the house again he paused for only a moment to examine the city street before going up the stairs. He was tired from the night before, huddled beneath the blanket as he sat in the big truck watching the road. His mind numb from the lack of sleep and his hands and face windburned and chapped from the drive down on the interstate. The Camry's one smashed window whistling all the way into Seattle. Mostly though, he didn't have anywhere else to go and he went up the stairs to the house with the singular hope that he would find a bit of rest within.

The stairs creaked underneath him as he climbed, the paint worn down from the constant rain, and the wood beneath showed green as an algal bloom. It wasn't a very nice place, but Patrick hadn't expected much and he went up the stairs with an even lower expectation of the man inside. The house only an address he'd been able to memorize in his time away, a series of numbers on an envelope that he'd dutifully addressed month in and month out for nearly half the time he'd been away in Monroe.

When he got to the door he rang the bell and listened. Somewhere inside there was a television going, and he heard a basketball commentator say, "It's up and it's good." Just around the corner of the house, parked in the driveway, was a new-model red Ford pickup. The only thing about the house that Patrick thought out of the ordinary and made him doubt he was at the right place. Everything else, down to the sagging eaves of the porch roof and the rotten railings, fit into Patrick's assumptions about the man inside.

Patrick pressed the bell again and listened for the chime. Nothing sounded and the basketball game kept going. Looking down the block he saw a few kids riding their bikes around in circles where the cross streets came together. The pavement beneath them almost black in the twilight and the lazy pull and swing of their laps seeming somehow, to Patrick, like vultures on the wing, circling high over some prey.

He sniffled with the cold and dug his hands into his pockets. He was dressed as he'd been the night before, in a padded canvas jacket and jeans. Work boots on his feet and a flannel shirt his son had given him. He watched the kids for only a moment longer before he turned and knocked on the door, listening for a second as the sound on the television lowered.

The only real time Patrick had ever spent in the city of Seattle was when his wife had been in treatment. He looked around at the neighborhood and tried to measure his memories of it then against what he saw today. Lines of waist-high chain link all the way down the block, dividing the sidewalks from the houses. Everything on this block simply built, worn away with time, but still holding. Craftsman-style wood frames over cement foundations.

He heard the latch go on the lock and then the door swung open. "Patrick?" a man's voice said as the overhead porch light went on and Patrick stood looking into the eyes of a man six foot in height, wearing gray sweats, his head shaved to the skin, but a grizzle of white coming through in places along his scalp.

"How's it going, Maurice?"

"People call me Maury out here," Maurice said. "Come on in, Patrick. I'd heard you just got out. I thought you were living with your son, though. I didn't expect to see you in the city."

Patrick followed Maurice in through the door. There were piles of mail and magazines everywhere. Most of the magazines showing glossy pictures of women bodybuilders on the front, tanned almost to the point of rawhide, wearing nothing but G-strings and tops only large enough to hide a quarter of their veined breasts from view. Patrick stood taking it all in while Maurice went into the living room and turned the television down, so that only an aura of subdued excitement emanated up out of the speakers, occasionally an air horn cutting through it all.

"Maury is the name of a sixty-year-old Jewish man," Patrick said.

Maurice looked away from the television and smiled. "Yeah, well, people don't want to hire a man named Maurice. Makes them think I'm a sixty-year-old black man."

"You are a sixty-year-old black man," Patrick said. He cleaned a stack of mail from one of the chairs in Maurice's living room and sat, his vision passing across the room in one sweep. One door leading off toward a kitchen, and another closer doorway that looked to go into a hallway and possibly some bedrooms. "You live alone?" Patrick asked.

"My grandmother left me the house when she passed a few years back."

"Rent-free living?" Patrick asked.

"Yep, I needed it, too. Like I said, no one was hiring an ex-con with the name Maurice."

"That why you changed it up?"

"Uh-huh." He was back to watching the television again.

"You got any work now?" Patrick said.

"Turns out no one is hiring a sixty-year-old ex-con named Maury, either," Maurice said, and then smiled, flashing a grin toward Patrick.

"You look like you're doing all right," Patrick said. "I saw the truck in the driveway."

"Don't be fooled by that. I leased it out. As long as I manage to make my payments it's mine."

Patrick tried not to let his eyes shift over the mess of a living room Maurice was seated in. "I guess you do have to look good while you look for a job, don't you?"

"Appearance is everything," Maurice said. He looked around on Patrick, running his eyes over him like he was appraising Patrick's worth. "You want something to drink? I know you're not supposed to imbibe, at least it's not encouraged, but who's really checking, you know?" Maurice laughed. He was already up and headed for the kitchen and when he came back he gave Patrick a tallboy. "You do okay in there without me?"

"Have you been reading the letters I sent?"

Maurice grinned again and looked around the room. "They're in here somewhere. Looks like you survived at least. How many years has it been?"

"Almost six."

"Shit, man. Time flies."

"Sometimes it does, sometimes it doesn't," Patrick said.

"Well," Maurice said, slapping two hands down on the meat of his thighs and looking around the room like he might find whatever he was looking for right there. "There ain't no business like ho business. You want to make a night of it, or what?"

"Not that kind of night."

"Don't be like that, Pat. You telling me twelve years away didn't get you ready for what's going down tonight? I mean what else are we going to do? You want to sit around and watch the wall? Because you know we did that for six years in Monroe and I'll tell you it's going to be just about as fun. Get your dick wet. Live a little. I tell you it's all I've been thinking about since I woke up this morning, and you showing up tonight makes it all the better reason."

"I'm not into that sort of thing."

"What?" Maurice laughed. "Women?"

"You know what I mean."

"Prostitutes? Okay, okay," Maurice said, raising his hands up, palms out. "The man says it's not his thing, it's not his thing. But how about we go down the street to this place I know and see what we can find. We've got to do something about that limp dick of yours. You've been living like a monk for the last twelve years and you don't want to cut it up a bit? You just got out of prison, brother. Let's live this night up like it ought to be lived. You feel me?"

"I didn't come here for this," Patrick said.

"Tell me about it at the bar," Maurice said. "Too much time in this place and I get claustrophobic."

THE LIGHT WAS fading when Morgan came out onto the porch. He put two hands to his back and worked the muscles till his vertebrae cracked. Then he sat in the chair and simply stared out on his land.

Drake had followed him to the threshold and stood waiting behind him in the doorway. "What are you doing?"

"Thinking things through."

"How's it looking?"

"Not good."

"I'm asking for your help," Drake said. "I don't have anyone else to ask."

"I know that," Morgan said. "But I just don't know what I can do."

Drake walked out and leaned on the porch railing with his hands down supporting his weight. He didn't say anything for a long time. "They have my wife."

"I can't tell you where Patrick is," Morgan said. "I just don't know."

"These men, you ever hear Patrick talk about them?"

"I heard Patrick talk about a lot of things. But I never thought about anything like this. You say one was bigger than the other?"

"Yes. His speech was a little slower, too. The smaller one seemed to be in charge."

"They said they were friends of Patrick's?"

"That's what they said."

Morgan shook his head. The sun was in the grass now, a low red light that seemed to emanate up out of the ground. "I don't know about that," Morgan said. "Your father didn't have many friends."

SHERI FELT THE car come off the pavement. The springs bounced down, and through the floor she heard the sound of gravel under the tires. Raising her head to look out through the small hole at the back of the trunk she saw the paved country road move away from her and the wheat grass build, the road narrow and the swish of the blades moving past the metal sides of the car as a wake of dust rose off the dirt with the car's passage.

She could tell it was late afternoon by the orange light filtered in through the haze coming up off the road and she could also tell which direction was west. She had grown up in Chelan County, dry as tinder in the summers and white with snow in the winter months. The land she looked on now reminding her of that area, grasslands all the way to the Rockies. Wheat and alfalfa fields, hops and industrial apple orchards, all of it to the east of Silver Lake.

With her neck muscles cramping and her eyes straining to catch anything that offered a clue to where she was, she lay there, bouncing to the rhythm of the springs. One pothole after another and the gravel pinging in the wheel wells. Her vision so limited that she could barely make out a thing but the road and the grass all around.

The car came to a stop and she heard the brakes grinding on their discs. The engine stayed on and a door opened. She felt the weight release and the car rise an inch or so. She didn't know what to do and she pressed herself back into the recesses of the trunk, readying herself for whatever might come.

The gunshot she heard tensed every muscle in her body and she rocked back into the darkness, hitting her head against the metal. Nothing had changed inside the trunk. Her world still only the single prick of light at the rear of the trunk lid. Outside only the sound of the wind as it worked through the wheat.

Straining, she heard a chain grate over metal and then fall away into the dirt. Next a gate was pulled open and then the car depressed again and the door closed. They were moving again and Sheri inched her way back toward the small hole of light and watched a cattle gate of some kind as it disappeared around the edge of the road. The wheels beneath continuing down along the gravel.

It wasn't till the car came to a stop again that Sheri felt completely trapped. Tree shadows had worked their way over the road and somewhere in the near distance the sound of water flowing could be heard. She didn't know where she was and her eye strained against the hole, trying to make out anything it could before the trunk opened and the big man who had come into her bedroom stood there looking down at her in a wash of light.

DRISCOLL SAT IN his office looking out over the city. He was seven stories up and through an opening between two of the downtown buildings he watched the bay and West Seattle farther on across the water.

The late afternoon sun was setting over the Olympics and no one but him was in the office. For the better part of an hour he'd sat bouncing a tennis ball against the wall beneath the window. He watched the ferries come and go. Their white bulk moving slowly past and then docking somewhere out of sight beyond the buildings. Occasionally a seagull would swing by, moving past the window seven stories up with its wings still and its head pivoting slightly as it went.

He threw the ball down again and watched it bounce first on the floor and then rocket up off the wall and back into his open hands. He did it three more times before he swiveled on his chair and sat looking at the closed door to his office. He leaned forward and placed his forehead flat on the desk, closing his eyes and breathing in the stale smell of the air. He hadn't been in the place for four days and for two days he'd worn the same suit and shirt.

There wasn't anything he could do anymore. He sat up and pushed himself away from the desk. His jacket lay folded over one of the chairs opposite and he took this up as he went out the door.

For about thirty minutes after leaving the casino and heading south on the interstate Driscoll had been in a kind of euphoria. He'd been right. All those trips to see Patrick—to question what part he played, what role he'd had. All those times Driscoll had asked Patrick just to come clean. To give Driscoll something—just get the killings of those two men off his conscience—and Patrick hadn't budged an inch. Now Patrick was running and it proved something to Driscoll that he'd known he wanted but had never quite been able to imagine.

And for thirty minutes Driscoll had felt satisfied. Driving on the highway, thinking it through, cars passing, cars being passed, suburb after suburb going by as he made his way south to Seattle, and then it occurred to him that Patrick might actually get away with it all.

Driscoll didn't have a license number for the stolen car. He didn't really have anything. And that's what he found himself with now— with less than he'd had four days before. He had almost nothing.

The elevator dinged and when the doors opened he was standing in the lobby level of the federal building. He walked through, the heels of his shoes the only thing to be heard as he made his way across the granite tile. Coming to the door he passed through a series of transparent safety-glass walls and metal detectors, and went out onto the Seattle street. A couple blocks later he sat at the bar of the downtown Sheraton. The bartender nodded to Driscoll and brought over an old-fashioned without even needing to be told.

"You in town this weekend?"

Driscoll rolled the glass around on the counter, watching the liquor coat one side and then the other. He looked up at the bartender. "Yeah, a new case."

"Anything good?"

"No, just a dead end. Thought I'd step out for a little. Get some fresh air."

The bartender nodded again. Silent acknowledgment was really all Driscoll wanted from the man. He existed. He was here. And by the time Driscoll had raised the glass to his lips the bartender was on to a group of executives who had come in out of the lobby.

Driscoll liked the place simply because there weren't any regulars. It was a big chain hotel where the closest thing, besides Driscoll, they got to repeat customers were the flight crews that stayed one night and then were gone again the next. The bartenders were all pretty good at shooting the shit and none of them ever asked anything too personal. Perhaps they just knew how to act when most of their clients might come in once or twice a year, or might never come in again. It was friendly without being prying and Driscoll liked it that way.

A year ago he'd stayed in the hotel for two weeks. The story he'd told them was that he was working a big case, but the truth was he was getting divorced from the woman he'd loved for twenty years. From the woman he still loved. But who didn't love him anymore.

Perhaps if Driscoll had spent more time with his wife or with his daughter instead of in places like this he'd still be married. Though, even thinking it, he knew he probably wouldn't have been. And the time he spent at the office, moving up the ladder, chasing things down, had really been the undoing of his marriage.

He tilted the glass back and finished the old-fashioned in one long swallow. His Adam's apple moving beneath his collar and a thin layering of perspiration collected at his temples. He set the empty down and signaled for another. Driscoll raised a cocktail napkin to his forehead and wiped it clean. He had no fucking clue. Over twelve years he'd worked on this case, picking it up and putting it down.

When the drink came he thanked the bartender and then watched him walk back down the bar. He sipped at his drink and thought it all through again.

Driscoll pulled up his phone and checked for missed calls. There were two text messages from the marshals, but nothing Driscoll could use. He toggled down through the contacts and found the number for his wife. He found his daughter's cell phone number.

Driscoll looked at the highlighted contact in his cell. He read his daughter's name three, then four times, and then he put the phone facedown on the bar and picked up the old-fashioned again. Beads of water had grown on the sides of the glass. The cocktail napkin on which it sat stuck to the bottom as he tipped it back and took another long swallow of the sugary bourbon.

For a long time after his marriage came apart Driscoll had wondered if they'd ever been happy, his wife, his daughter, him. Or maybe they'd never been happy and he just thought of them that way because it was easier for him to deal with. His wife and daughter like something out of a dream, half remembered the next morning, slipping slowly away with the coming light of day.

But the thought was too painful and when the bartender came by Driscoll ordered another drink. Driscoll had no fucking clue and he knew it.

MORGAN SET THE log and then hefted the ax, bringing the blade down into the wood and sinking the metal deep as the handle. He raised the log in this way and brought it down again, listening to the tear as the two sides came apart and fell aside. The work had been waiting for a week now and he went after it, breathing hard, while sweat beaded on his forehead and the back of his shirt grew wet with perspiration between his shoulder blades. He bent and hefted the two sides of the split to the pile nearby and set another. Pausing to wipe a sleeve across his forehead and look to the cabin.

He knew he was being a coward. He'd never set out to hide anything from his grandson, and now that's what he was doing. Patrick had abandoned them both and now Morgan was left trying to set it all straight. He thought of Patrick again. Where was he? What was he doing? Did he have any idea what was going on?

For a time Morgan just stood there with the ax in his hand, wondering about a great many things, and thinking about Bobby inside his house, back at the table with the letters, reading every page as if it was going to reveal some great secret, though Morgan knew there was nothing like that to be found, and the things that his grandson searched for were not so easily located.

After splitting the next log Morgan paused to sit. He ran his hand down into his jacket for his cigarettes. He brought out his pack and shook a smoke out. Placing it to his lips and then feeling the weight of the pack in his hand, he thought better of it, took the cigarette from his mouth, and then slipped the pack back inside his pocket. He smoked too much but it hadn't hurt him much till a year or so before. Whether it was old age or some cancer growing inside him, he couldn't tell, but he thought it was probably both, and he went on through his days with the weight of it over his shoulders like a lead harness, pulling god-knows-what behind.

He wiped a sleeve across his forehead again and looked at his grandson in there at the table. Sheri was missing and he didn't know what he could do about that, but he knew he had to try. "Well," he said, leaning one hand to the seat and angling himself up. "I guess I'm old enough."

He came up the stairs and stood on the porch looking in through the front window. He didn't know what he was protecting anymore. "Old," Morgan said, in a whisper only audible to him, "and now I've begun to talk to myself." He put a hand out and turned the doorknob. "What's new about that?" he said, answering his own voice.

Drake looked up at him as he came into the cabin. "I don't know if it will help but I want to tell you something about those men who took your wife," Morgan said. "I know them and they know me. The skinnier one is named Bean and the bigger one is John Wesley. They looked out for Patrick while he was inside. And for a long time I helped them by bringing whatever they needed from the outside."

B EAN CHECKED THE SIGNAL on the prepaid phone, the green light of the display open in his palm. A primordial glow showing on the lines of his face before he closed the thing in his palm and took a step away into the night. The day gone behind the mountains and the light from the fire barely visible through the small thicket of trees. He paused to take it all in, the country road a mile off but no car seen or heard for over an hour now. The place he'd picked for them close to a drainage stream, no bigger than a creek, the trees grown tall and thick around the water's edge.

He stood there looking it all over, the creek heard from time to time, and the wind shifting and moving the branches overhead. Smoke pulled one way from the fire and then another, gray as it rose, and then turned black, all of it lit from beneath and then fading away into the night sky above. At the fire Bean could see where John Wesley stood with a slender branch of willow in his hand, tending to the coals with his eyes fixed downward into the flames, and Drake's wife sitting there with her hands still taped together in front of her.

They hadn't talked more than to offer her some food. Cans of chili they ate cold with their fingertips. A few apples they'd stolen from Drake's kitchen. They ate and threw the empty tins into the shadows of the thicket. Only letting Sheri eat when they had finished.

Now Bean stood beyond the fire wearing the black suit, his legs knee-deep in the wheat field. The lapels of his jacket turned up to ward off the cold and the black material scuffed with dirt in places from the few days of work he'd used it for. He pulled the lapels closer around his neck and walked a few more feet through the grass, holding the lapels of his jacket to his skin and watching the empty space in the wheat fields a mile off where the road came through.

In his other hand he depressed the power button on the phone and listened to the music play and then when he was satisfied he turned the phone back on and watched the display light again. The same signal as before.

THE BAR MAURICE TOOK him to was a small neighborhood spot a few blocks up. Dimly lit with blue and purple neon lights all down the wall, and the windows tinted almost black. It was unlike any place Patrick had ever been, low ceilinged with a pearly light of neon on every surface. The beer was mostly in bottles and the liquor in plastic jugs. The customers a mix of the young taking shots at the bar—their heads tipped back and their nostrils flared with each progressive slug of alcohol—and the older crowd closer to Patrick's and Maurice's age. Mostly single men who looked to have come in after work for a cheap beer and a view of the younger crowd.

It wasn't the type of place Patrick had been expecting. Nothing like the Buck Blind back in Silver Lake, where he could grab a beer and have a discussion. Maurice's bar was loud and dirty. Patrick wanting nothing to do with it as he looked around the crowded room for the nearest exits while music pumped like an artery in his ears.

Still, Patrick tried to talk to Maurice about why he was there, but the music was too loud and the man simply nodded at everything Patrick said, watching the crowd behind them in the mirror. Every once in a while taking sips from a glass of whiskey. The place so crowded that Patrick hadn't noticed the girls behind them until Maurice turned to talk to them. Maurice introduced them each in turn, telling Patrick how he knew them. Patrick struggling to hear above the music, but the girls not seeming to care as they danced in place to the rhythm.

SHERI WORE ONLY a set of sleeping shorts and a tank top and she squatted next to the fire feeling the heat on her skin. She extended her bound hands toward the flames, feeling the fire on her palms. The night cold behind her and the frozen feel of her clothes any time they touched the skin. She was shivering with her teeth chattering and the tremors rolling up her spine almost as constant as the wind that came over the wheat fields.

Opposite, John Wesley sat on a log and watched the fire. He was at least a foot taller than her and weighed close to three hundred pounds. He looked slow and cumbersome in the padded flannel he wore. His jeans too tight and the bulge of his stomach showing where it came over the waistline and protruded pink and hairy from beneath his shirt.

The other man had gone to lie down in the car and she could hear the soft pull and give of his breath from time to time. She looked up at the big man and then looked away again. He hadn't taken his eyes from the fire in more than ten minutes.

Already the fire was dying, sputtering on the meager collection of fuel they'd managed to cull from the grasslands. The flames licking past the dried edges of wood while Sheri listened to the crackle of grass and sage. John Wesley watching the small twigs blacken, then falter, curling in on themselves like the last spasm of life in a dying spider.

She stood and turned to catch some heat on the backs of her legs, watching the night beyond the thicket of trees and listening to the drainage stream flowing past. Out in the fields the wash of a single car went past on the nearby road. It was the only sound besides the crack of the fire and the rolling waters of the stream she had heard in over four hours.

"This time of year it can get into the teens at night," John Wesley said. He'd risen from the log he sat on and he stood now looking across the fire at her. Her legs white from the cold and beyond the flicker of firelight echoing out through the trunks of the trees into the night. John Wesley took off his flannel and brought it around to her. "This will help."

He laid the jacket over her shoulders, and she felt herself jump and then tense, waiting for some punishment that didn't come. He was gone back to his side when she turned. The white undershirt he wore stained in the armpits and around the collar from days of wear. "Thank you," she said, crouching again so that the tails of the flannel fell over her thighs.

She turned and looked to where the car sat. The doors closed and the windows fogged with the heat from Bean's lungs. When she turned back she asked John Wesley if Bean was waiting on a call. "I've seen him look at his phone a few times," she said. "Is it my husband he's waiting on?"

"Something like that," John Wesley said. He picked up the willow switch and played with the fire.

"And you're looking for Patrick?"

"Yes."

He played with the stick for a long time, letting air into the belly of the fire and watching as the oxygen bloomed red with flame. When he looked up at her he asked, "Does it hurt?" gesturing to the welt at her cheekbone.

"No," she said, bringing her wrists up and laying the back of her hand to the swollen side of her face. "It's better now."

"I'm sorry about it."

She tried to give him a good-natured smile but it came out ghoulish across the fire. "I need to use the bathroom," she said.

"I can't untie you."

"You don't have to."

He rose and came around the fire and pulled her up with one hand and she felt the power as he lifted her onto her toes and then placed her down again. They walked out past the fire to the edge of the trees and she felt his arm loosen and then release. "This good?" he asked.

"Yes," she said. She looked around at him where he stood, only a couple feet off. "Can you at least turn around?" she asked.

He looked her over for a second and then half turned, his eyes faced away from her as she squatted. Working with her hands bound she had to shimmy the shorts down. Her bladder at the point of exploding and steam rising from between her legs as she peed, the blue light of the moon everywhere in the night and the wheat shifting like waves across a distant ocean.

She felt abandoned and set adrift. What mountains she'd been able to see in the last long beams of sun lost from view and the night beyond black as it had ever seemed to her. She squatted, looking over the wheat field like a sailor looking for land.

She thought of Drake out there somewhere. She thought of Patrick. She hoped for all of this to go away but she didn't know how it could.

Behind, the crack of a twig in the fire. She turned her head to look at John Wesley, the corner of his eye on her. "You done?" he asked.

She nodded and looked once more toward the open wheat fields. John Wesley waited for her to pull her shorts back up before reaching a hand to her arm. She dodged his grip and before she thought any more about it she was into the wheat, high-stepping as fast as possible and trying to keep low. John Wesley somewhere behind, crashing after her. The wheat cut at her bare thighs as she ran and the flannel John Wesley had given to her fell behind somewhere in the field.

"YOU'RE SAYING YOU know those men."

Morgan stood with his weight to the sink and his hands behind on the counter. He was looking back at his grandson where he paced the small room. "I've known them for a long time," Morgan said. "They looked out for Patrick while he was away—made sure no one messed with him."

Drake stopped and put his hands to the back of a chair, the window black with the night beyond. "And how did they do that?" Drake asked. He was not looking at Morgan, but at the old man's reflection in the window.

"It wasn't easy for Patrick. You should know that. I'm sure you've heard what it's like for a lawman in there."

"He promised them something, didn't he?" Drake hadn't moved and Morgan could see his hands tighten on the chair back, the knuckles grown white.

"He did."

"More than cigarettes and little things from the outside," Drake said. He turned and fixed his grandfather.

"Yes," Morgan said.

"And now they've followed my father into our lives. Into my life with my wife, and into our home."

"I don't think Patrick meant for it to happen this way," Morgan said.

"But it has."

"Yes," Morgan agreed. "Your father just wanted to get home. That's all there was to it. He wanted to make sure of that. I don't blame him for what he did. I don't even blame him for what's happened now. With all the wrong your father did it was always for the right reason. It was for you."

Drake stared back at his grandfather, his jaw held tight and the muscles tense against his temples. "For me?"

"That's all he ever talked about when I went to see him." Morgan gestured to the letters once again collected in their box. "You can read it right there. You can read it for yourself if you don't want to hear it from me."

Drake just shook his head. His body now half turned to take in the box of letters on the table. He was shaking slightly and there looked to be little control left in him.

"I'm sorry," Morgan said. "I'm sorry about how this has all turned out." He patted his shirt pocket, looking for his cigarettes. "From what you've told me already I don't even think Patrick knows these men are looking for him."

"Why's that?"

Morgan found his pack of cigarettes and thumbed one out. He replaced the pack again and began patting at his pockets once more, looking for his lighter.

"Why's that?" Drake asked again.

Morgan stopped and looked back at his grandson. "Because technically they're not supposed to be out of prison for the next twenty years."

"WHY DON'T YOU call him Maury?" the girl asked.

"It's not his name," Patrick said. "His name is Maurice." They were sitting on the couch in Maurice's house. The second girl was back in the bedroom with Maurice and occasionally—over the sound of the living room television turned, still, dully on—Patrick would hear Maurice say something and then he would hear the girl laugh.

"I'd be more worried about your own name."

"Why's that?" Patrick asked.

The girl considered the question for a time, as if weighing the outcome of her answer. "Your name is Pat," she said, smiling at him and putting a hand across his thigh. "Isn't it a woman's name?"

"It's short for Patrick," he said. He tried to move away on the couch, but felt the girl's nails tuck in under the inseam of his jeans and pull him closer.

"Pat, Patty, Patricia," the girl said.

"How old are you?" Patrick asked.

"Old enough." The girl grinned, keeping her eyes on his. She had one leg up and over him before he thought to move. Straddling him like some beast she meant to ride. "Maury says you just got out."

"That's right," Patrick said. He was looking up at her where she sat. His nerves going berserk beneath his skin and the warmth from the undersides of her thighs now pressed on his lap.

"Maury is a good guy," the girl said. "He's a friend of ours." She pushed in beneath his chin and he felt her nuzzle up under his jaw and begin to kiss his neck. His eyes not seeming to focus anymore, and an anxiety for the thing that he couldn't explain, but, at the same time, elated him.

He found his hands wrapped up behind her, reaching up the skin of her back beneath the clasp of her bra, moving one way against her skin and then retreating. Something pleasurable and animal about it all, the catch and pull of his palms against her bare skin, the dig of his fingertips as they moved over her ribs. He brought his hands around and clutched her sides, pulling her into him.

All of it feeling like something beyond his control, an act of God, a storm approaching, something there was no defense for.

He ran his hands over her back and sides, tight skin everywhere on her body that he didn't know what to do with, but at the same time felt bound up within and committed to—a man fallen into a river, fighting against the coming falls.

He'd been with only one woman since his wife died. A woman ten years younger than him and a teacher at the local school, someone who had worked with his wife, and who, at the time, taught his son. The whole experience rushed and awkward, something sudden in the backseat of a car after a night of drinking. No words spoken or heard, just the act in its barest form. Performed and then quickly pushed away, never to be spoken of at parent-teacher meetings or when their paths crossed on the street or in the grocery store.

It had been a mistake, and Patrick had thought about it often when he'd been away in Monroe. Dreaming up other outcomes and conclusions for that night, but never truly being able to put it behind in any better light.

The girl slid off him onto the floor, her two hands gripped on his belt and pulling him lower against the couch. The cool press of her fingernails inside his waistband.

He felt bubbled inside the room, like there was no outside world, and it was only here alone that he existed. The girl between his legs as her hands worked on his belt. He heard her laugh and he felt momentary fear as she pulled his pants from his thighs and over his knees. "Guess you are a Patrick," she said, laughing still, and then standing to take her pants down and then step out of them, one foot after the other.

In that brief second he tried to think of something to say, something he thought she might enjoy. But nothing came and he looked at her body there before him, two skinny legs, her body marked red in places by the pass of his own hands against her flesh. He sat forward and helped her with her shirt until she took it in one hand and pulled it off. So much bare skin, he thought.

"How old are you?" he asked again.

"Old enough to be your daughter, or your granddaughter," the girl said, watching Patrick, a cruel little smile on her lips. "Whatever you like. Whatever you're into."

His mind suddenly wanted to be anyplace but here. A desperation fighting inside of him to just get up and walk out of the house. Though he knew he never would, and that he was already committed to how things would turn out.

He closed his eyes and he felt her legs again on top of him. Different now, as she put her hands to his shoulders and eased him back.

SHE RAN UNTIL she couldn't feel her legs anymore. Cold as stone with the pale skin slashed red with blood from the blades of wheat. She slowed, crouching with her hands bound in front of her, fingers splayed into the earth for balance. The night air on her immediately and her own heat rising from her in a pale blue tangle of mist. Not a sound behind her but the wind working through the wheat.

The road was only fifty yards on but her thighs felt heavy on her legs already. She dropped to a knee, listening to the wheat move. No John Wesley; his footsteps faded away behind her as she ran, fading away until he wasn't there at all. Now she didn't know where he had gone. Whether he was behind her still or ahead of her, moving around on her as she rested.

For a full minute she waited. The cold of the night everywhere now. She looked to the road, just a matter of yards away and up a small rise. She knew it would be the easiest thing to follow.

She ran her eyes over the field one more time, left to right, watching the wheat bend in the breeze. Her heart beating in her chest and an elevated awareness to everything around. Turning, she went on, slowing four or five times as she went to look behind and listen to the wheat. In the night there was nothing to tell her which way to go, no mountains to show her the way home and the moon high overhead, fixed in the sky at its midpoint.

She came to the road almost by accident, stumbling out of the wheat into a small drainage ditch. The road raised slightly in front of her. With her two hands out in front she scrambled up the loose gravel onto the pavement. Keeping low she started to move down the road in the direction she thought they had come from.

She didn't have any way to tell if she was going the right way and for a second she turned to study the road behind. Nothing but the lightless night behind her, going on and on, her breath curling away in front of her face before it thinned into the air. The cold felt now where the sweat had begun to show and cool her skin.

She went on, the cuts on her legs tearing at her thighs and the sweat stinging her eyes. Her only hope was to find a farmhouse or town. Anything that would offer the least bit of protection.

Up ahead she saw a pair of headlights break over a low rise in the wheat and move toward her. Sheri slowed, jogging and looking behind her at the open road. She raised both hands in the hope she would be seen. The light from the car headlights now everywhere around her.

She watched the car draw to a stop twenty feet before her and the man inside get up out of the driver's-side door. His silhouette just visible behind the glare of the headlights. His head turned toward where Sheri stood, her arms still raised into the air.

"Thank God," she said, trying to catch her breath. The man moving out from behind the headlights toward her as she kept speaking. "I'm—" And then she stopped short.

"Good run?" Bean asked. He was almost to her now, the gun in one hand while the other reached for her arm.

She put a foot behind her, pivoting, her head half turned, and then something heavy hit her full in the face and the last thing she remembered was the numbing heat of her own skull hitting the pavement.

MORGAN CAME IN out of the cold carrying a pail of stream water in his hand. His right side burdened with the weight as he closed the door, then set the pail near the stove. At the window Drake was watching the road leading away up the hill. Morgan could see also that the boy had found the old double-barrel. The shotgun and a weathered box of bird shot there on the table behind Drake.

Morgan sat and rested on one of the dining room chairs. He picked up the box of shells and examined the cardboard. He hadn't used the things in a while. No reason to. Not enough time or energy left in his life to sit and wait for something to chance in front of him. And no one to give the meat to if he did. The rabbits and prairie dogs enough for him in the spring and summer. In the colder months his hands had begun to hurt. His fingers not as steady and the joints often aching, making the Arctic birds fat from their summer feeding harder and harder for Morgan to shoot.

Morgan knew Drake was still angry about it all. The boy had barely spoken to him in the last hour, not since he'd told him who the men were. Or, more aptly, who they were to the best of Morgan's knowledge. Killers through and through, and Morgan knew, too, that he should be scared of them, but he just wasn't. They had never been unkind to him in all his dealings. They had protected Patrick. And Morgan could not deny them his gratitude.

He set the box of ammunition down on the table and pushed it away from him. He looked up at Drake where he stood at the window. "What's this for?"

"They can come into your life just as easily as they came into mine."

"They don't know where I live," Morgan said. "They don't know about this place."

Drake stepped away from the window and sat opposite Morgan. He picked up the shells of bird shot and fed two into the bores of the shotgun. And then he placed the gun back on the table, pushing it with his fingers toward Morgan.

"What will you do if they come here?"

Drake brought out his service weapon and showed it to the old man. He put it away at the back of his waistband almost as quickly as he brought it out, looking away from Morgan until he could find his words. "I'm angry, that's all. I'm just angry and I have no place to go. I know almost as much now as I did this morning and that's nothing at all."

Morgan rested his eyes on the shotgun again but didn't comment. After a while he asked, "You and your wife have any children?"

Drake turned and looked at his grandfather and then looked away again. After a moment he said, "No," to the empty pane of glass.

Morgan thought to leave it, but he thought he'd see it through. "You ever wonder what it would be like?" Morgan asked.

Drake stirred but didn't say anything.

"It replaces all there ever was in your life and all there will ever be," Morgan said. "Even if you turn your back on them the feelings you have will still exist, knowing they're out there, knowing something that came from you is out there in the world."

Drake got up from the table and walked to the stove. Taking his time he turned on the propane and lit the small burner. He poured water from the pail into a pot and set it to boil. "What if you found out your child murdered someone?" Drake said. "What would you do then? Would you still love him?"

Morgan thought that over. He knew why the killers had come into his grandson's life. He knew what they'd been promised and how it was Patrick had come to possess what they were looking for.

Money. It had existed out there in the world for many years and it would exist out there in one form or another for many more. And it meant nothing to Morgan. Not a thing. "I still love Patrick," Morgan said.

"No matter what he's done?"

"I don't like what he's done. I don't think he was right or that many would forgive him. But, yes, it doesn't change anything in me."

Drake took two tin cups from beside the sink and then turned to his grandfather and gestured to the boiling water. Morgan told him where to find the tea and then Drake poured and brought the cups to the table. Both sat at the table with the hot tin between their palms. Finally Drake said, "You get lonely out here? No phone? No neighbors? No one to talk to?"

Morgan told his grandson about the woman at the post office. He told him about the meal they'd had. About the way they sat and talked through her lunch hour. He told Drake about the old veteran from Walmart and how the man—even with all he'd done in his life—had seemed dissatisfied. Like he had one eye on the past and the other on the afterlife.

"I'm worried about Sheri," Drake said.

"I know."

"I'm not a killer," Drake said.

"I know that, too."

"I've thought about it a lot in the last few hours. I've thought about what I will do when I find those men—just doing it, but I don't know if I can." He raised his eyes and Morgan could see the worry painted on his face. "I tried to shoot a man once," Drake said. "He put two bullets in me and sliced up my hand. I couldn't do it. I should have but I didn't and I think about that a lot. Reliving how it went wrong."

"You've got to let that go."

"My father told you about that?"

"He did."

After a while Drake asked. "Are you scared? Those men out there— you worry about what they might do when they have what they want?"

"No," Morgan said. "I imagine they're making their minds up about all of us, but I don't feel threatened by it."

"You think my father would feel the same?"

"I think if he knew you were here with me, Sheri taken by those men, he'd do something about it. I think he'd have to."

THE GIRL WAS gone when Patrick woke. He lay on the sofa looking up at the ceiling of Maurice's living room. Night outside and the occasional wash of headlights going past on the road. He didn't know what time it was but didn't think he'd slept for very long. With one hand he pressed the thin sheet Maurice had given him to his waist and swung his legs to the floor. With his other hand he searched the sofa for his underwear and then pulled them on.

In the bathroom he pissed a stream of urine that smelled of whiskey, his free hand held out on the wall for balance. From the window over the sink he could see Maurice's red pickup still parked there in the drive. The reflection of the streetlights shining brightly on the waxed paint.

Patrick ran the faucet and then cupped the water and washed his hands and face. He didn't know what he'd thought to accomplish coming here. He only knew that he'd needed to come, that he owed Maurice that at least.

When he was done he dried his hands and came out of the bathroom. The house dark and the clock on the stove telling him it was nearly one A.M. The door to Maurice's room cracked and Patrick stopped just beyond. Maurice a dark shadow on the white sheets of his bed. The gray pants pulled up and no shirt to cover his chest. Patrick pushed the door open a foot. "You awake?" he asked.

Maurice shifted and then looked up. "Some night, eh?"

"Yeah."

Maurice was smiling now, a big grin showing on his face. "You won't want to wash that smell off for days," he said. "There's nothing like it. You feel me, right?"

"I came here because I thought we should talk. I'm out now. I owe you. You took care of me in Monroe. I didn't want you to think I forgot."

Maurice pulled a cigarette from somewhere and lit it, offering one to Patrick.

"No," Patrick said.

"I didn't forget, Pat. I knew you'd come by. I'm glad you did."

"I need you to help me get the money. I need that truck out there."

"Sure, Pat. We can go in the morning. I don't have a problem with that. I know you came here for more than just a good time."

"It's a lot of money," Patrick said.

"I know it is."

"I just thought it would be on your mind."

"It has." He smiled again and then took a long pull off the cigarette and let the smoke roll up out of his lungs into the room. "You did have a good time, didn't you?"

Patrick watched his old friend. He hadn't moved but to light the cigarette and he lay there in his bed. On the nightstand beside him, Maurice's wallet, cell phone, and keys neatly stacked one on top of the other like a cairn of rocks marking a trailhead. "Yeah, the best," Patrick said. "Better than being in prison."

Maurice laughed again, looking around on Patrick. Smoke escaping the line of his teeth. "You're goddamn right," Maurice said.

JOHN WESLEY LIFTED SHERI'S head in his hand, turning her one way, then the other. In one hand he held a burning log from the fire. The flicker of light playing across one of Sheri's cheeks while the other cheek lay in darkness like a cool, worn-away river stone waiting somewhere in the recesses of a dried-out creek.

They'd picked her up off the road and put her in the backseat of the car. Now John Wesley waited for her to wake. Their fire fifteen feet off and the car door pulled open. And he could see that if she stayed with them for a day more she'd be broken. He hadn't meant to lift her off her feet with the punch but she was such a fragile little thing and she'd come up off her toes almost like it hadn't been him at all.

He turned and looked to the fire. Bean waiting there and the shadow he cast stretching away behind him into the trees. With one hand John Wesley closed the door, the log in his hand smoldering now and the embers beating to the pulse of what little wind there was. He'd never taken someone from their home, though he knew Bean had, and he wondered how it would turn out for all of them. The three of them now connected in some irrevocable way.

When he came back into the firelight, Bean was waiting for him, standing in the same place he'd been before. Half there and half somewhere else entirely. "Is she going to live?" A cruel smile on Bean's face as he said it and the lapels of his coat pushed together in one hand, while his other hand reached for the warmth of the fire.

"I think so."

John Wesley knelt and dug the log into the coals. When he stood again, Bean was holding the phone, the green light of the display flashing in his hand and the low pulsing sound of its vibration.

Bean depressed a button and held the phone to his ear. He listened for a time and then when he was finished, he looked over at John Wesley, the grin growing across Bean's face. "Yeah, man, I feel you," Bean said, and then closed the phone, already turning toward the car, Seattle a few hours' drive away.

PART IV

THE OLD MAN AND THE SEA

MORGAN WOKE HIM BEFORE sunrise. The dawn light at the horizon and Drake's grandfather bent over him with a hand to his shoulder.

Drake came up like a man surfacing from below, air pulled deep in his lungs with his first waking breath. He sat straight up in the chair, the muted blue light everywhere inside the small cabin. No memory of closing his eyes or even laying his head down against the table.

"You've been asleep almost seven hours," Morgan said, his hand taken back from Drake's shoulder. Morgan waited a moment and then walked to the stove and lit the propane burner. He placed some water to boil and then turned back to Drake, still there where he had left him.

Drake pushed himself away from the table and stood. He ran a hand through his sleep-mussed hair to smooth it down and at the same time walked to the window. Bending slightly to take in the light coming up over the far rise. "What time is it?" he asked.

"Almost six."

Drake looked around the room, everything the way he'd left it the night before. The shotgun on the table and the cast-iron stove there in the center of the room with the smoke pipe vented to the roof. The room seeming colder to Drake than it had at any point since he'd arrived the day before. He pulled up his cell phone and looked at the display. "Did anyone call?" he asked.

"No."

"Nothing?"

"I know them," Morgan said. "Until they have what they came for she'll be safe."

Drake watched the old man. The water began to bubble inside the pan and when it was ready the old man poured it into a shallow bowl. With a rag he cleaned his weathered face and ran the cloth beneath his neck. The excess water falling to the bowl while Drake tried to gather his senses for the day. "You shouldn't have let me sleep . . . ," Drake began.

Morgan looked up, placing the rag on the edge of the small wash-basin. "I want to show you something. Would that be okay? Something I think is important for you to see."

IT TOOK DRISCOLL a moment to figure where he was. With his head tipped back and his mouth open he soon found he was looking at the ceiling tiles in his office. He snapped his mouth shut and swallowed to wet his throat.

He checked his watch and then stood, putting two hands to his back as he felt his vertebrae pop. The office was just how Driscoll had left it the afternoon before. He tried to play back his night but he came up short. There were only glimpses of things said and done. Two more old-fashioneds, the brief memory of shots being taken with the bartender, and then at another bar a basket of fries eaten and then washed down with a cold can of beer. He ran back through it, trying all the more. A life seen through the slats of a fence while Driscoll paced one side, peering through at the night before.

He turned and took in the office. Everything was there, his jacket on the chair, his gun on the desk next to his keys and wallet. He walked around and brought up his jacket. Holding it with one hand he patted the material down with the other as he looked for his phone.

Driscoll had missed a call from the marshals and then another from the head of security at the casino. He listened to them both and then sat back at his desk and thought it through. One of the black-jack dealers, a woman working a double, had noticed her car was gone when she left around eleven the night before.

The marshals were angry he hadn't answered any of their calls, but Driscoll didn't care. A quick check with the Seattle police and the state patrol came up with nothing on the Toyota Camry and he knew they were all still clutching at straws.

From a drawer in his desk he took out a bottle of ibuprofen and swallowed four pills dry. He went to the bathroom and cupped water into his hands, drinking it like some lost wanderer come in out of the desert sun. When he straightened and saw himself in the mirror there were dark circles beneath his eyes and a layer of scruff had grown on his cheeks and neck. The shirt he wore was greasy from three days' wear and the top couple buttons left undone. No idea what had happened to his tie.

He came back to the office and stood in the doorway. In all the time Patrick had been locked away Driscoll had gone right to the source and now with Patrick missing he knew he had to find another source.

THE NIGHT COOL was still in the cottonwoods when Drake and Morgan came down off the prairie and threaded their way into the stand. The sound of the creek there at the base of the hollow and the first white tufts of spring beginning to show in the branches above. They crossed and went up the opposite side, coming out of the trees and into the grasslands again.

Drake carried the shotgun in his hand as his grandfather led. The old man holding a set of the wire snares and watching his steps as they came up off the creek. Drake with no idea what his grandfather meant to show him, or why it mattered. No word from the killers. Sheri gone away somewhere and Drake worrying over where that place might be and who was at the end of it.

"Before your father went to prison he used to come out this way to visit," Morgan said, the wheeze of his breath audible between words. "We'd set snares in the morning and then shoot some in the day. Then, in the evening, cook whatever we'd managed to pull from the prairie. Most times we'd leave a few snares till the next morning and Patrick would go home with a couple rabbits."

"He came out here?"

"When he could."

Drake walked with the shotgun faced outward and down as he had on so many other days with Patrick, following his father up the cut of a ravine so that they could find a high point to take in the terrain. The wood stock of the gun warmed by his hand.

As if sensing his thought, Morgan said, "I've been meaning to ask, don't you have something in your cruiser that has a little more wallop?"

Drake kept walking. He didn't want to tell his grandfather the two killers had emptied out the car. He was angry with himself for dropping his guard—for trusting Patrick. He still was. He didn't want to tell Morgan the only protection he had left was his service weapon.

What the killers had taken from him was worse than anything they could have taken from within the cruiser. When they came into his house they took any sense of security he'd had. The life he and Sheri had made for themselves was fractured. Sheri pulled one way and Drake the other. And he was thinking about this now, watching the steps he took, feeling the grass bend beneath his shoes.

They walked for another five minutes. Drake watched his grandfather's back. The grass as high as their thighs in places and the prairie rolling before them with the mountains far beyond in the west, the steam of Morgan's breath floating back over his shoulder as he picked his steps.

"Let me ask you something," Morgan said. "You had a good childhood, didn't you? You lived a good life. You played basketball and Patrick took you camping in the mountains. You had friends. School was good to you."

"Yes," Drake replied. They had crossed a long stretch of flat ground and ahead of them was a fence of wooden posts and barbed wire.

"He wasn't the man you think of now."

"He wasn't the man he is now," Drake said. "He was a sheriff and now he isn't."

"Occupation defines him, then?"

"You know what I mean."

"I think it's easier for you to keep him in the box everyone else keeps him in."

Drake wouldn't respond. Behind him, the tops of the cotton-woods had dropped below the horizon and the prairie seemed to go on forever.

"I know when he was caught it shook you up," Morgan said. "Everything you thought about Patrick was brought into question. And that scared you. It turned your life upside down. You blamed him for that, you still do."

"Yes."

"But yesterday when I asked you what would happen when you found him, you didn't know."

"I'm a sheriff's deputy and he's a criminal," Drake said, feeling his voice tighten, struggling with the idea.

"So you would arrest him?"

"He messed his life up. Not me. I don't have anything to do with it anymore."

"So you think he did it all for himself?" Morgan asked. They had come to the fence marking the end of Morgan's property. "You want to know what it was all about—the last twelve years your father was sitting in Monroe." Morgan bent and found a small strip of black electrical tape wound to the bottommost wire. He rose and walked east to where the sun sat a few inches past the horizon. He looked north and then squared himself. "The county road down there can only be seen from this spot. If you're not standing right here the grass hides it or, on the other side, the hills." He looked over at Drake. "Come over here," Morgan said.

Drake walked the twenty or so steps from the fence to where Morgan stood.

"You were five or six when your mother got sick and by the time you were seven she was dead," Morgan said. "You probably remember that pretty well, don't you? You think of her as a woman lying in a hospital bed with a bunch of wires connected to her. All you probably remember of her is the way the hospital smelled or what the waiting room looked like. If your father hadn't kept a framed picture of the three of you, you'd probably have to guess what color her hair was or what her face looked like when she smiled." Morgan stopped to gather his breath. He was looking toward the county road a mile away. Not a single car passing in the whole time they'd stood there.

"What you don't think about when you think of your mother," Morgan went on, "is how lovely she was—what a great person she was before she got sick." With one leg he swept his foot over the grass, parting it and sweeping the dirt. The grainy sound of bits of rock and dirt rolling across a hard flat surface. "Everyone loved her and when she got sick it didn't seem like it was really happening—it seemed like it couldn't happen to her. Because things like that don't happen to people like her. People with good hearts, with an easy laugh like hers or a face like hers, or any number of other things I still remember." He knelt and Drake heard the old knee crack, his grandfather now bent to the prairie floor, his fingertips lifting a weathered board, one and a half feet long and eight inches in width. The hole below big and square as the grave Drake had dug in the apple orchard behind his house.

Morgan bent forward and brought up what looked to be a small tackle box. Green, with the metal clasps and pins all rusted and stained with time. "Patrick missed your mom more than anything. Having her there meant one thing in his life, and having her gone meant something altogether different. He loved her and when she passed it scared him. She really could have done anything—been whatever she wanted, had any life she chose—and for her to go like that, at her age, it didn't make sense and it scared him more than anything he'd ever come up against," Morgan said, still talking as he brought the box up and placed it on the ground next to Drake's feet.

Drake knelt next to his grandfather and placed the shotgun away from him in the grass. He put his hands on the tackle box. "What's in here?" he asked.

"You know what's in there."

"I don't want to open it," Drake said.

"He loved you," Morgan said. "That's all it proves."

Drake undid one clasp, then the other. He bent back the lid and raised the small shelf beneath. A folded piece of paper with his name on it sat there in a plastic sheath. Underneath the letter, four stacks of bills. "How much is it?" Drake asked.

"Two hundred thousand, minus a bit Patrick asked me to bring him while he was in Monroe."

"This is for me?"

"When Patrick put it here he told me to give it to you on his death."

Drake brought up the piece of paper and slid it from the plastic. Drake's name written there on the outside of the paper in his father's hand. The first line written inside simply an apology. The next: "For the house and for whatever else you need it for." Then a final signature from his father.

The message was short and to the point, like anything else his father had done. Still, Drake flipped the paper over looking for more. When nothing else could be found he slipped the paper back within its plastic envelope.

"You probably won't believe me but Patrick was getting out when he was arrested. He was building up the money to pay off the house. He wanted to keep it in the family. He wanted to keep it for you."

"But he didn't get out," Drake said. "He went to prison for twelve years." His voice broke a little and he recovered himself. "He killed two men for this."

"I don't know what to say about that," Morgan said. "You asked me last night whether it's possible to still love a son who is a killer. I think it is."

"That's all you know about it?"

"I know what happened to those two men was an accident. It was a misunderstanding. Patrick was worried about it before he went and he asked Gary to come along and watch his back. Gary was too jumpy. He watched one of the men go for a cigarette and before the man could pull his pack from inside his jacket, Gary caught him at a hundred yards. The second man was a witness at that point."

"That doesn't make this okay," Drake said.

"I don't blame either of them," Morgan said. "Gary was watching out for your father and your father was watching out for you."

"Jesus," Drake said. "I don't want this. I never asked for this." His voice held low and the words only a whisper. Drake looked down at the money. "You've had this ever since?"

"Yes."

"Just waiting to give it to me?"

"Yes."

"So he's dead?" Drake asked. His eyes still on the open lid of the tackle box, the wind rustling the small folded piece of paper that sat on top; he didn't want to raise his eyes.

"I don't know," Morgan said. He looked away to the road, where a pickup was cresting the far hill and then descending once again, out of sight, beyond the grass. "I don't know where he is. I don't know if we'll ever see him again, but if those men get ahold of him before you do I know it will mean trouble for both me and you."

Morgan told Drake all there was to know. He told him Maurice's full name, how long they'd shared a cell for, where he lived now, how Patrick had asked Maurice for help, and how Maurice had been the one to make the connections with Bean and John Wesley. Patrick doing the rest, trying for protection and making promises he could back up with only the money as a reward.

Drake listened and when Morgan finished, Drake said, "So those men don't know you have the money?"

"Besides Patrick and myself you're the only other person who knows."

"You think my father would bring them here?"

"I don't know. It's possible."

"I can't believe this," Drake said. "All this time—" The anger in his voice cut into his words. "Do you know what it could mean for Sheri if my father isn't with Maurice?"

"Outside Silver Lake it's about the only place I could see him going."

Drake didn't have anything more to say. His grandfather didn't have the answers. But the anger was there still. He couldn't help it and he knew it wasn't his grandfather's fault.

"I had to show you this," Morgan said. "You had to know. It's your money."

Drake bent his hand to the small piece of paper and brought it up. He tucked it within a pocket of his coat. When he was finished he dropped the tackle box back into its hole.

"Telling the truth can be a horrible thing," Morgan said.

Drake thought that over. He thought about all the things he'd hidden away in his life—all the failings he'd had. "I lied to you last night," Drake said. "We had a child. A miscarriage. I buried it in a hole behind our house. I never told Sheri it was a little boy. I think about him all the time."

"Sometimes what you hope is at the end of the rainbow isn't what you thought it was going to be at all," Morgan said.

THE ASIAN MAN who came into the room to meet him was about thirty years old and had tattoos running up out of his shirt collar on both sides of his neck. Driscoll waited for him to sit before opening the file the warden had given him. The guard who'd escorted the inmate into the room now stood by the doorway about twenty feet behind.

"John Se," Driscoll said. He had the file open and he was looking down at the man's mug shot. The statement was not a question, but merely a fact. "You're in here for second-degree murder. Correct?"

He leaned back from the table and grinned at Driscoll. "Is it going to surprise you if I say I didn't do it?"

"It wouldn't surprise me at all."

"Well that is the fact," John said. "They have me in here because they picked me up for being an Asian male."

"Case closed," Driscoll said. "You Asians all look the same."

"Now you're getting it. I've been saying that for years."

"How long have you been in here?"

"Too long."

"How long do you have to go?"

"Too long."

Driscoll flipped through the paperwork a few times and then looked up at John. "You know it says here that several witnesses saw a man of your height and build cave in another man's head with the heel of his shoe. Says here that the tattoos on this perp's neck matched yours exactly."

"I don't know what to say to that. Neck tattoos are pretty popular these days."

"Not that popular," Driscoll said. "Not the best choice either, especially if you want to go around smashing people's heads in."

"How does self-defense sound?"

"I'm not your lawyer," Driscoll said. "I don't really care. All I care about is how much time you're doing in here and if you're willing to reduce that time by helping me out."

"Who are you?"

"DEA."

"They didn't tell me that." John looked behind him at the guard. "DEA?"

Driscoll snapped his fingers. "You have trouble keeping your eyes on the chalkboard when you went to school, John?"

John turned around and looked Driscoll over. "This is when you make the joke about Asians being good at math."

Driscoll didn't say anything. He had the two mug shots of the escaped killers facedown on the table in front of him. Their combined crimes included seven counts of murder, one count of arson, two counts of armed robbery, and one count of kidnapping. One of the men was guilty of killing his parents, his uncle, and his grandmother in their sleep, then burning the house to the ground to cover up the murders. "Until a week ago you were Patrick Drake's cell mate, weren't you?" Driscoll asked.

John looked back over at the DEA agent. "Pat? What does this have to do with him?"

"Two people were found murdered a quarter mile from where he was staying in Silver Lake."

"I don't know anything about that."

"No one is saying you do."

"Well, you can never be too careful, you know. I've been mistaken for things before."

Driscoll looked past the inmate to the guard who had brought him in. Perhaps just looking for some sign that John could give a real answer from time to time. The guard just shrugged, a smile beginning to show on his face before he dropped his eyes to his shoes.

Driscoll brought his attention back to the man before him. "You know these men?" Driscoll asked. He turned each mug shot over one at a time.

"I know them," John said. His voice diminished, pulled back somewhere into the shadows.

"These guys scare you?" Driscoll asked.

"What are you offering me here? I'm not too crazy about how this is starting to look if someone finds out I'm talking to you."

"The warden is the only one who knows what we're doing here. The guards all think I'm a lawyer here for a meeting with you. Well, they did until you yelled out to that guard back there."

"Sometimes my mouth gets me into trouble."

"I can imagine," Driscoll said. "What I can do is send that guard an early Christmas present this year. You know, the kind that makes sure he keeps his mouth shut."

"You're kind of dirty for a DEA agent."

"I can't protect you from any others you want to tell about this, but I can help you out if you're willing."

"Okay," John said. "What are you looking for?"

"What's Patrick's relationship to these two men?"

"That's a big question with a lot of zeros behind it."

"I know about the money," Driscoll said.

"Well then it makes sense that a lot of us in here knew about it, too," John said. "It wasn't common knowledge, but when you sleep in the bunk above Pat for as many years as I have, it gets out. Pat would have never said anything, but something like that gets out. He wasn't exactly running the show in here, but he wasn't wanting for anything, either. Pat wants something done, it gets done. Respect will do that, but mostly it's power, and in Pat's case that power came from the money he was supposed to have on the outside."

"He kept himself safe."

"That's all he did. Counting the days till he could get out."

"He never told you anything about the money?"

"I saw a bit of it from time to time. Someone was bringing it in for him. Just enough to keep people satisfied."

"So, you don't know where it is?"

"Would you tell someone where you'd hidden that kind of money?"

"Two hundred thousand isn't as much as you think it is these days."

"Who said anything about two hundred thousand?" John said. He leaned back in his chair and grinned at the DEA agent.

"How much?"

"I've got another nine years on my sentence," John said.

"You'll be out in four," Driscoll said. He was leaning into the table now, waiting on John. Behind him, the door opened and the warden appeared. He whispered something to the guard and then asked to see Driscoll in the hall for a moment.

"We're in the middle of something," Driscoll said.

The warden shot him a sharp look. "There are people waiting to talk with you, Driscoll."

John said something under his breath.

"What did you say?" Driscoll asked.

"Marshals," John said.

The warden was still waiting on him but he couldn't move. "How do you know about them?"

"They were here yesterday," John said. "I thought with how close you always seemed to Patrick, visiting him once a year, you'd have shown before them." John was smiling now, looking across the table at Driscoll, a wild look in his eyes.

The warden tried to get Driscoll's attention again but Driscoll waved him off. "Just give me a few more seconds." Driscoll waited for the warden to leave before turning to John. "You knew I'd come?"

"Patrick was like family to you."

Driscoll didn't look away. "He was something to me but it wasn't that."

"What happens when you catch up to him?"

"I don't know, but I can tell you it will be a lot better than what will happen if the marshals or those two killers get him first."

"Patrick is a good guy," John said. "He helped me when I first got here. Everyone needs someone like that, you know?"

"You paying for protection like he was?" Driscoll asked.

"No," John said. "I wasn't a sheriff either, though. I don't have the same kind of bills Pat probably does."

"He must have built up a pretty big debt by now."

"Twelve years," John said. "What do you think?"

"So what would you do?" Driscoll asked. "What would you do to find Patrick?"

"Are you serious about getting me out of here?"

"Like you said, I'm kind of dirty, but if it's within my power I'll do what I can for you."

John looked around to the guard, the low, muted hum of the halogen lights overhead. When John looked back to Driscoll he took his time, rolling his nails on the table as he thought it over. "I hope you can help Pat out. I really do," John said. "I wouldn't have told the marshals this, but when Patrick got here twelve years ago he needed someone just like I did."

Driscoll thought that over. "For a criminal you're not that bad."

"I'm not a criminal," he said. "I'm an innocent man."

"So you keep saying," Driscoll said.

PATRICK ROLLED OVER and put his feet to the floor. The sun was coming in through the front windows and the clutter of Maurice's house looked even worse in the day than it had in the night. He rested his elbows on his knees and cupped his hands together, running his fingers over his face. The smell of the girl still on his skin and a memory of the night before like a cruel act from his childhood he hadn't quite forgiven himself for.

He was hungover and when he got up to use the bathroom and splash water over his face, he could see Maurice still asleep in his bed, the covers pushed down to the footboard, and the man laid out full on his stomach still wearing his gray sweatpants. The windows covered up and the sun-warmed air in the room dead still and smelling of dust. His cell phone, keys, and wallet on the nightstand next to him.

He watched Maurice for a time and then walked away to the kitchen and filled a coffee cup with water and drank it full. He had one hand held down on the counter and the other around the empty cup as he looked out the window above the sink. He was thinking it all through again. The girl on top of him, the way she had felt, Patrick trying to resist what his body had wanted most. Something about it all not quite right, a nagging thought trying to break through the clouds. The cell phone on Maurice's nightstand not where it had been a few hours before.

He went back to the room and looked in on his friend. Careful not to wake Maurice, Patrick took the cell off the nightstand and brought it out to the living room. After toggling through the menu for a second he found the number Maurice had called at two A.M.

Fuck, Patrick thought. There wasn't one good reason he could think of for Maurice to call someone at that hour.

He stared at the number on the phone's display for the better part of a minute before he pushed the send button and listened as the call went through. On the third ring someone picked up. In the background the dull fuzz of a car in motion. No one spoke to him and Patrick listened without saying a word. He was thinking it all through again. He was thinking about Maurice last night and how he'd seemed so disinterested in anything related to the money. Money Maurice had been waiting on twelve years.

An ambulance went by on the main street a block up from Maurice's house, the sirens blaring and then fading away again as the emergency vehicle moved on. Ten seconds later Patrick heard the same siren begin to wail from the earpiece of the phone he held in his hand.

Patrick turned the phone off and moved for Maurice's room. No time. He put the phone down on the nightstand and grabbed up the truck keys. Maurice turned slightly on the bed but didn't wake.

With the keys in his hand Patrick came out the front door of the house and took the steps two at a time, jumping the last three and moving for the truck. He had the door open and the engine running almost before he knew what he was doing. With one arm pushed back over the passenger seat he reversed the truck out of the drive and locked the brakes, bringing the truck to a rough stop in the middle of the street. He put the truck in gear and floored the pedal. His eyes focused up on the rearview mirror and the main street behind. Nothing to be seen but the traffic going by as Patrick took the corner at almost forty miles per hour.

MORGAN RAISED HIS eyes and studied the sky. He held the last snare in his hand and the shotgun in the other. A dome of high blue from one horizon to the next and the sun distant and cold. For a while he just stood there watching the slight breeze work across the land, rolling over the far hills before it came washing over him.

Morgan looked over the path he'd taken. The grass shoots bent where he'd come through. But the trail gradually receding back into the landscape like footprints left in the sand of a beach. Nothing to say he'd been there fifteen minutes before.

After it was all done, after he'd shown Drake the money and explained everything to him and Drake had made whatever peace with it he'd needed to make, he asked Morgan if he felt like some sort of castaway out here. "All these rolling hills," Drake said. "You might as well be lost at sea."

Morgan thought that over. He was smiling already at the thought. Sharks circling, trying to take what they could from him. "If I was I'd be yelling at the heavens." He laughed, snorting a bit and trying to catch his breath. He felt relief. He felt like he'd held the money for so long without anyone to tell about it. And now he had and he felt good about it all.

"Still," Drake said, "I'd feel better if you stayed away from this place for a day or two. Go into town. Spend a few nights with that friend from the post office."

Morgan thought about that. He knelt and set the last snare. When he was done he rose and watched the hills again. Lost at sea. He looked up at the sky again. When night came there would be stars thick as buttermilk.

JOHN WESLEY HELD SHERI by an arm and rapped a knuckle against the door. Through a side window he saw Maurice rise from his seat on the couch and turn his head toward the window. He looked the big man over for a second, then turned and ran for the back. Twenty seconds later Maurice was at the front door again with Bean standing there behind him and the Walther pressed to Maurice's skull, just behind the ear. The door came open and Maurice stepped aside to let John Wesley and Sheri through. As he passed John Wesley thanked him and then came into the house and stood looking at all the magazines stacked in piles around the living room.

He sat Sheri on the couch and then turned to take in what he could of the house. Messy and unkempt, the room had spiderwebs in the corners and some of the magazines showed a thin filament of dust over their glossy covers. He picked one up and thumbed the pages. A good-natured smile across his face as he came to the pictures he liked.

Bean pushed Maurice into the living room and told him to sit. "I'm guessing Patrick isn't here," Bean said.

"Why's that?" Maurice said.

"Because someone called us from your phone and it wasn't you."

"How do you know it wasn't me?"

"You're wasting time," Bean said. He gave the gun to John Wesley and left the room. John Wesley looked at Maurice and then looked toward the direction Bean had gone. There was the sound of the closet in Maurice's bedroom being opened and the lamp on his nightstand being flipped; a dresser went over next.

"Come on," Maurice said. "This is my grandma's place."

Bean came out of the back hallway breathing hard. He looked around the room. "Your grandma like you? Likes looking at whatever the fuck this is?" He bent and picked a magazine off the closest pile. He put it down without comment. "Where's Patrick, Maurice?"

"He's not in the closet back there?" A smile on Maurice's face and his white teeth showing.

In less than a second Bean was on top of him. He beat him three or four times across the face in quick succession and then remained where he was, one knee into Maurice's belly. "Where's Patrick?"

There was blood on Maurice's teeth now, he was looking up at Bean and he was smiling a big grin. "You mean he wasn't behind the dresser, either?"

Bean beat Maurice with a savage intensity while John Wesley went into the kitchen and came back with some spray cheese and a package of crackers beneath his arm. The Walther now tucked in the back of his waistband. In his other hand John Wesley carried a bottle of water and when Bean rose from the couch, he used both hands to push his blond hair into place, smoothing his palms over it several times before John Wesley handed him the water.

John Wesley ate a cracker and watched Bean. He offered one to Sheri but she was too traumatized to move, all the way against the opposite side of the couch.

"He's not here," Maurice said, propping himself up on one hand to wipe at the blood on his lips with the other. "Don't you think I'd tell you if he was?"

"I don't know what you'd do," Bean said. "You tried to sell out your old friend for a cut of his money. I don't know what that is."

"I tried to help us out."

"So where is he now?"

"Shit if I know," Maurice said. "He took off with my truck, though, took it right out from under me while I was asleep. We did six years together and that's how he does me."

"You see the humor in this, Maurice?" Bean said. "You here on the couch saying how Patrick screwed you over."

"Shit, it's a dog-eat-dog world. You feel me, Bean?"

"But you don't know where he is now and you don't know where the money is?" Bean looked to John Wesley and John Wesley placed the crackers and cheese spread down next to the television and started going through the room closing all the shades.

"He could show back up here," Maurice said. His eyes tracked John Wesley as he made his way through the room, then they went back to Bean. "He doesn't have anywhere to go. He told me that."

Bean bent to the coffee table and shifted his hand through the mess there, searching through magazines and old fast-food wrappers. Maurice watched him and John Wesley continued to work his way through the room closing the blinds. He was at the window by the front door when Bean found what he was looking for and stabbed Maurice three times in the side with a ballpoint pen and then stepped back. A gasp was audible from Sheri but nothing more. She had risen up off the couch and stood now looking down at Maurice while Bean hovered over him, the pen held in his fist with his thumb pressed down over the blunt end. Maurice was crying and looking at his side where the blood was beginning to show.

"He's not coming back here," Bean said.

"He doesn't have anywhere to go," Maurice said, but even his voice sounded like it didn't believe him. He was shaking his head and holding a hand tight to his side. "Okay," he said, his other hand held prostrate in the air.

Bean moved toward him again and Maurice pushed himself off the couch and faltered a bit as he tried to get his feet beneath him. He was holding one hand to his side and when he turned away from Bean, John Wesley was there.

There was a brief sob and John Wesley felt the weight of Maurice's body fall against him, but there was little else for John Wesley to do but stand there. Bean drawn up behind Maurice and the blood now on the floor at John Wesley's feet as Maurice collapsed into him and Bean went to work with the ballpoint.

When it was done Bean rose and let the pen roll off his fingers and fall to the floor. Blood was on Bean's face and in his hair. He ran one hand through the loose blond strands that had come out of place but it only helped to smear the blood farther along through his hair.

John Wesley looked away and then went back to the television, where he'd left the cheese and crackers. He sat on the edge of the coffee table and ate them one at a time. Bean was in the bathroom and John Wesley listened to the water come on as Bean cleaned the blood from his hands and face.

Sheri had moved to one corner of the room, where John Wesley—eating crackers, making an effort to put cheese spread on each—watched her slide down the wall till she crumpled into herself on the floor, her knees pulled to her chest and her eyes buried in her bare arms. "He tried to hurt Patrick," was all John Wesley could think to say.

Sheri looked up at him. "What do you think Bean will do when he finds Patrick?"

"That's up to Patrick," John Wesley said. He looked away, running his eyes over the room, listening to the splash of water from the bathroom sink.

On the floor Maurice was still alive—just barely so. And when he started to pull himself little by little across the floor, John Wesley paused, his eyes oscillating between Bean in the bathroom and Sheri in the corner, then he looked to where Maurice had managed to cover a few inches of ground on his way to the door.

John Wesley wanted to say something to Bean but then thought better of it. Instead he got up from the coffee table and walked to where Maurice lay, struggling for escape, his chin upturned with the side of his face flat on the floor and his eyes looking toward the door. Each breath flaring his nostrils as he put one hand out and then the other, trying for a solid grip on the floor.

Bean came out of the bathroom with a towel in one hand and with his other caught Sheri by the throat as she tried to make a run for the back door. He should have been angry but he wasn't, the pulse of Sheri's neck felt in the skin of his palm as he made a slow turn of his head, taking in the room. John Wesley there beside Maurice, the blood spreading on the floor, and John Wesley crouched on his haunches like a little boy studying a snail making its way across a distance too far to travel.

G ARY WAS THERE IN the prison parking lot when Driscoll came out. The two U.S. marshals were there with him, too.

Gary stood next to the fence, smiling now and watching Driscoll as the guard showed him out onto the lot. The marshals a couple hundred feet away by their vehicle.

"These marshals have been looking for you."

"Looks like they found me," Driscoll said. "They ask you to come along? Help them track me down?"

"Thought you would have at least picked up your calls the last couple days," Gary said.

"I've got nothing for them," Driscoll said. His eyes moved over the two men at the other end of the lot and then came back to Gary. "It's not my case, it's theirs."

Gary grinned. "You worried they're going to take the glory away from you? All these years and nothing to show for it?"

"No," Driscoll said. "You're right. I don't have anything. I wish I did but I don't." The guard latched the gate behind him and Driscoll felt alone and exposed in the lot, the marshals both on their phones but looking to where Driscoll stood now. "Plus, there's always the worry that if I did have something the information might end up in the wrong hands."

Gary fell into step next to Driscoll as they crossed the lot, walking away from the prison gates. "These men are trying to find two

escaped convicts," Gary said. "I'm just doing my part. If they're looking for Patrick, and Bobby gets in the way, that's something I have to
live with."

"The way you lived with Patrick being in prison," Driscoll said.

"Be nice, Driscoll. Patrick went to prison for smuggling drugs. He
was the sheriff and he got caught. That's all."

"You got a job out of it, though."

"And so did Bobby," Gary said, his voice drawn tight and his jaw
rigid as they crossed the lot.

"I know you've been waiting on Patrick to get out," Driscoll said.
"Everyone except maybe Bobby has. And now he's the one in trouble."

"I don't know what you're talking about," Gary said.

"Yes, you do." Driscoll looked ahead to where the marshals had
taken notice of him. He didn't know what to tell them. Whatever Patrick's cell mate John had told them yesterday, it hadn't been enough.
Now he had something for them. Something that could help them all,
but Driscoll didn't know if he could share anything with them while
Gary was still helping them out.

He watched one of the marshals drop his phone to his pocket
and start to walk toward him. Driscoll pulled his own phone up and
looked at the blank display. He pulled up short with Gary still next
to him. Driscoll pretended to answer. "They don't really care about
Bobby, do they?"

Gary looked back at Driscoll, the marshal still fifty feet away.
"They've got a job to do and they're trying to do it."

"Just like you," Driscoll said.

"Yes, just like me."

PATRICK PULLED THE truck off at the exit in Everett. He was hungry
and he was having second thoughts. The diner he pulled up to had a
counter running the length of the restaurant and at the end near the
bathroom there was a pay phone. When he came into the place he

could smell the potatoes going on the grill in the back. He sat at the counter and ordered coffee.

No idea what he would do next and a fear growing inside him that all he'd done to get to this point would amount to nothing. The money he'd saved just another shackle around his life, holding him back from the hopes he'd had for the future. Now he wanted to get home to Silver Lake. He was worried about that dead space on the other end of the phone that morning. He was worried about what it might mean for his son and Sheri.

He waited for the coffee to come, looking the menu over and watching the grill man behind the counter. The potatoes were making his mouth water and he ordered a big skillet of hash browns with a side of bacon as soon as the waitress came back with the coffee.

The turnoff for Silver Lake forty miles to the north and he thought about this for a long time. Drinking his coffee cup dry and then calling for another. He didn't know what to do anymore. The phone at the end of the diner sitting there and a real need to just call Bobby and Sheri and tell them both what he'd been doing these last few days.

The only thing stopping him was the certainty that he'd be going back to prison the moment he made the call. He knew Driscoll was probably still out there looking for him. He'd switched cars three times since he'd left Silver Lake and he couldn't be sure of anything really, but he was almost positive whoever had been on the other end of Maurice's phone hadn't been the law.

He didn't know what to do and he looked behind him, out on the interstate going by just beyond the diner's big windows. He didn't know one damn thing, and he was a fool to have thought he did.

Up above, over the counter, there was a television going and he watched some soap opera play out in silence on the screen. Lots of people crying and a bunch of actors who looked like they'd never lived a day of their lives in the real world.

He looked away at the interstate again and then turned and watched the grill man. Patrick was jumpy and he looked it. Nothing he could do but try to sit still. The waitress came over with more coffee.

"You going far today?" she asked.

"No," he said. "Just up the road."

"Well, you look like you're worried the freeway is going to get away from you." She filled his coffee to the top and then stood there at the counter. "It's not going anywhere, honey."

Patrick gave a polite laugh. Even his laugh had nerves in it and he looked again at the interstate. He had to stop doing that. He thought of the money again and all the trouble it had brought him. "Just a reunion I have to be at this afternoon," he said.

"I hate those," the waitress said. "How long has it been?"

"Twelve years."

The waitress whistled and behind her the bell rang in the kitchen. When she came back with his food she said, "I hope you didn't leave anyone waiting at the altar."

"No, nothing like that. Nothing that special."

"That's good," she said. "I'm sure you'll do fine then." She asked him if he needed anything else and when he said no, she walked away down the counter and started pouring coffee for one of the other customers.

Patrick ate and watched the soap opera. Well aware that at any moment their perfect little world would start to fall apart around them, if it hadn't already begun.

JOHN WESLEY SAT NAKED on the coffee table staring at the fire-place. His skin had dried but the damp of the shower was still in his hair. Maurice was dead. Patrick was gone and they were running out of options. All they had now was Sheri and she wasn't much better than a mute. Her hands and mouth taped with some duct tape Bean had found, she lay on the bed in Maurice's room. John Wesley only able to see her spine where she'd turned away from him on the bed.

Gathering a few of the magazines together he approached the fire-place and squatted, crumpling paper in his fists and then rolling each new ball out onto the ash-stained cement. With a lighter he lit the col-lection of balled paper and watched it burn, feeding new pages from the magazine into the fireplace as it was needed.

Naked, he roamed the house looking for combustibles. When he passed the bathroom door he heard the shower going and the low croon of Bean singing to himself. Ignoring Sheri, John Wesley went on into Maurice's room and found a wooden shoehorn in the closet. Next he took a cutting board and a pair of wooden salad spoons from the kitchen. For a long time he stood in front of the small fire and fed the wood into the flames, watching how each new item stained and blackened in the heat. The feel of warmth so good on his skin.

When Bean came out of the bathroom in his suit, John Wesley was breaking down the dining room chairs one leg at a time and feed-ing them to the fire. Bean simply stared at John Wesley until the big man turned and smiled at him, then went back to breaking down the dining room chairs.

Bean left and went into Maurice's room and pulled Sheri to her feet. He brought her out and put her on the bloodstained couch and then went back into Maurice's room. He selected some clothes and laid them out for John Wesley. When Bean came back out into the living room he told the big man to go dress and then he went into the kitchen and poured himself a glass of water from the faucet, staying close enough that he could keep his eyes on Sheri. It was a beautiful day, he thought. Out the window above the sink there was nothing but high blue sky and the sun just past its midpoint for the day.

When he returned to the living room John Wesley was dressed and standing over Maurice. A look of horror on Sheri's face as she watched the big man squat and extend a hand toward the body. A skin had formed at the edge of the blood pool and John Wesley put a finger to it like a skater about to shove off across a half-frozen lake.

With four of the burning chair legs Bean went into Maurice's bedroom and placed them beneath the bed frame. When he was done he called for John Wesley and waited while the big man dragged Maurice in by his ankles. They were hoisting him onto his mattress when they heard the knocking begin on the front door, the smoke already starting to roll up from beneath the bed.

THE DRIVE FROM MONROE to Seattle was forty minutes if Driscoll kept the speed limit. If he ran the sirens it was thirty minutes, no accounting for traffic and the side streets he'd have to find his way through. He'd already lost enough time dealing with the marshals and Gary, and on top of that he'd taken his own time thinking it through—thinking what would happen to Patrick or Drake—before he made the decision not to tell the marshals what he knew.

He hit traffic merging onto the 405 and rode the bumper of the car in front of him for five minutes before Driscoll popped the sirens and sped past, one tire riding the grass and the other on the road.

He was being too cautious and he knew it. If Patrick's cell mate was right then Driscoll might already be too late. He ran up on a driver in the HOV lane and flashed his lights, veering around him and hitting ninety as he passed.

The big software buildings went by on his right as he came down the 405 and sped through Bellevue. Twelve years, he thought, it was a lot of time to pursue one case. Gary and Patrick both wrapped up in the same thing and neither of them talking. Now Gary was helping the marshals while Driscoll tried to avoid them. And he knew they wouldn't believe him, not after all he'd done to try to keep them away from this case.

Driscoll took the exit for I-90 and came around toward Seattle.

The speedometer at ninety-five as he hit the bridge across Lake Washington, the city just on the other side.

DRAKE STOOD ON the porch. Down at the cross street a group of boys on bicycles were turning and turning. He didn't know how long he'd watched them before he blinked. His eyes gone dry and a sense that he'd lost himself somewhere behind on the road over the mountains, or perhaps even before.

He knew standing there on the porch that he wasn't thinking straight. The sight of the money in the grave had shaken something up in him. Everything he'd learned from Morgan, Drake's own desperation to get Sheri back, and the anger he felt for his father all competing for space inside his mind. The thoughts crowded up, each yelling for the attention Drake didn't have time to give.

He wet his lips, searching down the street for some sign he was in the right place. No one came to the door and he bent to the side window and tried to see what he could, but there was nothing for him—the shades drawn across every piece of glass and the interior of the house a complete mystery.

At the end of the block he watched the boys turn once, then twice. Nothing on the street to say Drake was in the right place. All that mattered now was Sheri. The money was nothing to him.

Whatever Patrick had done, wherever he was, it just didn't matter to Drake anymore. A third of Drake's life had gone by without knowing who his father really was and he realized at some point it had stopped mattering to him. Patrick made his own mistakes and Drake chasing after him wasn't going to make them any better.

Drake looked to the windows again. Nothing to see but his own reflection in the glass—a slim figure standing somewhere between fog and light. His face as nondescript as a mannequin in a shop window. He stood staring at himself for half a minute before he turned, looking again toward the street, wondering if Morgan had been wrong about the place, when the door opened behind him.

By the time he got his body around, John Wesley already had him by his shirt and was dragging him through the doorway into the house. The smell of fire somewhere close by. Drake tried to get a grip but he found himself lifted from the ground and slammed into the wall once, then twice. The plaster cracking as his body bounced and he heard his service weapon clatter and slide away.

He lay on the floor trying to get his breath and then he was lifted once again. A brief feeling of falling as he went over. The floor coming up fast, blood all across the floorboards though Drake couldn't tell if it was his.

PATRICK THOUGHT ABOUT running. He rolled the bottom of the coffee mug around on the counter, listening to the sound. He'd finished off the hash browns and he was working on the bacon. Dredging it through a small pool of syrup he'd poured himself on the plate.

The waitress was away having a smoke and had told him if he needed anything to ask the grill man. Patrick watched the man work for a moment. His back was to Patrick, chopping something up on a cutting board. Patrick looked to the door again, and the interstate farther on. Again he thought about running.

For the first time in a long time he felt scared. He felt like those characters up there on the soap opera. Fragile. Unaccustomed to life outside the walls.

He pushed his plate away. The sound of it on the counter loud in the silence of the diner. The grill man turned and looked at him and Patrick brought out a dollar and asked the man for change.

He rattled the quarters in his hand as he came off the stool and walked back toward the bathrooms. Patrick stopped at the pay phone and dialed the number. It was the only number he knew by heart. A number that hadn't changed in twelve years and one he'd dialed a thousand times before.

He listened to the call go through. It was answered after the third ring and the voice there was familiar to him, but not the voice he was expecting. "Luke?" Patrick said.

A brief pause while the deputy cleared his throat. "Gary told me to wait around and see if anyone called. I didn't think it would be you, Pat."

"What do you mean you didn't think it would be me? Where's Bobby, Luke? Where's Sheri?" Patrick leaned into the phone; he had the receiver held tight to the side of his face and his eyes scanned back over the diner. "I don't understand what you're saying to me. Why are you at my house?"

"They're missing. It looks like they were taken, both Gary and Driscoll are out searching for them."

"Together?"

"Two marshals were here. Gary went with them and Driscoll is on his own."

With his free hand Patrick pinched two fingers over his eyes until the blackness swam behind his lids. He didn't understand what was happening. "Marshals?"

"I thought you knew. I thought that was why you were calling. They killed a girl in town. Stuffed her in the back of a car with another man they'd killed the day before," Luke said. "It was in the news last night."

"What are you doing at my house, Luke?"

"I'm sorry about this, Pat."

"Again," Patrick said, "why are you at my house, Luke?"

"Gary told me to wait—I thought you'd have seen it on the news—in case Sheri or Bobby showed or the two men came back."

"Who?" Patrick managed to say. He was holding the phone tight, the plastic growing slippery with his own sweat.

"They'd been following you since you got out. The marshals said it was two prisoners you knew in Monroe. They got transferred a week ago and killed one of the guards in transit. I'm sorry," Luke said. "I thought you would have known all this."

"I guess I haven't been paying that much attention."

"None of us knew anything about it till the marshals showed up. I guess they thought the men had gone over into Idaho or up to Spokane."

"What kind of car was it?"

"What do you mean, Pat?"

"The car they found the bodies in."

"It was a black Town Car."

He told Luke to hold on. He took the phone away from his ear and let it dangle by his thigh. He heard Luke call his name several times but Patrick wouldn't answer. From where he stood he could see Maurice's truck out there in the lot. The interstate just fifty yards farther on.

THE HOUSE WAS burning. Driscoll stopped the Impala in the middle of the street and was out of the car and up the stairs before the heat turned him away. The temperature too much and his hand raised across his face as he backed away to the sidewalk. Flames already beginning to show at several windows toward the back. The drapes in the front on fire and the glass panes crashing to the porch.

All down the street there were people beginning to come out of their homes. Several of them on their cell phones. Driscoll looked around at it all. The rush of the flames heard now like a constant wind. Neighbors gesturing with one arm raised toward the flames as they tried to make their voices heard over the crackle of wood and heat.

Driscoll came back to the car and put his elbows down across the roof, cradling his face in his hands. So close, he thought, always so close.

In the distance he heard the sound of fire trucks. He turned and looked back toward the house. Flames were beginning to come through the roof. This is the house, he thought. This has to be the house.

Up on the main street the first fire engine made a wide turn to get the corner. He knew he should stay. Already the neighbors were looking to him like he was the first part of some rescue. Only Driscoll knew he wasn't and that if he stayed he'd have to answer the question of what he was doing there in the first place.

Up at the corner the fire truck had come up short on its turn and was reversing out into traffic to bring the big square body straight so it could fit down the side street. He dropped down into the seat and brought the transmission into drive. Several boys on bicycles staring at him as he went past, moving fast with the grille lights of his Impala pulsing a silent flash. The big red body of the fire truck pulling to a stop in front of the house all he saw before he went around the corner.

He parked a block down and sat there. For a full minute he sat there staring out at the street through the front windshield. "Fuck—fuck—fuck!" he yelled, beating his fists against the wheel in quick succession.

When he looked up at his own reflection in the rearview mirror he saw the blood in his face, the skin pulled red with tension. He felt the beat of his Adam's apple as he swallowed, wetting his throat, and the slow rise and fall of his chest. His hands now resting, useless, palms up on his thighs, with his head played back against the headrest.

He looked back in the direction he'd come from. How did he even know Patrick had come here?

"Because the house is burning," he said, speaking aloud like it wasn't he who had asked the question.

"It could be a coincidence. It could mean anything."

"But it doesn't mean anything, it means something," Driscoll said.

Driscoll pulled himself up in the seat. He had his hands gripped on either side of the steering wheel. He hadn't seen the Toyota Patrick took from the casino lot anywhere on the street. Maybe Patrick never came this way. Maybe John was wrong about Maurice. Maybe he was wrong about Patrick.

Driscoll looked up again at his eyes in the mirror. He was tired.

He could see that. He was failing. Failing Bobby and failing Sheri, but mostly he was failing himself.

The house was burning and the Toyota Patrick had stolen from the casino lot was nowhere on the block.

Ten minutes later he found the Camry parked five blocks away. The window was broken out on the driver's side and Driscoll opened the door and sat in the old Toyota examining the wire harness pulled free below the steering column.

Driscoll shook his head, almost like he didn't believe it himself. Where the fuck was Patrick?

Two more fire trucks went by while he sat there and he was staring up at the empty space where they had been when his cell phone rang. He checked the display. It was a number he didn't know and after a second he picked up the call.

"Agent Driscoll?" a voice asked.

He answered, listening, waiting for the voice to go on.

"It's Luke, the deputy from Silver Lake. Patrick just called and he wants you to call him back."

B EAN SAT SHOTGUN WHILE John Wesley drove. Drake's cruiser radio was turned on and Bean listened as the codes came in but as far as he could tell none of them had anything to do with them.

He'd taken the jacket off Drake and gone through the pockets. One cell phone, a set of keys, a wallet, and a note in a plastic envelope that looked to be from Patrick to Drake. He read the note twice. When he was done he looked up and watched the road for several beats and then read the note again.

He looked to the back, where Drake lay unconscious in the rear cage, bleeding from a split of skin over his right eye. His face badly bruised where it rested against his wife's lap. And Sheri sitting there with a look of hate on her face and her hands still duct-taped.

He pursed his lips and kissed the air, watching as Sheri turned away.

John Wesley came to the on-ramp for the interstate and looked to Bean for direction.

Bean studied the note in its plastic envelope. "It's time we got a few things straight," Bean said, looking to the back, where Sheri sat.

MORGAN SAT OUT ON the porch for a long time before he went in. He made fry bread in the pan and then got out some of his preserves and ate the sweet jelly slathered on the warm bread. Except for the warmth from the propane burner the house was cold and he walked back outside to sit in the sun and take in the land.

A muddy patch of earth sat halfway up the hill from the rains two days before. Stained into the gravel. He leaned back in his chair and brought one leg over the other. Up above a hawk was circling over something in the fields and he thought of his snares and wondered if it was something he'd caught.

He was tired and his lids dropped once, then again. The hunting jacket buttoned over his chest and the collar turned up. When he came awake he didn't know what time it was and he had to take the hour from the sun. The hawk gone from the sky.

He lit a cigarette with a match and then sat there till the paper felt hot between his fingers. He mulled it over for a while before he went back inside and found the box of bird shot Drake had left out on the table. He looked this over and then crossed to where he'd put the shotgun away. He broke open the breech and looked in on the two shells. He closed the breech and found his truck keys.

PATRICK SIGNALED THE grill man and asked for the bill. A minute later the grill man came back with the waitress behind him.

"Sorry," Patrick said. "That reunion just got moved up and I'll be taking off soon."

"Don't worry about it, honey." She was at the register now and she put in the figures and brought up the total. When she came back over he could smell the cigarette smoke on her. "I hope it all turns out for you."

"I hope so, too." He brought out a few bills from his wallet and laid them over the counter. It was enough to cover the total and then some. He didn't have anything left in his wallet but a few old receipts and expired credit cards. The leather still smelled like the lockup. "Can I have a refill on the coffee?" he said.

She poured the coffee and he watched her as she did it. She'd probably be the last good memory he had in this life. After she was done he toasted her with his mug and saw the little smile come across her lips before she went to check on the other customers.

He was waiting on the phone at the other end of the diner to ring and he wasn't surprised when it did a minute later.

He answered and Driscoll said, "I bet you weren't planning on talking to me."

"I wasn't planning on ever hearing from you again."

"Then you should have stayed where you were."

"I think you know I didn't have that option."

"You're talking about the two men who came by your house?"

"And others," Patrick said. He held the receiver close, his back turned away from the diner.

"Maurice?"

Patrick didn't say anything. He was still thinking about what Maurice had tried to do to him. All that time inside and Maurice had tried to cut him out of the deal.

"You still there, Patrick?"

Patrick listened to the empty sound of the phone in his hand. He could tell Driscoll was driving. "I'm here," he said.

DRAKE WOKE IN the back of his cruiser. He lay there with his knees pushed up against the seat. His head hurt, the pain centralized over his left eyebrow. The skin hot and swollen, he held his eyes closed and he listened to the breath enter through his nose, feeling it swell in his chest and then release. When he opened his eyes he realized what had happened.

Above, through the back windows of the car, he saw telephone poles passing one after the other, the wires falling and then rising again in a never-ending series of waves. He felt the late sun on his face, and the pants he wore were hot against his thighs. But it was fading now, like it had been hotter at one point in the day. There was blood on him, too, on his pants and crusted to the front of his shirt. He could feel it under the material and on his skin.

It was only when he tried to move that he found his hands had been duct-taped behind him, and it was this movement that brought the realization of where he truly was. His wife's thigh under his head, and the two killers in the front, Sheri looking down on him, her eyes unwavering, and Drake thinking maybe he'd been too late, maybe she was dead. And then she blinked and Drake watched a single tear roll down her cheek.

"Reunited at last," Bean said.

MORGAN PUSHED OPEN the door and listened to the bell chime. He turned and closed the door, wooden with glass at its center. He looked out on the county road and his truck there in the gravel drive. The last time he'd been to the store there had been snow on the ground and he remembered how his truck had left muddy tracks all the way off the road and onto the drive. No more than a couple cars in the lot. Just as there were now.

The clerk was waiting for him at the counter when he turned. The clerk wiped a paper napkin across his lips and brought it away with the slight stain of mustard. Morgan knew the man's name but simply nodded to him as he went down the first aisle, passing the Popsicle case and magazine rack on one side and the chips and soda pop on the other. He came to the back of the store and looked in on the dairy coolers there.

"You're early," the clerk said. He had taken another bite of the sandwich he was eating for a late lunch and he wiped at his mouth again, standing there at the counter watching Morgan.

"How do you mean?"

"Just early," the clerk said. He took another couple bites. Finished the sandwich and then said, "You usually don't come in till the end of the month."

Morgan nodded at that and then looked away. The store was a mash-up of kerosene, fishing hats, T-shirts, beer, chips, hot dog buns, work pants, shoes, even horse feed and birdseed. Anything and everything was sold there and if they didn't have it they could get it in a week. Morgan liked that about the place and he went down to the next aisle and looked over the fishing supplies. He'd never taken it up but he thought maybe he would someday. The green tackle box with the money inside the only piece of gear Patrick or Morgan had ever owned.

He came up the aisle and looked over the wares behind the counter. Cigarettes and lottery tickets, an old Budweiser shirt and matching hat that had hung in the store for as long as Morgan could remember. "What do you have for deer shot?" Morgan asked. He was looking over the ammunition now, about ten rows of boxes were dedicated to it and he was examining the various measurements and sizes on the boxes.

The clerk turned and looked to the place Morgan was studying. He selected two boxes and then brought them back to the counter. He laid them out for Morgan to see. "I never took you for much of a deer man, Morgan."

"I'm not," Morgan said.

He paid and left through the front door. The bell chiming again. When he started up his truck he could see the clerk staring at him through the glass door. Morgan reversed out and then brought the wheel straight. He ran the engine a bit hard and he heard the gravel pinging in the wheel wells.

A quarter mile on he pulled over and just sat there with the engine running. "Damn it," he said.

When he came back into the little town he could see the shades were down at the post office and he checked his watch and then looked at the shades again. The woman's car was still in the lot and he pulled in next to her and then went up the stairs. It took her a minute to pull back the shade and then undo the lock. "Oh, hi," she said as he came into the small office. A little counter where she sat with the sorting room behind and about twenty wooden slots on the opposite wall for mail.

Morgan looked around the office. There was room to stand but little more. If he took more than a couple steps in any direction he'd come to a wall. "I was in town," Morgan said.

"I see that." She was smiling at him a bit. She wore the blue fleece vest with the eagle on the breast but little else to say she worked there. Her hair was slightly curly and the blond dye had started to go out of it, but it was still there in certain patches. Her figure was plump in the way Morgan liked; he thought about the rabbit stew again. He liked the way they had sat together and she had broken the bread with her hands and used it to clean out her bowl.

She looked him over. The counter flipped up behind her. "I have some mail for you, I guess." She turned and went back into the mail-room, bringing the pass down behind her. For a moment she was gone. The sound of her somewhere in the back as she rummaged for the right box. "I needed something to read and I almost opened one of your packages. Looks like you got a few good books here." She came back to the counter and set the box down on the floor. She brought up the mail and placed it on the counter between them.

He looked it over. "How can you tell they're any good?" he asked.

She was smiling at him again. "I peeked."

"That's a federal crime."

She didn't say anything back to him. He was stone-faced and she was looking up at him and trying to decide what he meant. "I just thought—"

He broke into a laugh and he saw the relief go across her face. "Go ahead," he said, opening the package up right there. "I'm happy to let you read any of them first."

She took one of the books off the stack and looked it over, turning it front to back and then reading the rear flap for a time. She held it close to her chest like a schoolgirl and it made Morgan smile to look at her.

"Are you sure?"

He nodded and then began to collect his things.

He was at the door when she said, "That was nice, wasn't it? You and me a few weeks ago."

"Yes," he said. "It was."

DRISCOLL CAME INTO the diner parking lot at full speed, grille lights going, and the dust kicked up from his tires rolling past him as he came to a stop. Patrick sat there on the tailgate of a red pickup with his feet dangling over the lot. He wore the same canvas jacket and jeans Driscoll remembered him wearing at the Buck Blind. While the two days of white growth on his head and face made him look ten years older.

The Impala was parked at an angle, blocking the truck. Patrick still sitting there watching him as Driscoll got up from his car. "Raise your hands," Driscoll said. He watched Patrick do it and then he told him to slide off the tailgate and turn around. Driscoll came around the Impala and pressed him then, bending one of Patrick's arms back and then the other. The handcuffs out in one of Driscoll's hands as he held Patrick's wrists with the other.

With Patrick turned on the tailgate, Driscoll went through his pockets, throwing anything he found onto the tailgate. Inside the diner there was a waitress and a cook staring out at them. The waitress had a hand to her mouth as if something had jumped out at her.

Driscoll set Patrick down again on the tailgate, letting him lean on the metal. His legs straight out and his hands behind him in the cuffs. "Hello, Driscoll," Patrick said.

Driscoll ignored him and ran his hands down one leg and then stood and patted down the other. When he was finished he rose and stepped back. He was looking at all that he'd taken out of Patrick's pockets. Keys and a wallet, and a receipt from the diner inside.

Driscoll pulled Patrick up and started to walk him to the Impala.

"Easy," Patrick said.

"You don't fucking get it, do you, Patrick? Bobby's gone and so is Sheri. You deserted them."

"Slow down," Patrick said. He made his best effort to turn and look at Driscoll but Driscoll had a good grip on his arm and levered him against the metal body of the Impala before Patrick could say more.

"Something happens to them it's on you," Driscoll said. He opened the door of the Impala and put one hand over Patrick's head and put him in the backseat. He slammed the door as soon as Patrick was inside and then he went back to the truck and went through the cab.

In the glove box he found the registration and read the name. He stood and walked to the back of the tailgate and cleared Patrick's things from the bed and then closed the tailgate. Inside the waitress and cook were still standing at the window looking out at him.

He looked the registration over again and then he walked back to the Impala and sat in the driver's seat with his eyes up on the rearview.

"I called you," Patrick said.

Driscoll held up the registration in his hand. "You're a selfish son of a bitch."

Patrick fixed on Driscoll's eyes for a moment in the mirror and then he looked away. "What the fuck, Driscoll?"

"Bobby and his wife are missing because of you," Driscoll said.

"You don't give a shit about anyone, do you? No one matters to you. No one should ever trust you. I just came from your buddy's place. The house is still burning."

Driscoll waited. He watched Patrick mull that over, he watched the muscles beneath the man's cheeks tighten. When Patrick turned back he said, "You come all the way up here on your own, Driscoll? No one to watch your back? No one to say this ever really happened?"

"I came because you said you wanted to turn yourself in."

"Where are the marshals?" Patrick asked. "You trying to keep me for yourself?"

"I'm trying to save your son and your daughter-in-law," Driscoll said.

Patrick looked up at the mirror. "I know you," he said. "I know why you came out to see me every year—deep down somewhere you think we're the same in some way."

"You don't know what you're talking about."

"Your marriage," Patrick went on. "Your daughter. You think I didn't hear about your family?"

"That has nothing to do with you." But he knew it did. He knew in some way he needed something to show for all the time he'd taken away from his family—all the work he'd put in on this one solitary goal.

"I think you should ask yourself who deserted who," Patrick said. "I think you should ask yourself if you're trying to save Bobby or if you're trying to save yourself."

DRAKE LOOKED DOWN the long hallway, light fading away into the darkness beyond. He sat in a solitary dining room chair with his wrists still taped behind him and John Wesley's hand resting like ten pounds of meat over one of Drake's shoulders. Three minutes had passed since Bean took Sheri away down that hall. A door far down opening and only a sliver of light visible now as Drake strained to hear what he could from the darkness.

"What is this place?" Drake asked.

"Just the first place we found," John Wesley said.

For a long time they'd driven east into the fading light. The night moving up through the sky and the sun disappearing behind. When it was over Drake hadn't been able to tell where they were, or even how far they'd come, and he looked around the house now searching for some beacon of information to help him get a bearing.

Two silver candleholders sat on the table, their wicks burned almost to the metal and the wax pooled at their bases. Everything in the house seemed like something from a forgotten time. The hutch sitting there across from them with the old china plates displayed along its surface. A pile of mail by the door, built up and then toppled across the floor in a collection that seemed to take in weeks. The night out there beyond the windows like a fine silk cocooning them all within the house.

But more than any of this it was the slight odor, acrid and deep, that hung in the air that bothered Drake the most. Just beyond comprehension. Like the basement door had been left open and the fetid, black air was slowly beginning to infect the house. Like some unlucky soul had fallen and lay there still. And for the first time Drake wondered if John Wesley had meant it was the first place they'd found tonight, or if it was the first place they'd found a week before when they killed the prison guard and disappeared.

Down the hall there was a muffled scream and something crashed to the floor and moved away, the sound fading until there was only silence again. Drake tried to rise from the seat but was pressed down. He heard the scream again and he knew it was Sheri and then he heard Bean say something Drake couldn't make out. The sound of a human body being dragged kicking across a floor and then the sound of bed springs depressing under the body of another. And then the screaming started again and did not stop.

Drake fought to get his feet beneath him but there was no moving out from beneath John Wesley's hold. With his eyes centered down into the darkness he couldn't do anything but listen.

"Bean wanted you to know you can stop this at any time." John Wesley was bent down beside Drake now, speaking to him like he was speaking to a stubborn child. "It's just money. It's just money and nothing more."

Drake wished he'd taken the money, he wished he'd hidden it somewhere new. But he hadn't wanted anything to do with it then, standing there with Morgan, looking down on it like he was looking down on something that had never had the chance to live—a life that had come and gone too soon and now was better left behind. He didn't know. And he sat there struggling under the weight of John Wesley's hand as his mind wrestled with the fact that if he was going to keep Sheri alive he would need to give them something. He would have to tell them whatever he knew, directions possibly, Morgan, the property. If he hoped to keep his wife alive he would have to lay it out like crumbs for them to follow, little by little, feeding them and buying time. Because eventually, he knew, there would be nothing left to tell.

"I'M THE ONE who called you, Driscoll," Patrick said again. He sat with his back resting on the rear bench seat and the yellow lights of buildings and streetlamps passing by in the night outside his window. "I'm the one trying to make things right."

"I don't want to hear it," Driscoll said, looking up at the rearview again. Patrick only a shadow, an outline of a human being.

"I called you for a reason, Driscoll. I didn't call Gary or the marshals. I called you."

"Once you're in the lockup downtown we can talk."

"You want to be right," Patrick said. "I understand that. After all these years you want to prove you were right all along."

Driscoll didn't say anything. He was watching the interstate ahead. At sixty miles per hour they'd reach Seattle in thirty minutes. "You deserted your son twelve years ago and now you've done it again," Driscoll said. "You just don't change."

"You're right. I did those things. But I did them for a reason. You should understand."

"We're not anything alike," Driscoll said. He could feel the blood rise in his face for a moment and the words strain at his lips.

"No," Patrick said. "I thought maybe we were but I see now that we aren't."

"Good."

Patrick shifted in the back so that he could look out the window, watching the lights of a mall until they were gone. "I messed everything up," he said. "Do me just one favor. Bobby and Sheri are out there somewhere. If they're looking for me I want them to know where I am."

Driscoll looked up at the mirror. "What if they're not looking for you? What if they were taken because of you?"

"Then I want you to let the men who took them know where they can get their money."

BEAN FLIPPED DRAKE'S PHONE open and looked at the text. He smiled a bit to himself and then held the phone to the cage for Drake to see. "What do you think?" Bean said. "Should we call him?" He was having fun with the idea, rolling it around in his head like a marble. Patrick had been picked up by Agent Driscoll, which meant one way or another Patrick was going back in.

He turned and looked behind but Drake had already gone away from him and was looking out on the fields. They drove on the county roads now, keeping to the speed limit, taking Drake's directions turn by turn and avoiding the highway. What trees they saw on the sides of the road were squat as the grass, everything else nothing but black ink spilled across the landscape.

No one had said anything in a long time. Sheri off to herself now, her head leaned to the window, looking groggy. Bean knew he hadn't done much to her except throw her around a bit. Perhaps a little too hard at times. Just a little roughhousing, nothing more than he'd do to a dog that had snapped at his hand. Some liked it that way, they saw it as fun. Others didn't, and Bean was still deciding which one Sheri had been.

"What will we find out here?" Bean asked. He spoke to himself, looking to the back to see if Drake was listening.

Bean toggled down until he found the text message again. A single line from Agent Driscoll to Drake, "I'm with Patrick." He put the call through and waited. When Driscoll picked up he told him to put Patrick on. "Hello," Patrick said, and then, "Hello? Hello?" Bean was enjoying himself. He liked listening to the desperation grow in Patrick's voice.

Bean said Patrick's name and then listened as Patrick tried to get his bearings. "Hello . . . Hello? Hello?"

"You didn't think you'd hear from us so soon," Bean said. He looked to the back and got a thrill to see Drake watching now, listening to Bean's half of the conversation, trying to appear as if he wasn't straining to hear what Patrick had to say on the other end. "I wanted to let you know we're okay now. Me and John Wesley are just fine. I thought we should clear the air on that one."

"That's good," Patrick said. "I'm glad to hear it."

"Well, I don't want to take up too much time," Bean said. "I just thought we owed you a call. We're sitting here with the deputy and his wife. I wanted you to know that. I wanted to make it very clear to you."

"I think we all want the same thing."

"How do you figure?"

"I owe you," Patrick said. "You know it. I never forgot."

"I'm not so sure about that," Bean said. "But you know, I can call you back in a couple hours. Don't want to take up too much of your time."

"Wait," Patrick said. "Just hold on. Let me say something to Bobby. That's all. You understand, don't you, Bean?"

Bean looked to the back. It was obvious to him that the deputy hadn't heard anything of what his father was saying. He held the phone off his ear now and he met Drake's eyes. "You want to tell your father you love him?" Bean asked. "After all these years I know he'd like to hear it." Bean held the phone to the cage and watched Drake come forward.

"I don't know," Drake said. "I guess I just want to say we'll have to go fishing some other time." He raised his eyes to Bean and then slipped away from the cage, back to his corner, where he looked out the window again.

Bean studied him for a time. The sound of Patrick breathing on the other end of the line. Bean considered it all, wondering if the risk had been worth it. And then deciding it had not, he closed the phone.

For a long time he sat and watched the centerline come toward them out of the darkness, one yellow dash at a time. "Fuck the speed limit," Bean said. "Let's just get there."

H E'S GONE," PATRICK SAID. He'd come forward in the backseat with his hands cuffed behind him and his ear to the phone. Now he fell away, leaning his weight to the rear seat and watching the road ahead.

Driscoll brought the phone back and stared at the screen. The whole call had taken less than a minute. "The man who called from Bobby's phone?" Driscoll asked.

"He's one of them, the more dangerous of the two. He's one of the men who came into Bobby's house a few nights ago."

Driscoll couldn't decide how to go on. He had Patrick now. It didn't seem like any of this should be happening. "They didn't want you?" Driscoll asked.

He saw Patrick thinking it over. "They don't need me anymore," he said.

Driscoll looked up at the rearview. "What do you mean by that?"

"I thought if I called you it would all go away," Patrick said. "I thought they'd give up on me, or they'd come for me. I didn't think they'd have Bobby or Sheri. I never thought it would happen like this. I mean I knew it was a possibility but I just didn't—I couldn't . . ."

"As a former lawman, you of all people have to understand why I'm taking you in."

Patrick shook his head. He was looking out the window. He wouldn't look at Driscoll. "You've waited a long time for this," Patrick said. "And you're going to take me in for a stolen car?"

"It is what it is."

"That drug money," Patrick said. "I stole it. I'm telling you right now. I'm confessing it to you. You want that, don't you? You want to be right after all these years."

Driscoll had him in the rearview. "Don't bullshit me."

"I'm not. I'll show you where it is. Everyone will know it was you who figured it out. That's what you want, isn't it?"

Driscoll looked up at the mirror again. Patrick was waiting on him. Driscoll thought about the years he'd wanted only this, about the years he'd spent avoiding his family, sacrificing relationships with his wife and daughter so that he could put himself in this moment. And then he thought about what it would mean when there were no more excuses—when one day he might finally go home and sit at the table with his family and have a dinner. And he wondered if he was too late or if maybe there was still time.

"What's it going to be?" Patrick said.

THE DOOR TO the woodstove was open partially and Morgan sat with his back to it, his legs up on another chair and an old blanket stretched from his lap to his feet. He was faced toward the door, and out the window, he'd watched the sun descend and then thirty minutes later the light completely go out of the sky. Now only the reflection of the kerosene lamp on the table could be seen in the glass, suspended there in the darkness of the window, and his own shadowed ghost on the periphery.

The books he'd received in the mail were stacked close at hand on the table and he looked at them from time to time but didn't move from his seat. Again, he thought of the woman and then just as quickly pushed the thought away.

On the floor lay a tin plate with what remained of his meal—taken early in the day, almost as soon as he'd come through the door. Just a bit of fry bread with some cooked meat and some tomatoes he'd grown and then dried over the past summer. He was looking at this, thinking how he needed to get up and wash the plate, when he saw the small pink nose pop from beneath the counter on which he cooked.

He'd seen the mouse before. The sound of it there behind the counter, trying for whatever crumb he'd dropped. And now he sat as still and quiet as he could, watching first the nose appear and then the head. The mouse as big as his thumb and colored brown as the winter fields.

It came out from under the counter and then stood, sniffing the air. The small whiskers twitching and the little claws clutched in front of its chest like a dog watching a ball raised high overhead.

For a time the two of them sat there, the mouse on its haunches and Morgan in his chair. Then as if Morgan was not there at all the mouse moved in a straight line for the plate. The miniature body low as it came across the floor and the black eyes focused solely on the leftover crumbs of Morgan's meal.

Morgan didn't stir and he watched the mouse come up short, testing the air again, and then, satisfied, move the remaining foot toward the plate. It sat there on the tin for a minute, holding one of the larger crumbs between its paws, working the bread down like a man eating corn off the cob.

It finished the crumb and moved on to the next. The mouse close enough that Morgan could hear its claws skittering across the tin. He watched and waited. There was no rush and he didn't want to scare the mouse away.

The animal ate a third crumb and then went sniffing around the edges of the plate. Finding one it came up on its back legs again and stood gnawing at it. Morgan didn't move, but he saw the ears of the animal turn up. The mouse gone rigid for a moment, standing there, nose poised in the air and ears flaring one way and then another. The tin was the only thing to sound as the mouse flitted back across the floor and disappeared behind the counter. Crumbs left uneaten on the plate and Morgan looking now toward his own reflection in the window glass.

THE KILLERS HAD PARKED the patrol car just beyond the ridge and they went on foot to the summit, looking down on the small cabin. Bean carried the Walther in one hand and Drake's service weapon in the other. John Wesley carried the shotgun they'd taken from Drake's cruiser a couple days before. They stood watching the smoke feed up into the air in a blue moonlit plume. Nothing else to see at the base of the slope except the shift of the cottonwoods in the wind.

They stood without speaking and studied the terrain. When they were done they went together down the slope and separated as they came upon the light spilling from within the cabin onto the grasslands.

THE DOOR SWUNG OPEN on its hinges with such force that it bounced back almost completely, leaving a sliver of the night visible beyond and the bulk of John Wesley standing there. Without moving from his seat, Morgan raised the shotgun from beneath the blanket and emptied one barrel into the wood frame of the door, catching John Wesley in the left arm. Splinters of wood all across the floor and the big man taking a step back with the deer shot in his flesh. A look on his face that Morgan could only guess was complete surprise.

John Wesley faltered a bit and then came forward. With his good arm he pushed the door open and stood looking in on Morgan. Morgan's feet now planted on the floor, the woodstove behind him, and the old bird gun still in his hands. The bore smoking slightly and the blanket fallen to the floor.

John Wesley looked to the window over Morgan's shoulder and in the same moment Morgan saw a piece of his firewood come through the window. Glass all over the floor and the stove wood rolling to a stop, Bean just beyond clearing the remaining glass from the frame with his pistol.

When Morgan turned back to the door John Wesley was raising his shotgun. Morgan pulled the trigger and the second shell of deer shot went full into the big man's body, laying him out on the floor.

Morgan was running before he knew it.

BEAN WAS HALFWAY THROUGH the window when Morgan took off. All he'd wanted was a chance to talk with Morgan. He didn't want to kill the man, at least not until he'd gotten the money.

He had one hand on the sill and a leg through the opening and he was trying to keep his cool. But the only friend he had in the world, John Wesley, was laid out there on the floor and he wasn't moving. Bean got the other leg over and he went through into the room just as Morgan came off the porch. Off balance and running, Bean raised the Walther and took aim.

Morgan there ten feet from the stairs, the light from the open door spilling onto the prairie. Morgan moving for the shadows. Bean pulled the trigger and felt the gun buck slightly. Morgan fell out of the light and into the darkness. Bean had no idea if he'd hit the man or not.

He came down off the porch with the pistol still pointed out on the prairie, Drake's own service weapon now tucked into the waistband of his pants.

Grass moved in the wind, and farther on the sound of the high thin branches of the cottonwoods clacking together. Bean's eyes trying to adjust. He came to the edge of the light and stood with the gun in a sweep of the land.

Nothing but the high grass to see.

For what felt like an hour he stood there looking out on the night. And then he backed away, his finger still held down on the trigger, the gun warmed in his grip. He came back into the cabin and sat for what seemed a long time with John Wesley. Bean's legs crossed and the tail of his suit jacket spread behind him on the floor. One hand with the Walther in his lap and the other laid palm down on John Wesley's back. The big man still warm and his face away from Bean, cheek down on the floor.

Nothing Bean could do.

Bean was rocking slightly and watching the open door and the night beyond when he rose and left his friend behind on the floor of the cabin.

DRAKE AND SHERI PUT their backs to the seat and kicked at the cage. Drake counted down the time and then both of them shot out their soles at the cage a final time. Nothing moved. The car sat there rocking slightly on its springs and the sound of their breath was the only thing to be heard there in the darkness.

He looked over at her but there was little to see. The silver light of the moon luminescent on her features, the bruises the men had left nothing but dark marks on her white skin. "I'm sorry," he said.

"I trusted Patrick, too," Sheri said. "It wasn't just you."

They'd heard three shots come from over the edge of the hill and then nothing for a very long time. He moved and kicked at the glass of the side window, feeling the body of the car shake. The bottom of his foot felt numb from the twenty or more times he'd tried to push through the rear cage.

He stopped to catch his breath. The night cold had seeped into the car. His lungs pumping in his chest and the steam rising, then disappearing in the air before him. Free to move, he went to the window and looked out on the night as if he might find some help there.

All he'd told the two men was that the money was down there. There was no other choice. It was all he could think of to buy time, and he looked out on the crest of the hill, hoping Morgan had taken his advice to clear out for a day or two. Just go on into town and see if his friend could give him a place to sit this all out. But the guns going off down the hill suggested otherwise.

Sometime on the ride over he'd managed to get his hands free and he'd loosened the tape from around Sheri's wrist as soon as the two killers had disappeared from sight. Now he tried to pry away the clear glass-like polycarbonate separating the front seat from the back. All of it supported on a metal frame that had been bolted to the floor at his feet. He didn't have anything but his own strength to rely on and his strength wasn't enough.

WHEN BEAN FOUND Morgan he sat at the bottom of the cut with his back to a cottonwood trunk and his legs splayed out on the ground. He'd broken the bird gun open and it lay on his lap with the chambers exposed and the two empty shells in the dirt to his right. There was a pain in his shoulder like a knife blade any time he moved and he sat there trying to calm it away with one hand raised to the meat at his breast and the other out on the ground like an anchor.

He looked up at Bean as he came out of the trees, moving down the slight incline to where Morgan rested. Bean carried a pistol before him and he stopped five feet away from Morgan, the barrel of the gun aimed off to the side. Morgan could see Bean was looking him over and making his judgments.

"You were just sitting up waiting for us," Bean said. He moved a little closer, squatting so that they could look each other over at the same level. The gun still in his hand.

"I've been sitting up waiting for years now," Morgan said. A wave of pain passed through him and he closed his eyes tight. When he opened them again Bean was still there. Morgan gave him a smile.

"John Wesley is dead," Bean said.

"I expected he was."

"We could have just sat down and talked."

"I know how those talks go with you," Morgan said.

Bean looked from the open breech of the shotgun to the empty shells in the dirt by Morgan's thigh. "You and Patrick, huh?" Bean laughed a bit to himself, looking back the way he'd come from. Light up the hill where the cabin bled a thin gray tone into the night air. "I would have thought you were too old for something like this."

"Turns out I'm not," Morgan said. He moved a bit, taking his hand away from his chest, and watching the way Bean looked him over. The man hadn't moved except to kneel there in front of him.

"You were always good to us, Morg," Bean said. "I didn't mean to shoot you."

"You didn't."

"Then what's wrong with you?"

There was sweat growing on Morgan's forehead and upper lip and it felt cold in the night. "Just old," Morgan said. "Just sitting here catching my breath."

Bean gave a disappointed smile. He rose and slipped the pistol into the waistband at his back. For a second he stood looking down the stream and then he turned and fixed Morgan again with a stare. "Where's the money, Morgan?"

"There is no money."

Bean knelt again, pulling the suit jacket away where it bunched between his stomach and thighs. Morgan watched him and thought of how the man reminded him of some gunfighter in a novel, pushing the jacket back over the grip of the gun before taking his paces.

"I read the note from Patrick to his son," Bean said. "I have the deputy and his wife back there in the car. I can tell you right now it's you or him."

Morgan thought that over. The pain was coming over him in waves, and he thought again about the woman in town. He thought about Patrick. He didn't know what to think. Morgan's heart doing the stutter-step inside his chest.

With one hand Morgan felt around on his jeans until he found the spare shells in his pocket. He knew Bean was watching but he didn't care. His hand was slow and it shook too much but he got one shell out and then another. The two shells in the palm of his hand and a dry rasp now felt on his tongue as he tried to push himself up.

"Don't," Bean said.

Morgan got one shell in his fingers and fed it down into the bore. He was working on the other one when Bean put his hand out and cupped his palm over Morgan's fist. The two frozen there like that, Bean kneeling before Morgan and Morgan sitting there with his back to the cottonwood trunk.

"You're an old fool," Bean said.

Morgan looked up at him. The words not coming and a dry heat seizing up in his chest just above the heart, his insides gone solid and heavy as cement.

THROUGH THE CRUISER windshield Drake watched the pale indent in the sky. His grandfather's cabin out there just beyond the ridge and no shot or sound for more than thirty minutes. He sat forward on the edge of the backseat—one hand to the cage—watching the place Bean and John Wesley had stood. There was nothing for him to do. His arms ached and his legs felt swollen from trying to kick out the doors and windows. His bad knee pulsing like a metronome.

The keys had been left in the ignition, but the car was not on. There was no light but that of the stars and what little escaped from the cabin beyond the ridge. Drake's eyes had long since adjusted and he could see now far away over the grass. Watching the way the moon came down silver and glossy over the fresh shoots of spring. Far away he saw the occasional headlight break over the top of a hill on the county road and then go away again.

"What do you think?" Sheri asked.

"Morgan?"

"Yes."

He didn't know what had happened to Morgan and he went on watching the ridge before him and thinking about the morning.

Drake leaving Morgan to go west over the mountains and the old man simply turning to walk back out into the grasslands to set his snares. Every day seeming to repeat itself like the one before.

"I can't say," Drake finally said, though he knew it was probably too much to hope for. And he thought what little time they had left owed a lot to Morgan.

It took Drake a second to notice the figure come up over the ridge, the head visible first, backlit by the pale light of the cabin. Then the shoulders came into view. A black figure standing there looking at the cruiser. He watched and waited. Drake's face still at the window and then when the man turned in profile to look out at something far away on the county road, Drake saw it was Bean.

The chill went down Drake like ice on the skin. He fell back against the seat, covering Sheri as much as possible. Listening now to Bean's footsteps as he came down off the ridge and made his way to the car.

Drake looked around but there was nothing for him to use. There was nothing he could do but wait it out and hope somehow to escape notice. Though he knew it wasn't a possibility and Bean knew exactly where they were.

Drake heard the shuffle of gravel under Bean's shoes and then he didn't hear anything anymore. The warmth of Sheri's body under his, the strangled breathing as they both tried to make themselves as small as possible. Drake looked up and Bean stood outside the door, just his body visible through the glass, the Walther tucked into the front of his pants next to Drake's own pistol. The black sides of his jacket outlining the white belly of Bean's shirt.

Drake's eyes ran along the walls of the cage but there was no escape. Both he and Sheri moved all the way across the seat, as far away from Bean as they could get. Nothing to prevent Bean from just reaching in and pulling them out one at a time.

But then Drake saw what had taken up Bean's attention on the county road. Blue and red light now beginning to flicker on the white of Bean's shirt. Drake rose and looked behind down the gravel road. The first halo of flashing light showed over the horizon and then the grille lights came into view over the far ridge.

The car was a long way off but it was moving fast, running down the road with the gravel popping beneath the tires. Drake turned and saw Bean had backed away into the grass. He stood there now with his body toward Drake, both guns loose in his hands by his thighs, and his face turned to the oncoming blaze of light.

Drake watched Bean until he took one step back and then another. He was looking at both of them now, the guns still in his hands and the light growing on his face. Drake watching Bean there in the grass, his legs dipped into the prairie like a man wading backward into a swimming pool, first one foot, then the other.

And then Bean was gone. A few hesitant steps before he turned and disappeared over the ridge, the black jacket waving behind him as he cut down through the grass and went from sight.

PART V

THE HOUSE IN THE WOODS

D RISCOLL WALKED OVER FROM the Impala and told them a body had been found in Maurice's house. Drake and Patrick were sitting on the stairs and Patrick looked up when Driscoll mentioned the house but didn't say anything. Driscoll went on and told them the coroner was waiting on a set of dental records to make a positive ID, but the body looked to be Maurice's.

After a while Patrick turned to Drake. "Did you see anything when you were there?"

Drake looked over at his father and then looked away again. There were flashlights moving out over the grass. Driscoll had called two marshals in and they worked as a team with four deputies from the local sheriff's department, their flashlights swelling up over the landscape and then moving off again. "I don't know," Drake said. He shook his head. He didn't want to tell his father about it.

They were sitting on the front stairs of Morgan's cabin. Patrick's wrists were cuffed behind him and Gary, Driscoll, and Sheri stood in a half circle around them. All with their arms crossed to ward off the cold.

There had been three shots. The first two—Drake guessed—were from Morgan's bird gun and the last from a pistol. Thirty minutes later Bean had come up the hill and stood next to the cruiser. Drake was thinking about it now. He was thinking about it all and trying to put it back together but nothing seemed to fit.

The first thing they'd seen when they'd come down the hill was John Wesley where he lay just inside the door. He'd taken a load of shot to the shoulder and then another load in his chest and stomach. He was dead and Drake looked around the small cabin for any other sign. The bird gun was gone and so was Morgan. There was a piece of firewood on the floor and the broken glass of the window fallen all around it. The iron stove still had some warmth to it but the room was cold with the window busted in and the door open on its hinges. A single chair had been knocked on its side, another one close by the stove sat alone.

Patrick was still waiting on some sort of answer from him, but Drake didn't have anything to say. He was angry with his father. Just yesterday he'd sat on this same porch with Morgan like nothing would happen. Drake somehow believing this, knowing now how wrong he had been.

The difference between what he wanted and what would actually happen complete as two passing worlds up there somewhere in the stars. Mostly, though, Drake was angry with himself for letting Patrick convince him they could have some kind of normal life; drinking beer on the back porch and watching the apple orchard with the smell of barbecue and smoke in the air.

The saddest part about it all was that Drake still wanted those things. Only now he knew they would never be. For a long time Drake watched the flashlights out there in the grass. The deputies were taking their time, working their way down the hill with the night wind moving the grass. Soon they'd be into the cottonwoods and up the other side. He wondered how far they would take it.

"Was it Maurice?" Patrick asked.

Sheri stirred. "I'm sorry, Patrick. I know he was a friend of yours."

Drake wouldn't look at his father. Anything his father touched seemed to turn to blood on the floor—pools and pools of it.

He shook his head and looked up to Sheri. He didn't know what there was left to say. Nothing was how it was supposed to be and Drake pushed himself up and walked the few steps toward her. He hugged her, holding her close, her chin resting on his chest and her forehead to the bottom of his jawline. Drake kissed the top of her head, feeling one of the welts that had risen close to the bone, and then taking her hand, he asked her to step away.

In that moment he didn't care anymore. He didn't care that his father was sitting there on the stairs watching them. He didn't care about Driscoll or Gary or what they might want. Drake only wanted his life with Sheri to go back to some form of normality, though he could honestly say he didn't know what that might be anymore.

They were careful not to go too far—only to the edge of the cabin light. They sat and watched the deputies out there as they moved over the grass. Drake kept his hand on hers. The warmth of her body felt close to him.

"What happens now?" Sheri asked.

"I don't know," Drake said. He looked back to the cabin. Driscoll, Gary, and Patrick there. He felt her hand tighten on his.

After a while she asked, "Why doesn't Gary or Driscoll go help the marshals?"

"I don't think either one wants to leave the other one alone with my father."

Sheri's eyes shifted over the small gathering at the foot of the stairs. Drake saw her waver there for a second and then look to Drake. "Twelve years ago Patrick did it, didn't he?"

It took Drake a while but eventually he nodded. He watched her take that in. He waited for her to say something and when nothing came he asked her about Bean.

"I don't want to talk about it."

Drake didn't know what to say. He knew he had to ask but the asking was painful and he was having a hard time forming the words. He looked away from her now toward the search party out there in the grass. The flashlights were farther away from them, almost at the cottonwoods. With his eyes still out on the rolling hills, he said, "I just need to know if you're okay."

"He didn't do anything to me."

"And the house? The place that they took us—could you find your way back there?"

"I don't know," she said. "I don't think so."

"No," he said. "I don't think I could, either." He turned to take her in. She wouldn't look at him now.

"Are you asking if he hurt me?" she said.

"Yes."

"Not in that way," she said. "He took something from me that I don't think I'll be able to get back for a long time."

Drake waited. He didn't want her to go on but he couldn't stop her.

"I'm telling you he didn't rape me. He didn't get off on that. He wanted to make sure I knew I was helpless. He wanted my security. He took that all away from me. And now he's out there somewhere." She paused. "It's almost worse that way," she finally said.

He turned, looking away for a time before coming back to her, watching as the search party lights reflected on her pupils. "Are you okay?" he asked. "Are we okay?"

"I don't know," she said.

PATRICK RAISED HIS head when the shouting started down by the creek. He stood and Driscoll put a hand to his shoulder but then removed it after he saw Patrick wasn't trying to run.

They covered the ground together, Patrick in the lead with Driscoll and Gary following close behind. Drake and Sheri cutting across the grass toward them. All of them in the near black of night until Gary brought out a small flashlight and flicked it on.

Already Patrick could see the men standing around the base of the tree. Their own flashlights illuminating the scene with a strange glow, the tall thin shadows of tree trunks shifting across the landscape as one deputy or another moved his light to take in the cottonwoods behind.

The incline was difficult with his hands cuffed behind him and Patrick slipped, falling to his side so that the meat of his shoulder would take the fall. He lay there with one of his legs beneath him for only a second before Gary had him up, asking if he was okay. Patrick didn't spare the time to answer. He'd seen the legs there on the other side of the tree trunk now. The tips of the boots he knew were his father's and the old bird gun there on the man's lap.

Patrick came down and stood looking at his father. There was one fresh shell loaded into the shotgun and the other was still in his palm. He seemed to be staring at something just past them all, and for a long while Patrick looked out on the darkness beyond the cottonwood stand and tried to make out what it was.

DRISCOLL WALKED OUT onto the porch and then came back inside again. The paramedics had come and taken John Wesley and Morgan away. The blood was still on the floor where the big man had lain for the last couple hours. Drake brought his eyes up and took in Driscoll where he stood in the doorway of the cabin looking them all over. "You ready, Patrick?"

Patrick didn't show any notice of Driscoll. He was watching the far hill where the ambulance had gone.

"You taking him in?" Gary asked. "I'd like to come along if that's what this is."

"That's not what this is," Driscoll said. "Patrick owes me something."

Patrick came out of whatever trance he was in. He looked to Drake and Sheri first and then he looked at Driscoll. "I said what I did to get us here."

"I don't think so, Patrick."

"Think whatever you want," Patrick said. "Bobby is alive because I did what I did. All the rest, it's all the same as it's always been. There's no money. There never was."

Driscoll reached inside his coat and brought out the note written in Patrick's hand. It was still in the plastic envelope. He walked it over to the table and set it before Patrick. "This was in the front of Bobby's cruiser. Are you going to tell me you don't know anything now?"

Patrick was studying the note on the table, his hands cuffed behind him and his back at a slight arch as he bent to take in the old note. He started to laugh, softly at first and then louder, and when he looked up at Driscoll he said, "You really don't have anything, do you?"

"Where's the money?" The words were fast and spit came up out of Driscoll's mouth as he spoke. He was leaning into Patrick now, staring him down.

"We can take him in together," Gary said again, his voice weaker now, but still trying. He was sitting opposite Drake, and Drake could see the sheriff's eyes dart from one man to the other.

Driscoll straightened and returned to the open door, looking on the land out there that was now probably Patrick's. The remaining deputies and lawmen were still searching the area for Bean. Driscoll's back was to them and Drake couldn't tell what was going through Driscoll's head. Patrick was going back in regardless. There was no getting around that.

Drake was alive. He knew what his father had done for him. Sitting here with his wife and his father when he might not have been. But still, the note was on the table. The money didn't belong to any of them. And maybe that was the problem.

"I can show you," Drake said.

THEY CROSSED THE prairie with the moon full above them. Drake in the lead, followed by Sheri and then Driscoll, Patrick lagging behind with his hands cuffed and Gary bringing up the rear. The two men far enough back that their voices could not be heard over the sound of the grass swishing at their feet.

"How much is it?" Gary asked.

Patrick looked over his shoulder and then went on walking. He was having trouble seeing where to put his feet. Drake carried a flashlight and so did Gary. But the light would probably be better if both turned their flashlights off and they just used the moon. "You know how much," Patrick said.

"All of it?"

"Two hundred thousand."

Gary quickened his step. He was just behind Patrick now and every few steps he felt Gary's shoe catch the back of Patrick's heel. "It can look like an accident," Gary said.

"I don't want that," Patrick said.

"It's been twelve fucking years," Gary said. His voice elevated.

Driscoll turned and looked back at Patrick but there didn't seem to be any recognition in the man's face.

They were still walking when they came up over a small rise and Patrick saw where the fence sat in a line along the hill. "It's going to be okay," Patrick said, speaking over his shoulder to Gary. The thought that they'd soon stop and then there wouldn't be another chance to talk for a very long while. "No accidents," Patrick said again. "I didn't do all this to watch it all fall apart in front of me. You're going to have to take care of Sheri and Bobby now. They're going to need you."

SHERI RODE SHOTGUN and Gary drove. It was past midnight and they'd left Morgan's cabin an hour before. Neither of them had said much to the other since they'd left, Sheri only telling Gary what roads to take and where to turn. She was reading the directions off an app on Gary's phone and the display gave the front seat of Drake's cruiser an intimate closed-off feeling that Sheri could only avoid by opening her window. The night air blew by at sixty miles per hour. The far lights of farms the only thing to be picked off the Eastern Washington prairie.

The turn for Silver Lake was a few miles ahead and she put the window up. The heaters had been turned on full and she switched them down and then flicked on the phone. The small blue icon that was them and nothing else around for thirty miles.

"How far?" Gary asked.

"Two miles." She put a hand to the dash and messed with the heater for a while, trying the various settings. Though she knew them almost as well as her own car. Just doing what she could to pass the time, all the while studying Gary from the corner of her eye.

Gary wet his lips and then glanced her way. "I'm proud of Bobby."

"I'm proud of him, too," Sheri said. She didn't know where this was going but she'd been the one to suggest it. She'd been the one to tell Drake she didn't mind going back to Silver Lake with Gary.

"Not a lot of people would have given up the money like that."

They rode in silence for a long time after that. Gary took the turn and the road began to wind into the mountains. Silver Lake another hour away. The smell of the evergreens growing as they went and the air turned crisp and cold. High up on the peaks she saw the snow in the mountains. This place was her home, though it had not always been. And she tried to imagine where she would go or what she would do if she ever left.

After a time, she said, "Patrick wasn't alone when he took the money, was he, Gary?"

"No," Gary said. He glanced her way and then returned his eyes to the road.

"All this time," she said.

"I know."

She waited, listening to the wind pass by outside the window. "You've been the sheriff as long as I've lived in Silver Lake."

"I know that, too," he said.

She watched the high, blue mountains and when she turned back she asked, "Should I be scared of you?" She was watching him but he wouldn't turn to look at her.

"No," he said. And then after a while he asked, "Should I be scared of you?"

She didn't know how to answer that. All the years they'd known each other, all the help Gary had given them over the years. None of it fit.

She looked his way. "Tonight could have gone a lot different," she said. "I don't know if this is the right way to say it but I guess I think you did the right thing back there."

"How's that?"

"Bobby gave up the money but I think in some way you did, too."

THE FIRST LIGHT chased them up the mountains and they drove now in the western shadows just beyond. Drake sat with the green tackle box between his feet on the floor. Patrick, with his hands cuffed, was asleep in the back and Driscoll drove. For a long time Drake sat and watched the undergrowth pass by his window and then when he tired of it he turned and looked to the back, where Patrick slumped against one of the doors, his head bent to the window and his eyes closed.

"You know what they say about a guilty man," Driscoll said.

Drake nodded. "I know."

Driscoll raised his eyes on the rearview mirror and then brought them back to the road ahead. "When we come into Bellingham I'll drop you at the hotel and then take Patrick in for holding."

"I'll go in with you."

"You don't have to."

"I want to," Drake said. He didn't know how to feel about it. He never thought he'd be the one to take his own father in, but he was.

"I'm going to take the money in as well. I'll be handing it over in Bellingham. It's their case still."

"I understand."

"Are you sure you don't want to go by the hotel first? The guys in Bellingham are going to want to talk with Patrick. It might be a while."

"I'll go with you," Drake said. "They'll want to talk with me as well."

"We don't have to rush anything."

Drake thought that over. He didn't say anything more and Driscoll didn't try to talk him out of it.

They drove in silence and by the time they came out of the mountains Drake was asleep, only waking when Driscoll pulled the Impala to the front of the Bellingham Police Department and turned the engine off.

Patrick was up, and Drake wondered how long his father had been sitting there, his eyes on both of them while Driscoll drove and Drake slept.

Driscoll asked for the money, and then, when Drake handed it over, he ran his eyes between father and son and then went on inside the department.

"He's wondering if I'm going to let you loose," Drake said, speaking over his shoulder to Patrick.

Patrick didn't respond. Out on the street a school bus had stopped and the doors slid open. A group of elementary students waiting with their parents and then when the doors slid closed again Drake and Patrick watched the parents walk away, some talking to each other for a time before splitting and going on again toward their individual houses.

Patrick cleared his throat. "We'd both be in Monroe if you let me loose."

"I'm sorry about the way this turned out," Drake said.

"There's nothing to be sorry about. I just wish I could have seen your grandfather, you know?"

"I feel responsible." Drake had his head down, his eyes on the place the money used to be. Morgan was dead and in some way Drake was a part of that.

Patrick shook his head. "You know you're not responsible for any of this. Drug smuggling, the money, the deaths of those two men, or your grandfather. I know you want to believe you are. I know that's why you became a deputy but it's just not your fault. I've wanted you to know that for a long time and I've wanted to say that to you for just as long and I guess now I have. You understand? You're not responsible for my mistakes."

Drake sat looking out on the front of the department. Driscoll would be back soon and Drake didn't know when he'd see his father again.

Patrick leaned forward and Drake could feel him close behind. "Say something."

There wasn't anything Drake could say. The emotions were spinning around inside of him like a tornado. Nothing ever settling. He knew his father wanted him to let it go but he just couldn't.

SHERI GOT THE phone on the second ring and listened to what Drake had to say. By then it was afternoon and Drake had already given his statement to the Bellingham police. He'd slept a few hours at the hotel and one of the detectives had told him he'd give Drake a ride home in an hour or so.

Sheri hung up without saying more than ten words and when she walked to the front window she saw Luke out there in his cruiser, watching over her. It was Gary who'd insisted on it. With Drake not home yet it was just a precaution, Gary had said. Bean out there somewhere still.

She turned and walked away from the window. Everything was the same as it had been when Bean and John Wesley had taken her from the house. Even the cereal bowl was still there in the kitchen sink. She looked this over and then after a minute she cleaned the bowl and spoon and set them on the rack to dry.

She straightened the kitchen first and then the living room. Ten minutes later she walked down the hall and stopped in front of Patrick's room. The door was open and she stood there for a long time looking over the crib and changing table, the walls painted to look like a sunset.

Drake's voice on the phone had sounded tired. It was how she felt, worn out, scrubbed down. For forty-eight hours she hadn't known if she would live or die.

She had not known how it would turn out for so long, and now she did. Her life with Drake. Her life here in Silver Lake.

She stood in the doorway for a long time before she turned and went back to the kitchen. When she came to the second bedroom again she carried an empty cardboard box with a wrench and a screwdriver inside. She removed the tools and set the box on the bed next to Patrick's things.

The first thing she packed was Patrick's clothes, taking them from the changing table drawers and folding them before putting them in the cardboard box. When she was done, she set the box in the hallway and came back into the room. It took her thirty minutes to break down the crib, loosening the bolts and then removing the sides so that each lay flat against the wall.

Sheri did it all with a quiet determination. There was no pausing or break in her labor. It was just her and the room. Two separate bodies that had once been and now were not.

THE DETECTIVE WHO'D agreed to take Drake back to Silver Lake was waiting for him in the front drive of the hotel. A plastic container of 7-Eleven nachos in his lap that he ate chips from one at a time. He nodded to Drake and when Drake was seated in the car he wiped one hand clean with a napkin and drove out of the lot still eating chips with the other hand.

The man was twenty years older than Drake and from talking to him earlier, Drake knew the detective had been one of the first to respond to the two bodies found at the gravel lot outside town. The case Driscoll said Patrick was involved with.

The detective had been a young guy then, the incident one of his first investigations. Now he was aged past his middle and moving into the last years of his service. He talked and drove at the same time. Pointing out various places he'd made busts and pulled drivers over to find sandwich bags of meth in their glove compartments.

Halfway to the highway Drake stopped the man and asked him to turn the car back.

They made it to the gravel lot just as the sun began to set. The detective sitting in the car and telling Drake what had changed and what hadn't. He gestured to an open spot just twenty feet away. "That's where they were shot," he said. The detective made a gun out of his fist. Bucking it with each shot. "Pop. One goes down. A clean shot to the temple, cracked his skull right down the middle. The second man turns to run. Pop, pop, pop. He gets cut up as he moves. Makes it maybe four steps and then falls right there." The detective was still holding his trigger finger out on the scene, letting it quiver there in the air before him. A spot of nacho cheese on his fingernail. He brought the finger back and put it to his mouth and just sat there looking the lot over. "We found the bodies behind one of the big rock piles over there."

"Where was the shooter?" Drake asked.

The detective pointed out the spot. It was about a hundred yards off. "Twelve years ago there was one of those big yellow excavators right there. The shooter was probably back behind it in the shadows."

"Were they shot at night?"

"That's what we figured."

Drake opened the car door and got out. The evening cold around him and the lot out a ways from the city, built up against a few acres of wetland. Farther out, the white trunks of a stand of birch trees, the leaves just starting to sprout. He walked over and stood in the spot where the men had been shot.

He turned and looked to where the shooter would have been. Nothing there now but an empty space between two piles of gravel. He knelt and looked at the ground, running his hand over it and feeling the grit against his skin, expecting somehow that his fingertips would come back stained with blood. Still kneeling, he put a hand to his bad knee and pushed into the muscle, feeling the dull, familiar ache of his old injury. He imagined the shot. He felt the force of the bullet and the tear it made through human skin.

By the time he stood, the detective had come out of the car and was waiting a little ways off watching Drake. "The thinking on this has always been that there were two men. One waiting where you are now to distract the two victims, then the other back there in the shadows covering them all."

"What did my father say when you interviewed him today?"

"Denies it ever happened. Says he's not the one. Says we had it wrong all those years before and we still have it wrong."

"Even with all that money?"

"Funny thing about it is I always thought it was going to be more. Two hundred thousand is a lot of money but it doesn't seem like enough to kill for."

"What happens now?" Drake asked. He was trying to put it all back together in his head. He was trying to picture his father here twelve years before.

"We've got statements from you and your father but it's really not enough without the gun, or any direct proof your father was here. We can't hold him. Driscoll will move him to the federal building in Seattle tonight and I'd guess it will be the last we see of your father. He'll be back in Monroe in a week."

"Even the money isn't enough?"

"It's drug money. It's not like the bills were marked."

Drake looked to the spot where the shooter had been. He paced it out, walking over and then looking back at the detective.

When he was finished he came back to the car. "It seems like a pretty good shot."

The detective nodded. "It was." He watched Drake where he stood. "They're saying your father will be out again in a few years. That worry you?"

"Honestly," Drake said, "I really don't know."

"And this other guy, your father's buddy from Monroe. He's still out there, too. He's out there now."

"The money's gone," Drake said.

The detective grinned and opened the driver's-side door. "Like I said, it always seemed like too little."

BEAN SAT AT THE edge of the wood and surveyed the clearing before the small house. His face dirty and his hands crosshatched with slivers of dried blood from the rock and grasslands he'd traveled through much of the night. Somewhere along the way, he'd lost the jacket and his white shirt was stained gray with a mixture of dirt and sweat. The collar a jaundiced yellow where it rested against the exposed skin of his neck.

Most of the night had been spent making his way through the fields, grasslands and prairie giving way to wheat fields and then back to prairie. When the day came he followed small creek beds that had gone dry or still trickled with water and worked his way across the country in a zigzagging fashion, using what tree cover he could find to hide him from view.

Now, almost twenty hours later, he had come to the house at the base of the mountains. He sat watching it for a long time as he tried to make up his mind. The light fading and no sense that Drake or his wife had been able to lead the marshals back this way. Though Bean knew he and John Wesley had been careful enough coming here the night before.

He waited, watching the light fade till it sat over the fields in a blue haze of floating pollen and spring seedpods. The light catching it all like the filament of weeds in a stream.

After a long while he rose and crossed the clearing. His muscles cramped from his rest and his body aching. He came to the house and went along its side, peering through the windows at the darkness within.

The smell had grown worse in the day since they'd left and Bean put a shirtsleeve to his nose as he came through the door. He left the door open and walked into the house. When he came to the basement door he eased it open on the hinges and stared down into the depths at the cement floor below. He couldn't risk the use of a light switch and after a time he went down the stairs. The sound of his shuffling through the darkness the only thing to be heard from the top of the stairs.

After a minute he was back again, standing in what little light fell from above, one hand held to his nose and the limp body of a woman supported on his opposite shoulder. He came up the stairs and walked, carrying the woman through her house and out into the yard. He dumped her there and then went back for her husband. The two lying faceup in the grass. Both in their early seventies, the blood drawn from their faces and the bruises John Wesley had left on their necks now only a slight yellow.

For a long time Bean simply sat there with them. He'd needed their house after he and John Wesley had made their escape and now he needed it again.

In an hour he'd have the couple in the ground, and in another hour he'd sit resting in their tub, windows open to let in the night air, cleaning the last couple days of trouble from his skin.

For MOST OF THE day Patrick sat in the holding cell watching the clock on the wall. He was alone in the cell and it had been two hours since anyone had come by to tell him anything. The empty dinner tray the only thing to say anyone had ever been there at all. Far down the hall he knew an officer sat at a desk but he could not see him, and besides the occasional murmurings of a drunk in a cell two or three doors down, Patrick felt very alone. More alone than he'd ever felt in prison.

He checked the time again. The clock in a metal cage, painted white like the walls. Gray cement floors all the way down the hall and into his cell. A single bench for him to sit on and not even a sink or toilet for Patrick to use if needed.

He stood and walked to the bars and tried to look down the hallway but there was nothing to see, not even a window. He looked to the clock and wondered if the sun had set, or if it was still twilight outside with the pale pink of sunset still in the air and the saltwater smell of Puget Sound drifting like far-off music.

He walked back to the bench and sat again. He'd been told he was going south that night, down to Seattle, where he'd be processed and then eventually sent back to Monroe. He set his face in his hands and rubbed the coarse hair on his cheeks, working his fingers up across his skin until his hands sat behind him, yoked across the back of his neck.

Fucking Bobby, he thought. He shook his head in disbelief. Smiling to himself as he brought his head up and stared for a beat too long at the overhead light. He was proud in a way. It had been a lot of money. But Patrick could see now that Bobby didn't need it, probably never had, and in that way Patrick was proud of him.

He sat there and watched the hands of the clock go around and around. An hour later he heard a far door open and then something being said to the officer down there. There was the sound of rubber soles on cement and farther on the clack of hard-soled dress shoes. When Driscoll showed he was wearing the same rumpled suit from earlier in the day, the top button on his shirt undone and no tie. The service weapon visible beneath his coat. Two officers came before him, one with the keys and the other holding a shotgun in one hand while reaching for the cuffs on his belt with the other.

"You ready, Patrick?"

Patrick stepped back from the bars, the movement inherent now to who he was. Barred gates opening from one cell to another. He looked out on Driscoll and said he was. The door came open and the officer handed the shotgun to Driscoll and came forward with the cuffs. Patrick letting the man get the bracelets on him.

With the officer leading him, Patrick went down the hall, glancing over into the cells as he passed. The drunk now lay out on his own bench, snoring with his pants wet at the crotch and a pool of liquid beneath him on the floor. Patrick heard the other officer swear and then the keys came out and the door to the drunk's cell was yanked opened. It was the last thing Patrick heard before they came out of the holding area and made their way to a side door. Driscoll followed while Patrick walked. The officer still leading and Patrick glancing up to check the time before they went out the door and the cool of night came over them like a soft cotton sheet.

Driscoll's Impala sat there in the loading dock and Patrick heard Driscoll fumble for a moment with his keys. There was nothing around but a line of cars parked fifteen feet away, the headlights facing them, and the blue light of the overhead halogens giving the area a washed-out feel. Moths and small winged insects playing in the light as a single spider dangled from a web catching what it could.

He heard Driscoll grumble about something and then two high beams were on them in a flood. Bright and encompassing as a nuclear explosion. Patrick tried to raise a hand to ward off the light but found his hands pulled down by the officer.

The best Patrick could manage was to close his eyes, the light pink beneath his eyelids and then the rapid pop of gunfire very close and the thump of bullets finding contact. Two bodies dropped to the ground on either side of him, and he no longer felt the officer's hand holding him back.

DRAKE CAME IN FROM the garage and found Sheri in the kitchen. The box of Patrick's clothes had been put away atop a stack of other boxes. Now he crossed the living room and went in after the sides of the crib. It took him two trips to bring the four pieces outside to the garage, leaning them carefully against the wall with bits of cloth nestled between each layer to keep the paint from scraping.

He closed the garage doors and padlocked them. Luke still out there in the patrol car and Drake's own cruiser now back in the drive. For a while he stood looking in at the inside of his house, golden with light. Sheri putting dinner together in the kitchen and the overhead lights in the hallway leading back into the house.

Drake nodded to Luke and then mounted the stairs. He paused at the top and looked out on the forest. He wondered how long Gary would have Luke or Andy sit outside the house. The two patrol cars in the drive reminding Drake of the crimes committed and how Sheri and he were living in the aftermath.

He opened the door and went inside.

When he'd come through Silver Lake earlier that day he saw the small memorial set up for the girl who had been killed. Flowers and ribbons placed beside the door to the doughnut shop. Candles that were no longer lit but that Drake could see had burned through the night and sat melted in an uneven mass on the pavement. A single picture of the girl, framed, showing her the year before when she was a senior at the local high school. He was thinking about this now, and thinking about Morgan and the way they'd found him sitting against the tree with his eyes on the darkness.

Drake took a seat at the kitchen counter and watched Sheri pour a steaming pot of water into the sink, straining pasta while a red sauce simmered on the burner. He tried to put the days together in his mind but they fell apart in front of him. He wanted to feel something about it all but he kept returning to a selfish thought, that Sheri was still alive, that he was. He looked out on the patrol cars there in the drive. He wondered how the foot of their stairs would look with candles burning, with ribbons and flowers. He wondered if anyone would have cared. He didn't know if he had the answer.

They hadn't talked yet about the crib or the way Sheri seemed to be packing the house away little by little. She had only asked him to clear the room, to put the things away in the garage. Drake thought about this as he set the table. He thought about Patrick's bed in there and how he'd break it down after dinner and put it away with all the rest. Leaning it against the crib. And for a long time he looked away into the darkness out back of their house, trying to locate the small dirt patch where their child was buried, but he didn't see it and Sheri called his name and told him to pour two glasses of water and grate a small block of cheese before she brought the pasta over.

They sat in silence and ate the food. Neither had had much to say the entire day. Several times now Sheri tried to speak but the words failed her and she looked away again or twirled her fork through her pasta.

"Is this the life we wanted?" she finally asked, the pasta gone from Drake's plate and the red sauce all that remained against the white porcelain.

He looked up at her and there was nothing to take away from her face. The eyes steady as they appraised him, her chin held tight and the lips solid and unmoving.

"I don't know," he said, looking around at the house they'd made their own.

"Is this the life *you* wanted?" she asked.

Drake didn't know what to say, but he knew if he asked the same question of her she would have an answer for him. Somewhere along the way it had all gone crooked for them and he stared back at her and knew what his answer would be, and he hoped it wouldn't take them long to find their way back to where it all went wrong.

ANDY WAS AT the front door in the morning, and Drake rose from bed and pulled his boxers on and then some sweats. He got to the door just as Andy started down the steps to go around and try the back door.

"Gary says he wants to see you," Andy said after Drake had the door open.

"What about?"

"Don't know, he just got me on the radio and told me to tell you to go into the department."

Drake looked behind him into his house, the living room still in shadow and the door to their bedroom left open slightly. "Sheri's still sleeping."

Andy looked past Drake like he might see her back there but then when he didn't he raised his eyes and told Drake not to worry, he'd be just outside.

Drake wore his deputy browns and his star. He drove into town in his own patrol car and put on his belt just before coming into the department. He wore his hat and he didn't even have time to take it off before Gary called to him from the back office.

The first thing Drake noticed was Agent Driscoll sitting in one of the seats before Gary's desk. Gary motioned to the other one and Drake sat, taking his hat from his head and placing it in his lap.

"Aren't you supposed to be in Seattle?" Drake asked.

Driscoll sat up a bit in the chair and put a hand to his side, wincing for a moment and then recovering. "That was before someone broke my rib with a rubber bullet. I was just telling Gary here all about it."

Gary looked over at Drake. "Someone jumped Driscoll and an officer just as they were taking your father out of holding."

Drake looked from Gary to Driscoll. "He's gone?"

Driscoll smiled. "Let me get down to it." He was still holding his hand to the injured rib.

"Please do," Gary said.

"One of the officers who brought Patrick back to holding after he made his statement let Patrick make a phone call."

Gary watched Drake's face and said, "Driscoll says Patrick called over to the Buck Blind."

"Well, your father made a call into the bar specifically, not the restaurant," Driscoll said. "You two know all the regulars down there, don't you?"

"You're talking about half the town of Silver Lake," Gary cut in.

"Weird thing about it is the rubber bullet. They're used by city police for riot control."

Gary shifted and fixed Driscoll with his eyes. "I don't like what you're saying. I don't know why you're talking to us about this. Just go by the bar and see who answered the phone."

"You're right, Sheriff. After I got out of the hospital last night I called over there and got no answer."

"It can get busy down there," Gary said.

"Yeah, that's kind of what I was wondering. I worked in a restaurant when I was a kid. Some little Italian place, and I remember how it was. You start juggling too many things at once and eventually you're going to drop something. I guess the bartender just dropped that phone call."

"Do you even know if Patrick talked to anyone?"

"The officer said he did but he wasn't close enough to hear who he might be talking with."

"So you think it was some regular down there? One of Patrick's old smuggling buddies?"

"That's the guess."

Gary laughed, leaning back in his chair and crossing his hands over his belly. "You just love this place, don't you," he said. "You're almost a regular as it is. I expect you'll be buying your lake cabin soon enough."

Driscoll smiled back at Gary. "We could have one of those old-time cabin-raising parties. Isn't that how it's done around here? We help each other. You'd help me, wouldn't you, Bobby?"

"Sure I would, Driscoll."

"Agent Driscoll living in Silver Lake," Gary said. "Sounds like fun."

Driscoll tried to laugh, but just ended up wincing and putting a hand to his ribs again. "Feels like someone is kicking me every time I try and take a breath," Driscoll said.

"I bet," Gary said. "It could have been a lot worse."

"Don't I know it, at close range the bullet lifted me right off my feet."

Drake nodded. He was trying to catch a break between the two men but he hadn't been able to find it yet.

"I'd never been hit like that," Driscoll was saying. "I imagine it looked like one of those big boxing swings we used to see on television when me and you were younger. You know, the big heavyweights going at it. One punch and the guy's bottom jaw is up in his brain and his feet are sailing into the air. Lifting him right off into outer space. Man, I miss a good fight like that sometimes. Now we have all these featherweights dancing around the ring."

"It's true," Gary said. "Things used to be different. No one can take a hit like that anymore and any time I watch a fight these days they always end up hugging on each other."

"The young fighters have some finesse. But they've got nothing behind their punches. No offense, Bobby."

"No offense taken," Drake said. "I'd rather watch finesse any day than see two big guys slamming away at each other."

"Yeah, well, to each his own," Driscoll said. "What I wanted to get down to here is who Patrick called and how they got their hands on rubber bullets made specifically for the police."

Drake could see Driscoll looking around at all the hunting pictures that lined the office. Gary holding up the head of a big buck. Gary kneeling next to a moose somewhere up in Canada.

"You shoot, don't you, Sheriff?" Driscoll asked. "You probably work in a variety of different situations. You might even know where someone would be able to buy that type of bullet."

"Agent Driscoll, you're getting real serious all of a sudden."

"Try getting shot, it will switch your whole perspective around."

"I'd prefer not to," Gary said. "I like my perspective just the way it is."

Driscoll didn't say anything for a while. He was staring at the wood backing of Gary's desk. "Where were you last night, Gary?"

"I was actually at the Buck Blind for most of the night."

"One more thing for me to talk to the bartender about," Driscoll said.

"For fuck's sake, Driscoll, just come out and say it."

"Last night you shot me with a rubber bullet and helped Patrick escape custody."

"Can you prove any of this?" Gary asked.

"I hope you have some sort of alibi for last night," Driscoll said.

"You're flying too close to the sun," Gary said.

Driscoll winced and stood, his hand to his side. He looked around at Drake. "You should know who you're working for. He's just as bad as your father only he hasn't been caught."

Drake held Driscoll's gaze for a long time before looking away. He heard Driscoll turn and go, the department door closing a few seconds later.

Drake ran his eyes over the office. No one but them. "How much of what Driscoll said is true?" Drake asked.

"About your father and me?"

"Yeah."

"Not a word of it," Gary said.

"You were at the Buck Blind last night?"

"Most of the time."

"What does that mean?" Drake asked.

"I mean I got up to piss and I went home at some point and ate a Lean Cuisine," Gary said. "What else do you want me to say? We're like family, aren't we, Bobby? You know you can trust me."

Drake gave him a hard stare and then stood. He took off his belt and then his badge. He put them on the desk. "No offense, Gary, but I don't think I can do this anymore."

THREE DAYS AFTER Drake turned in his badge, he and Sheri went back east of the mountains for Morgan's funeral. The town came out and the reception was held in the only restaurant, a barbecue and burger joint on the county highway with a single room and outside a front patio underneath a tent. Drake and Sheri shook hands with everyone and thanked them for coming. An older woman tried to give Sheri a novel she'd borrowed from Morgan but Sheri didn't think Morgan would mind if she simply kept it.

"It was a heart attack?"

"Yes," Sheri said. She thought of the old man she'd only met once. There and then not there at her wedding. She tried to think if she knew much more than that but nothing came.

The woman held the book for a time, sitting across from Sheri on one of the benches. And then when Drake came over to tell Sheri they were going on to the property, the woman said, "He just seemed so alive."

"He was," Drake said.

ALL OF MORGAN'S things were still there in the cabin when they stopped off, and Sheri watched as Drake went through the possessions. From what Sheri knew of Morgan he'd lived alone, simply, with nothing more than the woodstove and a few pots and pans to keep him company.

She watched Drake and while he read through one or two of the letters sitting out on the dinner table, she walked back into the bedroom and leafed through the books. A whole wall had been dedicated to them and the color of the bindings gave the uniform wood tones of the cabin a special quality that nothing else on that prairie seemed to have.

When she came back out of the bedroom, Drake was boxing the letters away. "You okay?" she asked.

He looked up. "I thought this place would feel different. But it feels the same."

"Isolated?"

"Yes, I feel like Morgan is just going to come up out of the cotton-woods any moment."

She looked away at the fields outside. The door and the window had been patched with pieces of plywood. "You worry what's going to happen to this place once we leave?"

"No," he said. "Not really."

"And Patrick? There's been no word?"

"He's not coming back here. Morgan's will left this place to him. It's Patrick's and I don't know where he'd go but it wouldn't be here." He picked up the box and brought it out to the car.

While he was gone Sheri started to collect what dry goods she could find. A box of baking soda, a jar of flour, a can of Crisco in one of the cupboards next to a hidden bar of Hershey's chocolate.

Outside she heard the car door clap shut and then a second later the split of a log. She came out onto the porch and for the next hour she watched Drake break down a collection of cottonwood sections, stacking them up in an even pile at the rear of the cabin like Morgan might come up out of the cut to use them.

It was night by the time they left. The letters the only thing they took with them.

FOR A WEEK Drake cleared brush from their orchard, pruning back the dead branches and forming the apple trees. In the mornings or in the afternoons he gave Sheri rides to work with their only car and then waited through the day for the call telling him she was ready to be picked up. Occasionally, Luke and Andy came by the house, though they didn't have to anymore.

The two deputies helped Drake to take down the remaining bits of the old alder fence Patrick hadn't gotten to. When they finished they helped Drake stake metal posts and run barbed cattle wire. At the front where the drive met the lake road they installed a wide metal gate that sat on a hinge and had to be unlocked with a key.

Besides the trips Drake took to the Buck Blind he didn't speak much with anyone. Only occasionally seeing Gary when Drake came and went. It was Gary who told him about the dead calf one night while Drake sat eating a burger at the bar. The wolf didn't kill the calf outright; it had nipped and bitten at the calf's flanks, leaving the calf bloodied and weak by morning. The rancher noticed it all too late and the calf was dead by noon that same day. "It's a shame about that wolf," Gary said. "They're saying they'll have to shoot her now."

"Who's saying that?"

"Fish and Wildlife. They're telling Ellie to use the collar and track the wolf down. But she won't do it."

"I'll talk to her," Drake said. He ate a couple more fries and then pushed the plate away. Gary sat watching him and after a while asked, "What are you doing out there at your place? Building a compound?"

"Just getting the place in order. Trying to do something with the land."

"You're going to sell the apples?"

"Yes."

"And the fence Luke and Andy helped you with?"

"After everything I thought it would be nice to feel safe again. For Sheri to feel safe."

"I can put a car out there again. If that's it."

"That's not what I mean," Drake said.

Gary looked at him and shook his head. "Talk to Ellie," he said.

RAIN KEPT THEM out of the mountains for two days and then when the sun came out on the third day they tracked the signal up an avalanche chute, white in places with snow. The sound of the spring melt running underneath the rock. They came up onto the open ridge with sweat stains on their shirts and their thighs aching from the ascent. The GPS telling them the wolf was somewhere in the valley beyond.

The trees began again after about a hundred feet and they made their way through the trunks as they descended. Coming out into a clearing they found the wolf lying just a couple hundred feet farther on. Crows lifting from the body as they came closer and the GPS collar still attached.

Ellie came to the animal first, crouching with the backs of her thighs resting on her calves. The spring grass had grown tall through the clearing and it surrounded the wolf on all sides, stretching away toward the forest where the mountain went on dark beneath the trees.

Drake slipped the day pack from his shoulders and laid it in the grass at his feet. He took a step closer, watching the way the clearing rolled away before them. Grasshoppers flitted off, the brief clap of their wings heard as they tried to stay afloat through the air. He hadn't realized Ellie was crying till he came closer and saw the tight pulse of her shoulder blades working beneath her shirt. He put a hand to her back and she jumped, pulling away and standing.

On the ground Drake saw the wolf had been shot through the head, the right foreleg badly mangled by a metal trap.

"They killed her," Ellie said. She had recovered a bit and she stood a few feet off. The redness still in her eyes.

There was nothing for Drake to say. He was kneeling in the same place Ellie had, looking down on the wolf. Someone had tried to cut the GPS collar away but the knife used hadn't been sharp enough for the job. He put a hand out and ran his fingers up through the fur, gripping it in his hands for a moment before letting go. The meat had begun to go bad and he could smell it.

The wolf had pawed up the ground around where the trap had been, tearing the grass and leaving a small patch of exposed earth that had grown muddy with the rain. There were paw prints everywhere, bits of fur, and in one section near the wolf's left hip, the partial indent of a boot. Ellie had already seen it and Drake examined it for a long time before he stood. Ellie already scanning the tree line like she might find the killer out there in the shadows.

The light was fading in the sky and Drake checked his watch. It would take them an hour to hike back down and by then the sun would be completely down. "We'll come back tomorrow," Drake said. "I can help you with the tracking."

Ellie turned and looked back at him. She was kneeling near the edge of the forest where the grass ran out and the shadows began. When Drake came over to her he could see another boot print, much clearer than the last.

"Looks familiar, doesn't it?" Ellie said. "Looks a lot like one of the prints from those poachers a few weeks back."

Drake knelt and examined the indentation in the mud. "Probably a day old. The edges are clean." If it wasn't for the GPS collar Drake knew they never would have found the wolf at all.

"Tomorrow," Ellie said.

"Yes."

"First thing."

"Okay."

BEAN STOOD WATCHING THE empty road. Fields of soybean ran along one side. The line of wire fence running down it and out of sight on both sides. He turned and looked up the road, just the same as it had been for ten minutes. Nothing but the deep shadows of the mountains farther on, avalanche chutes turning from rock to snow as the elevation grew and the trees thinned to clusters and then nothing at all. The light beginning to fade in the west and the road Bean stood on taking on a slanted otherworldly look that seemed to tilt away from him as he waited there.

The couple's property was back a few hundred yards on a gravel access road. The trees opposite the soy field hiding the house from sight. Weeks before they'd taken the couple's car and then ditched it as soon as they came into Seattle.

Where Bean stood he was visible to both lanes of traffic, an empty red gas tank he'd found in the garage at his feet.

By then he had lived a week in the old house at the base of the mountains. Waiting for things to die down and for whatever decision he was going to make, but that he hadn't been able to make until that point. A few days before, eating canned soups and stale bags of cereal in front of the couple's computer, he'd come across an article in the Seattle paper.

The article was brief, only a recap of a much larger article he assumed had run earlier in the week. The money listed at two hundred thousand and all of their names mentioned one way or another, Bean still at large. And the amount of money Patrick had always told them much too small. He scanned down through the article, making sure he had the facts right. Somewhere out there Patrick was still running around, and the money Drake had led them to somehow not enough.

He read the article five times before making up his mind and now he stood alongside the road, clean shaven and looking respectable in a set of clothes he'd taken from the house. No car or truck for ten minutes.

While he waited, he picked gravel from the side of the road and targeted the fence posts, playing a game with himself to pass the time. He was juggling a collection of these rocks when an RV showed on the horizon, the body just visible in the twilight and the headlights turned dimly on.

As the RV came closer he stepped a foot into the road and began to wave his arms over his head. He wore a blue sport coat he'd taken from the man's closet, cotton khakis, and a white undershirt. With his hair combed neat and pulled back over his scalp, he looked like a man who'd lost his way in the country, or abandoned his car in search of gas.

He continued to wave and the RV came to a stop a few feet past where he stood. Bean arrived at the window as it came down and looked up on an older man wearing a white shirt and clear wire-rimmed glasses.

"Where's your car?" the man asked, speaking through the open window, his hands still on the wheel.

Bean smiled. He'd forgotten the gas can and he looked back at it now. "A mile or so down the road."

The old man at the wheel nodded like he understood. "I can give you a ride into town if you like. I was just out tooling this baby around. It wouldn't be more than twenty minutes."

Bean smiled again. "That's real good of you," he said. He jogged back to the gas can and scooped it up in his hand and then returned to the RV. He heard the door unlock as he approached and with one hand holding the gas can he slipped Drake's gun from inside his waistband and shot the driver at point-blank range through the open window.

The man slumped into the wheel and the horn sounded, but Bean reached a hand in and pushed the driver's body back, resting the bloody scalp against the headrest. With the engine still idling and the RV in park he opened the side door and came up the stairs into the RV. The thing was big as a bus and built with a dining area on one side and a kitchenette on the other; in the back a small bedroom with cupboards lining the ceiling and a small flat-screen mounted in one corner.

He went down through the RV looking the place over, Drake's gun in his hand and the Walther resting in his waistband at the small of his back. The bathroom was empty and the rear bedroom held only a mattress and single mirror. There was no one else on the RV.

When he came back to the front he saw that the man's blood had sprayed a good amount of the dash and part of the passenger seat, but the windshield was relatively clean. He put Drake's gun on the passenger seat and then bent to look through the glass at the road ahead. Nothing to see, not even a farmhouse or an approaching car.

Taking the driver under his arms Bean dragged him off the RV and into the forest, where he covered the body with dead branches and bits of moss. The white shirt stained red in places seemed now almost a piece of the forest itself.

He came back out from beneath the trees wondering how fast a vehicle like that could get up over a mountain pass and down into Silver Lake. The door stood open before him and he put a hand out on the railing and pulled himself up the stairs.

IT WAS NIGHT BY the time they got the wolf down off the mountain. Ellie gave Drake a ride to the Buck Blind. He came in through the front entrance and watched Sheri carry two plates out of the kitchen and set them on a table. She came over and they kissed and then she sent him into the bar for a beer.

Drake nodded to Jack, the bartender, as he took a seat. Ten minutes passed before Gary came in and Drake looked to the bartender, wondering if Jack had called him or if it was just coincidence.

They sat and drank their beers and made small talk. After a while Drake brought up the wolf.

"Where was it?"

Drake told him. He described the avalanche chute and the ridge above. He described the small descent into the valley through the trees and the clearing farther on. "We're going to go back tomorrow. There was a boot print up there."

Gary sipped from his beer. "So someone did your job for you?"

"Someone who didn't have the authority to shoot her." Drake leaned back from the bar and looked over at Gary. "What size shoe do you wear?"

Gary shook his head. "You're serious?" He was smiling and he lifted his beer and then, reconsidering, put it back down again. "You know I work for the people—no matter what the law says. That includes you, too, Bobby."

"That's what you're saying."

"That's all there is. Besides, it doesn't matter, does it? You went up to kill the wolf and the wolf is dead. What else matters?"

Drake thought it over. He didn't know if it mattered or not. He was starting to have a hard time telling the difference.

"Sheri's usually off around this time, isn't she?"

Drake nodded. He glanced over his shoulder toward the dining room. "Usually," he said. "Seems like maybe there's just a couple more tables."

"You come and pick her up every day?"

"I try. There's just one car now so I usually drop her off and then come get her at the end of the day."

"But today you were up in the mountains?"

"Yes, so Sheri dropped me at Fish and Wildlife and then came to work. We'll probably do the same tomorrow."

"You know, it's nice you're helping out," Gary said. "You're always welcome to come back, you know?"

He didn't have anything to say to Gary. He'd made his decision. He knew he couldn't go back on it and in a couple minutes Sheri came over from the restaurant and approached Drake and Gary where they sat at the bar.

"You ready?" she asked.

Drake said he was and got up from the bar. He was collecting his wallet and cell phone from the bar when Gary said, "You know they caught Bean earlier today."

Sheri—who was half turned toward the exit—stopped and looked back at Gary. "You sure?"

"I wanted to wait till both of you were here. He wasn't caught, really. He was shot as he tried to steal an RV from a man over in Chelan County."

Drake stood watching Gary where he sat. "Dead?"

"Doesn't get much deader."

"How?" Sheri asked. "I mean, who shot him?"

"A ten-year-old boy—the grandson of the poor son of a bitch who was driving the thing. The sheriff called me forty minutes ago and gave me the info. The driver pulled over to help Bean out. Bean was carrying a gas can or something and the driver stopped to offer him a ride. Bean shot him right there and dragged the body off the RV and hid it off the side of the road."

"And the boy?" Drake asked.

"Hidden in the bench seat of the dining area," Gary said. "The sheriff said the grandfather was just taking the boy out for a little drive. They didn't live more than twenty miles away."

"That's horrible," Sheri said.

"Bean left a gun behind sitting on the seat when he dragged the driver from his RV. I guess he figured he was alone."

"I can't believe it," Drake said.

"Looks like you can stop building a compound out of your place."

Drake shook his head in disbelief. "Ten years old . . ."

"I'm sorry I didn't tell you sooner," Gary said. "I just thought it would be better if you two were together."

"It's fine," Drake said. He looked to his wife and saw her eyes had gone watery. "It's okay," he said, trying to comfort her. He thanked Gary and after a little while he led Sheri out through the bar.

At the door, just before they left, Gary called after him. "I'm a size ten if you're still wondering."

Drake nodded. He put a hand to the door and propped it open for Sheri, the night air out there like a cool balm on the skin.

AT HOME THEY made dinner together and for a long time neither said a thing. At ten they watched the evening news and the story came on first thing. The cameras showed an empty road and the RV, a big thing that looked like a tour bus, wrapped with yellow police tape. Several of the Chelan County deputies working in the background to guide what little traffic there was.

An interview with the sheriff followed and then one of the two marshals made a statement for the camera. The news moved on to an Easter egg hunt somewhere in North Seattle that weekend, followed soon after by the weather and the local sports. Drake watched it all in silence as he sat on the couch.

For some reason little of it surprised him and he got up and went back into Patrick's room. Without bothering to turn on a light, he sat at the desk in front of the computer. Sheri hadn't come into the room much since breaking down the crib and removing the changing table. Now there was only the bed that Drake still hadn't gotten around to.

He swiveled on the chair and looked over the mattress and frame. His father had made the bed and it looked untouched. On the desk where Drake sat there was a paper from a week and a half ago. Someone had brought it by—either Luke or Andy—and Drake had taken the time to scan the article, looking to see what was said and what wasn't.

The story was a full page of text, cut up throughout the front section of the paper. It detailed the three days Patrick had gone missing and ended with Patrick's escape from the Bellingham Police Department. They'd contacted Drake but he'd offered no comment, hanging up before the reporter was able to ask a second question.

Now Drake stood and walked to the bed and knelt, feeling around underneath for the box of Patrick's things. He slid it out and brought up the folder and then crossed the room to the desk again.

For about five minutes he stood leafing through the articles, the light from the hallway the only thing to assist him in his study.

It was when he started to rip the article from the newspaper that Sheri came to the door. He looked over at her but didn't say anything, simply continuing on with the article. When he was done he collected the pieces and folded them to fit in the manila folder with the rest of the newspaper articles, and then he placed the latest and, he hoped, the last within.

Only when he put the folder away and the box back under the bed did Sheri ask if he was saving it for Patrick.

"I'm not sure anymore," Drake said. He stood half in the light and half in the dark and for a long time he stayed that way.

THE BOOT PRINTS were still there in the morning. Ellie waited for him as he looked them over for the second time in two days. The edges around the imprints had crumbled away a little more but the shape and size of the boot was still easy to recognize.

"There's nothing off this way except for forestry land and a few hundred acres of clear cut," Ellie said. She was looking at a topographical map and lining up a compass. The boot tracks were visible every few feet, sometimes in the mud but mostly as a scrape in the forest floor—a patch of dead pine needles displaced or the scuff of a boot toe against a rotten log. It was hard going and at times they backtracked, looking for a sign before going on again. The trail leading them on, farther and farther into the woods, where even Drake felt he had never been.

They traveled light, each with a day pack loaded with supplies. In Drake's bag he carried a flashlight, a thermal blanket, some matches, a compass, binoculars, a radio Ellie had given him, and the spare ammunition to the .270 strapped over his shoulder. Ellie had the same except for the service weapon she wore in a holster over her right hip.

In an hour, they'd lost the track five times and spent just about as much time going back over their own footprints as they'd done following the original. After a mile and a half they came to a small creek where Drake saw the track pause, the boot prints in several places as if the person they followed had stopped to drink from the stream. While Ellie surveyed the map, Drake circled the area, coming across a second track. The boots about the same size but the tread slightly different, and this close to the stream the indentations clear in the wet earth.

He came back up the stream and found Ellie. "I don't think this person stopped here just for the water."

Ellie rested with one thigh supported on an egg-shaped rock. She looked up as soon as Drake came back and didn't break eye contact till he was finished. She was holding the map in her hands still and Drake wondered if she knew where they were, because he certainly didn't.

"Whoever was out here came to meet someone else."

"Do the two tracks go on together?"

Drake looked behind him. The second track came on about fifty yards farther down, followed the first for a time, and then broke off again. He couldn't be sure without following one or the other but he didn't think they had traveled more than a few hundred feet together.

"What do you think?" she asked.

"I'm not sure what to," Drake said. He was looking up the stream, listening to the wind high up as the trees swayed above. A yellow finch flitted out of the brush, catching the light and then disappearing back within the forest shadows. "What size boot have we been following?"

"I don't know." Ellie placed her own foot next to one of the prints and then looked up at Drake. "I can't be sure. What do you make of it? It looks like a woman's eleven or twelve."

"What's that in men's?"

"A nine," Ellie said. "Maybe a ten. I don't know if I've ever thought about what the size difference is between men and women." She was waiting for Drake to say something and when he didn't, she said, "What are you getting at?"

"Nothing," he said. "Just thinking about something Gary said to me last night."

"Gary?"

"Yeah," Drake said. "It's nothing, really. I wear a size ten. I can't make any more of this than you can."

Ellie brought the map over so that they could both see. She laid it out on a rock and marked their position with her finger. "This stream runs back down to the lake eventually. It looks far away but that's just because it follows the back side of the ridge. It really isn't too far—less than a day's walk really."

Drake looked it over. "But like you said, there's nothing out here."

"How does that second track look to you?"

"It looks the same as the first," Drake said. He was getting frustrated with it all. They were out in the middle of nowhere and he was having a hard time putting two and two together.

"Does it double around on itself?"

Drake looked up from the map. He thought back. The trail had come up the stream and met the first and then after a while peeled off. It could have but he wasn't sure.

"But they do split apart?"

"Yes."

"I've got the map," Ellie said. "I'm going to keep on with the first. I want you to follow the second and see where it goes. You can use the stream as a guide. It runs into the southern part of the lake in about four miles."

Drake looked back at her in complete disbelief. "I don't think that's a good idea."

"I'll be fine," Ellie said. "This is the job. Mostly we work alone, you know that."

Drake shook his head. "If you find someone I don't want you doing anything."

She smiled back at him. "I'll use caution," she said. "I'll radio you every thirty minutes. How does that sound?"

"Better."

She took out her water and drank a quarter of it and then put it back in her bag. "Four miles," she said. And then she put the map away and lifted the backpack onto her shoulders and went on across the creek. Drake watched her for a time as she picked the tracks out of the soft forest detritus.

When she was gone from sight he lifted his own bag and cinched the straps down over his chest and waist. Twenty minutes later he was still following the creek, the boot prints heading southeast toward the lake.

At thirty minutes he stopped beneath a ledge of rock cut away from the mountains by the creek. A deadfall straddled a pool of water where he could see trout skimming the surface for mosquitoes, bits of twig and pine bark collected on the down-creek side of the pool.

He rested and got out some of his water. When thirty-five minutes had passed he tried the radio and got only static. He waited and tried it again. Ellie came through sounding breathless.

"You okay?"

"It doubled back across the creek," she said. There was static for a moment and then her voice came through clear. "The trail is headed back up the ridge, right back to the clearing where we found the wolf."

He thought that over. "Back toward town?"

"Exactly," she said. Her voice sounded a little stronger and Drake imagined her a couple miles up the stream, and probably a thousand feet higher than he was. "You keep going," she said. "I might lose you when I come over the ridge. I'll follow my trail and if it just leads me back to the truck I'll swing around and get you when you come out at the southern part of the lake."

"Okay," he said. "It's just leading me that way as it is."

"Radio again in thirty minutes."

He replaced the radio in his bag and then stood with the backpack in one hand. He put one strap over his shoulder, removed the rifle from his other shoulder, and then put the other backpack strap on. For a long moment he stood looking out on the forest as it climbed gradually away from him and the mountain farther on. Besides the wind and the gurgle of the stream there was absolute silence and he felt a shiver travel up his spine and wring itself out on the fine hairs at the back of his neck.

He strapped the rifle up over his shoulder again and began to walk. Two hundred feet on he came to a wet boot print still dripping down one of the rocks.

The rifle was off his shoulder and in his hands before he knew it and for what felt like ten minutes he crouched next to a large boulder with his breath shallow in his lungs and his ears tuned to every swaying tree branch above.

He tried the radio again and got only static. He didn't know what that meant but he guessed maybe Ellie had made her way up over the ridge and was headed to the truck. With his heart thumping he looked down at the boot print again, the water evaporating where the speckled light of the sun came in from the canopy above. He leaned out from around the boulder and looked up the slight grade at the shadowed forest beyond. Nothing at all to see.

When he turned back the print was just a wet dot on the rock. It could have been anything and this is what he tried to tell himself. The rifle in his hands and the knowledge that whoever had stepped across the creek had done so only a few minutes before.

He came out from behind the boulder in a sweep of the forest. The rifle held to his shoulder and the sight magnifying the far shadows. There was nothing to see but the dense growth of the forest.

Careful with his feet, he made his way up out of the creek bed and followed the fresh trail over the floor of pine needles. He moved with the gun in his hand, resting as he came to each new trunk and then waiting, listening to the blank silence of the surrounding wood. Somewhere far off a chipmunk beat a series of strained calls, chattering in a harsh cacophony before going silent again.

Drake moved out from behind the tree and went on. The trail he followed faint but still there.

He came up a small rise and crouched to survey the forest beyond. Evergreen trees and sword fern; a full minute passed before he saw the brown tarp, colored the same as the forest floor.

Circling to his right he came on the tarp from uphill. The plastic stretched over several support branches that ran down from a larger bough that had been nailed crudely into two trees about eight feet apart. The tarp making a kind of lean-to, with one side open to the forest and the back side shielding the small residence from the creek.

Drake tried the radio again and got nothing but static. He waited and tried it again. Still nothing. He was about two hundred feet off with a clear view to the open side of the lean-to. A blue bucket that looked to contain stream water was there. Inside he thought he could make out the roll of a sleeping bag and a few more items.

He raised the rifle again and searched the area. There was nothing to be seen and he ran the sight back over the lean-to, appraising those items that he hadn't been able to make out with his naked eye. A rechargeable lantern with a crank sat toward the back, several tins of food, a couple magazines, and one book that Drake couldn't see from his angle, and then around the edge of the sleeping bag Drake saw something that made him drop the sight from his eye, refocus, and then put the sight back.

There was a kind of metal box, bright red with only the battered corners showing beyond the rolled sleeping bag. He rose from where he'd crouched with his rifle and came on toward the lean-to, checking his blind spots every few steps. Once even stopping to sweep the forest when, far off, he heard a stick break, and then the forest go silent again.

He came to the lean-to with the rifle raised. Nothing more than what he'd seen through the scope. With the barrel of the gun he nudged the sleeping bag and then dragged it away, revealing the red toolbox beneath, the paint scored away in places to reveal the gray metal. Rust showing in other places where the box had sat in the elements.

He'd seen this box before. Or at least he'd seen one like it. He crouched and ran a hand across the metal. The same dings and dents he remembered. A few new ones that he didn't.

Feeling something behind him he turned and watched the forest. No movement but that caused by the wind. When he was sure he was alone he let the rifle down onto the floor of the lean-to and with both hands he raised the edge of the toolbox and looked inside.

Empty. Nothing in the thing at all.

He rose and scanned the forest floor looking for a sign. The water in the bucket was fresh and clear and the pine needles were wet in places where the water had slopped over the edges and stained the earth.

Far out somewhere he heard another branch break and he was running, following the sound as he weaved through the trees, letting his feet navigate the uneven dips of the mountain. He moved farther from the creek, stopping once as he fought to catch his breath; he couldn't hear the water anymore. Nothing but forest behind and ahead of him, nothing except brief glimpses of the sun through the trees above to tell him his direction.

At some point he dropped the bag, the backpack falling behind him as the slope began to run downhill, the rifle now solely in his hands. He was another five hundred feet on when he thought of the radio inside but he didn't stop or go back. Up ahead something crashed through a thicket of devil's club and he saw the green, maple-like leaves swaying.

He raised the rifle and sighted but only the leaves were there to dance in front of him. He went on, coming to the thicket, and then he was through and out into bright sunshine. The light blinding him as he took a fall over a young pine lying lengthwise across his path.

He came up holding his knee and gritting his teeth. The pain intense and the fallen pine only one of thousands that lined the clear-cut mountainside he'd emerged onto. He bounced up onto his good leg, still holding the rifle in one hand, and balanced himself with the other.

Somewhere below he heard a rock fall, tumbling through space, and then clapping into another, where it shattered into several smaller pieces. He raised the rifle. The running figure of a man visible through the scope as he jumped one tree stump and then vaulted the fallen trunk of another. Drake called out, telling the man to stop, his voice carrying in the open space. But the figure kept running, a backpack bouncing as he went. The bald crown of skin and the sun reflected in a glare.

"Stop," Drake yelled, letting the voice carry. He held the rifle, the butt to the meat of his chest, just below his shoulder, and his eye searching down the scope.

The man didn't stop. It was more like he slowed. One foot in front of the other, his pace slackening like an old coal train shifting away its power. The man standing there, backpack over his shoulders, sweat showing now on the back of his neck. The beginnings of a mane of hair grown in around the edges of his scalp. And Drake knew it before the man turned around. It was his father. And he knew, too, what had been in the red toolbox and what his father had meant when he'd written Morgan to take care of *his* half.

Drake knew it all now.

He held the rifle, sweat beading on his forehead and creating paths down his skin, waiting for his father to turn around. And then when he did, Drake felt his finger tighten on the trigger. He felt the tension there. The way the trigger yearned for release.

Patrick stood looking back at him. A hundred yards away. And then he raised a hand and waved. He didn't say anything, he just stood there looking back at Drake, white hair grown in around his face and at the sides of his head. And Drake watched—he watched the hand go up high over his father's head. He watched the palm open, the fingers extend, and it was like his father was saying hello, or saying good-bye, only Drake didn't know.

The hand stayed that way for a long time, outstretched above Patrick's head until it, too, fell away and Patrick turned downslope.

For a few seconds more Drake watched as his father moved away over the open landscape. The rifle still clutched into the meat of Drake's chest. The crosshairs following his father, Drake knowing for the first time in a long time that whatever this was—sighting his father through the scope of a rifle—it simply wasn't his job anymore.

ACKNOWLEDGMENTS

The first wolf pack to be documented in Washington State in sixty years occurred in 2008. As of March 2014, there are thirteen established wolf packs in the state. Under Washington's wolf management plan, a pack of wolves is defined as two individual wolves traveling together. Three of the thirteen packs now roam the eastern slopes of the North Cascades. And one additional pack can be found just outside the U.S. border at the end of the North Cascade range in Canada.

I am in no way an expert on wolves. But like many in the state of Washington I have watched their population grow, wondering what will happen to the wolves as their territory meets that of the ranchers, farmers, and others who now populate lands once inhabited by wolves and other large predators. In 2012 the deaths of seven calves and one sheep in the northeastern part of the state, along with many injuries to livestock in the area, were attributed to wolves. The Washington Department of Fish and Wildlife ultimately killed seven members of the Wedge Pack in northern Stevens County.

The return of wolves to Washington State remains part of a critical debate.

FOR OPENING THEIR mountain home to me I want to thank Alan and Susan Rogers. You gave me much needed time not only to begin this novel, but also to finish a draft a year later. To James Scott and Taylor Rogers Scott, thank you for making me feel like family. I owe you both more than I can ever say.

To my agent, Nat Sobel, I am extremely grateful you found my work in a small literary journal out of Virginia. It's been an amazing five years. Thank you also to Judith Weber, who, along with Nat, read multiple drafts of this novel. Without the two of you *Sometimes the Wolf* wouldn't have become anything close to what it is today.

To David Highfill at William Morrow, this is a dream. Thank you so much for continuing to support artists like me. And (along with Cormac) thank you for one kick-ass title! I owe a great deal to Jessica Williams, who has been there at every step of the process. To Laura Cherkas, thank you for once again doing a fine job of copyediting. To Adam Johnson, who designed the cover for this novel as well as for *The Carrion Birds,* I have you to thank for another beautiful cover. Thank you to everyone at William Morrow/HarperCollins for helping this novel along. I hope you are as proud of it as I am.

I owe a huge debt to Simon & Schuster UK. Ian Chapman, you are a champion of the publishing industry and I'm so grateful we've now had the chance to work on three novels together. I hope there are many more. To Clare Hey, you published my first story in the UK and now you're my editor. It couldn't have worked out any better. Thank you so much for your keen eye.

I want to thank the friends who read drafts of this novel, inspired me, or simply offered sound advice. There are many of you, but the few to whom I owe the greatest thanks are Zachary Watterson, Debra DiDomenico, Dan Coxon, Chip Cheek, Lizzie Stark, Carter Sickels, and Jennine Capó Crucet. To Marc Divina, thank you for ridin' dirty and going crabbing in the middle of the day. To Drew Nicklas, thanks for all the crazy Montana stories. Who knew bears liked alcohol so much? And to Adrian Johnson, keep on keeping on, you feel me?!

A huge thank-you goes out to all my foreign publishers and

agents. I really couldn't do any of this without you. To Joel Gotler, thank you for opening the door to a world I never dreamed of. And to the filmmakers who picked up my first couple novels, Mark Tonderai and Andrew Lauren, I want to say thank you. Just knowing you're out there keeps me working all that much harder.

Finally, I wouldn't be here without my parents, who once upon a time saw fit to ground me for half the summer, part of the punishment being an eighty-mile hike through the North Cascades coupled with the assignment of reading ten books and then giving reports on them. Still not sure whether the punishment fit the crime, but I'm grateful all the same.

This novel and the novel before are dedicated to my parents, but all of them are always, always, for my wife, Karen. I couldn't do any of this without you.

BOOKS BY URBAN WAITE

SOMETIMES THE WOLF
A Novel

Available in Paperback and eBook

"As muscular and laconic as anything by Cormac McCarthy, yet it crackles with humanity. A-"
—*Entertainment Weekly* on *The Carrion Birds*

Sheriff Patrick Drake tried to lead an upstanding life until his wife passed away. He did okay for a while, singlehandedly raising his family in a small mountain town. Then he was hit with money troubles, fell in with some unsavory men, and ended up convicted of one of the biggest crimes in local history. Twelve years later Patrick is on parole under the watchful eye of his son Bobby, who just happens to be a deputy sheriff in his father's old department. Bobby hasn't had it easy, either. He's carried the weight of his father's guilt, forsaking his own dreams. Yet no matter how much distance he's tried to put between himself, his father, his grandfather, and the past, small town minds can have very long memories. But trouble isn't done with the Drakes—and a terrifying threat boils up from Patrick's old life. And this time, no one will be spared.

THE CARRION BIRDS
A Novel

"A hell of a good novel, relentlessly paced and beautifully narrated."
—STEPHEN KING on *The Terror of Living*

Available in Paperback and eBook

Ray Lamar has made some mistakes. He's good at hurting people—the dead wife he failed, the young son he abandoned, the victims who stand in his boss's way. But Ray's tired of being that man. He wants to go home to Coronado, New Mexico, to see his boy and make a new life far from the violence of the past. One last job will take him there. All he has to do is steal a rival's stash. Simple and easy. Ray knows there's no such thing as easy, and that simple plan has quickly become a catastrophe. Now the runners who have always moved quietly through this desert border town want vengeance. To stop a bloodbath and maybe save his own soul, Ray must figure out how to make it right. But for a man like Ray Lamar, there is only one way. A soulful tale of violence, vengeance, and contrition, *The Carrion Birds* is an elegant depiction of one man's last chance to make things right.

"As muscular and laconic as anything by Cormac McCarthy, yet it crackles with humanity."
—*Entertainment Weekly*